TAKEN
TO THE
GRAVE

BOOKS BY M.M. CHOUINARD

TAKEN
TO THE
GRAVE

M.M.CHOUINARD

bookouture

Published by Bookouture in 2019

An imprint of StoryFire Ltd.

Carmelite House
50 Victoria Embankment
London EC4Y 0DZ

www.bookouture.com

ISBN: 978-1-78681-826-3
eBook ISBN: 978-1-78681-825-6

For Hubby and the FurCrew

CHAPTER ONE

Professor Michael Whorton swore aloud as he narrowly avoided slamming his face into his office door. He gritted his teeth and reminded himself to lift the knob, then shoved his shoulder against the glass. The building was only two years old but was already falling apart, a tribute to the university's poor planning and money allocation. The resistance gave and he strode inside, tossed his briefcase onto the front-most section of his desk, and pulled out his laptop. The power strip he'd ordered still hadn't come, so he crawled under the sideways-U-shaped desk to plug it in, and spotted some sort of playing card just out of reach by the door. Typical—probably shoved under by some moronic student who hadn't thought far enough ahead to bring actual paper for their frantically scribbled grade-change plea. He shook his head. How was he supposed to give a shit when they didn't?

The landline behind him rang. He swiveled the chair around to snatch up the receiver. "Michael Whorton."

A rustle crackled across the line.

"Hello?"

The rustling intensified.

"Hello? Speak up or call back."

He reached forward to hang up the phone, but a hand gripped his shoulder, and pain ripped through his right side. The hand withdrew just as suddenly, the momentum of the release dropping him forward onto the desk.

Michael struggled to right himself and push the chair around, hand reflexively grasping his side. As the rotation finished, his eyes met his attacker's, then registered the satisfaction there. Fear squeezed his chest as he realized what was happening.

He grabbed for the desk to brace himself, but his hand, now covered in blood, slipped along the edge, and he tumbled to the floor.

"Hel—"

Before he could finish the word, his attacker's foot crushed his face into the floor. "No, no, no. We can't have you calling for help."

The foot rolled, shifting the top of Michael's head forward.

The air around him compressed, and something sharp sliced into the base of his skull.

CHAPTER TWO

The recognition that registered in his eyes before I killed him made it worthwhile.

I'm not a cruel person. I don't enjoy other people's pain. Quite the opposite. I help strangers and I rescue animals and I always try to do the right thing.

And this, without question, was the right thing. Otherwise, he'd have spent the next however many years ruining more lives. Our world is a vile, despicable place because of people who believe they can do whatever they like, hurt whoever they like, with no thought for the consequences to other people. Or, more likely, without care for the destruction they cause to other people. And unless they physically harm someone, there's no remedy for it, no way to get justice. They wreak havoc and laugh themselves to sleep knowing nobody can do anything about it.

This was the only way to put a stop to it. That's why I did it.

So, no, I didn't enjoy killing him.

But I admit, the expression on his face was satisfying. No, far better than satisfying—it was glorious to watch the haughty, superior demeanor evaporate, and show the true soul beneath: the craven, insignificant fool consumed by his own ego. So sublime to watch the ersatz victory he'd savored snatched from him, replaced by his pound of flesh. Glorious, because all of that confirmed he knew what he'd done was wrong, and that he deserved to die.

So, yes, I admit I'm glad my face was the last thing he saw. And if there's a hell, I hope that image is burned onto his retinas for all eternity, as the flames relentlessly engulf him.

CHAPTER THREE

"You know, you never explained to me why you quit the lieutenant job," Bob Arnett said over the lid of his coffee.

"I didn't think I had to," Jo Fournier answered.

"Try me."

Jo's glance flicked to the unrelenting inquisition in Arnett's brown eyes, then looked back to the rainbow of leaves swirling over the colonial-lined street. She'd known him for nearly twenty years—wow, that was a mental slap to the face—since she first became a detective, and hoped their years of partnering had pushed them past the need for this discussion. If they managed to pick up the smallest shifts in each other's expressions and use them as road signs during interrogations, why couldn't he pick up on her cues now?

Answer: he was ignoring them.

"Get a haircut," she said.

"Which one?" He laughed. The joke was almost as old as the partnership. His hair, black when they'd first met, was more salt than pepper now, and always managed to look just a bit scruffy. "But seriously."

"Did it occur to you that I missed our partnership too much? That I couldn't face the day without your engaging wit?" Subconsciously motivated by the hank of hair sticking out above his ear, she tucked a chestnut lock behind her own.

"No." His eyes bored into her.

"You're smarter than you look." She laughed. "The job just wasn't for me. Why's that so hard for everyone to understand?"

"Because people don't walk away from upgrades in money and power."

She sighed mentally, and shifted in her seat. "Why's this coming up now all of a sudden after all this time? Boring weekend?"

"Partly because I waited, nice and polite, for you to tell me yourself, and it never happened. But mostly because Garber just quit and the position's open yet again. Rockney asked me if I thought you'd consider it."

Jo braked her turn onto Oakhurst University Ave for a pedestrian, and used the pause as an excuse to delay. He wouldn't like part of the answer, and wouldn't understand the rest. Hell, *she* didn't fully understand it.

"Part of it was the politics. I'm not like you, my friend. I *mind* being hated."

He chuckled. "And the rest of it?"

She returned the pedestrian's wave and resumed the turn. "Rockney promised I'd be able to keep my boots on the ground, but that was a pipe dream. The Jeanine Hammond case confirmed what I worried about all along. Profiling behind closed doors when we could squeeze out a minute here and there? That's not what I went to the academy for."

"I *knew* you never let that one go." He shook his head and chugged his coffee.

She bristled. Partly from annoyance, but mostly because he was right, she hadn't let it go. They'd closed the case, which had involved at least six murdered women, but only because the killer had shown up dead on the other side of the country, purportedly a suicide off the Golden Gate Bridge. Although everyone told her she was crazy for looking a gift horse in the mouth, she'd been convinced at the time that there was more to the case, and she was convinced of it still. She'd learned everything she could about the killer's past, and requested reports on all Golden Gate Bridge suicides several times a year. She wasn't sure what she was looking for, but analyzed them until she went cross-eyed, certain something would eventually emerge.

But she wasn't going to admit that to Arnett. "It just brought my issues with the job to a head. Anyway, enough about me. Laura's shingles any better?"

He narrowed his eyes at her, but turned back around. "Yeah, it looks like they'll be gone for good shortly. We were supposed to go on a romantic camping trip this coming weekend to celebrate, but apparently Kylie's moving back in, and Laura wants to be there to help."

Jo resisted the urge to comment on Laura's propensity to over-accommodate, a sore spot for Arnett that had contributed to on-going problems in their relationship. "Have I mentioned lately how glad I am I don't have kids?"

"Uh-huh. And you'll keep mentioning it until your mother lays down another guilt trip, and then I'll catch you googling how-to-freeze-your-eggs again." He smiled.

Jo laughed and rolled her eyes. "Something go wrong with Kylie's job?"

"Depends what you mean by *wrong*. Turns out writing dialogue for video games isn't the be-all-end-all she hoped it would be."

Jo shook her head in a show of solidarity. The younger of Arnett's two daughters, Kylie, drove him batty. She'd dropped out of university—the very one they were approaching—after her freshman year, convinced that real-world experience was the path to success. The problem was, she wasn't sure *what type* of real-world experience. This was the death of her third fledgling career, in less than two years. "Patience. She's finding herself."

"So Laura keeps telling me. What the hell does that even mean?"

"Damned if I know. But then, I can't remember a time I didn't want to be a cop." Jo pulled up behind the two campus police vehicles and the Oakhurst PD squad car framing the entrance to Dyer Hall, which housed the biology department. "Huh. I don't think we've been here since they built this."

Oakhurst University had undergone a recent renaissance. The founder of UniversalApps, a software giant, had bequeathed a hundred million dollars to his alma mater six years before. That caliber of donation catapulted a university's raison d'être, because it was the kind of money you invested rather than spent and then lived off the yielded interest in perpetuity. So, since then, the university set about redefining itself as a top-tier research school. That meant new programs, new priorities, and more than a few new buildings.

Jo and Arnett strode past a crowd of students held back by caution tape, and stared up at the structure.

"Yeah, well. I hope the vic's the guy who designed it," Arnett said.

Jo considered the glass-and-cement planes, discordant among the surrounding red-brick federal buildings. "It's intended to be quote-unquote *green*. To let in as much natural light as possible. And the cement and metal don't need paint, so there's no toxic run-off into the environment."

"Ugly as hell."

She bobbed her head from side to side, trying to find the beauty in it. "You're not wrong."

They took the elevator to the third floor, and spotted more caution tape as they stepped out. As they strode toward it, the office in question came into view, door open and forensics team inside. A completely filled sign-up sheet for today's office hours, *Tuesday 1 p.m.–3 p.m.*, hung under the nameplate.

They stopped in front of the uniformed officer guarding the tape, whose badge identified him as M. Sheehan. Young, possibly right out of the academy, with a muscular frame and a blond buzz cut. He eyed Jo up and down, and she shoved down a flash of annoyance. Even in a progressive New England university town like Oakhurst, she regularly ran into people who were nonplussed by a female detective. Admittedly, her five-six, one-hundred-ten-pound frame didn't cut an impressive figure, but she'd been told one too many times that her green eyes and wide smile were *too pretty* for a policewoman, so her solution was to head off the bullshit before it got started.

She met his eye without blinking. "I'm Detective Josette Fournier, and this is Detective Bob Arnett. We have a stabbing?"

His face flicked to Arnett's and back, then shifted to a professional blank. "Yes, ma'am. Professor Michael Whorton. A student showed up for office hours and found the door closed, with blood seeping out from under it." He pointed to the coagulating mess.

"The student's name?" Jo asked.

Sheehan consulted his notes. "Rosanna Trenton."

"Where is she now?" Jo asked.

"Department offices on the first floor, being treated for shock."

"Has the next of kin been notified?"

"Yes, ma'am. The vic's wife is somewhere in Maine on a business trip. They notified her. She's finishing up there and driving back as soon as she can, sometime tomorrow."

Arnett was incredulous. "Finishing up?"

Sheehan shrugged. "Garcia talked to her. He didn't get the sense she was all that broken up."

Jo peered into the office. Small, about ten feet by ten. The door was made entirely of glass, but Michael Whorton had plastered the inside with copy paper to occlude visibility. Between the two medicolegals working the scene she caught glimpses of walls lined with bookshelves, and a U-shaped desk that lined the back and right walls then jutted out to bisect the room. A laptop sat open on the desk displaying a stock shot of the Grand Canyon on the screen, next to stacks of papers and a briefcase. Shades covered the solitary window.

She recognized one of the individuals through the hazmat-esque scrubs. "How'd the tournament go, Janet?"

Janet Marzillo turned and shook her head. Her current obsession was Texas Hold 'Em, and she spent a fair amount of time in free online games. She'd taken her first shot at the real thing in Atlantic City a few weeks before. "Almost too easy. First time out, and I made it to the final table. Then I got flustered and overcommitted, and had to bluff my way through a mediocre hand that rapidly turned to guano. But, I placed high enough to win back more than my entry fee, so there's that. How's that new boyfriend of yours?"

"Boyfriend? I've been dating him three weeks." Jo rolled her eyes.

"Two more than usual," she said.

Arnett choked back a laugh, and covered by craning his neck to examine the room.

Jo smiled, but changed the subject. "Any information for us yet?"

"We still have quite a bit to do. You want to kit yourselves out and join, or wait?"

"We don't want to get in your way, and I can see most of it clearly from here. Just give us the short version for now," Jo answered.

Marzillo's sassy smile rearranged into focused concentration. "Vic was stabbed first in the side, then at the base of the skull, which almost certainly resulted in instantaneous death. Which is strange, because if you have the sort of savvy for a kill like that, why bother to stab the man in the side first? As best I can tell, the killer had a clear shot—looks like the vic was on the phone, back to the door, and the killer came up behind him." She pointed first to the landline dangling over the side of the back desk, then to a bloody handprint. "My guess is he tried to stand up after the first strike, then fell down before the attacker stabbed him in the neck, because there's no blood flow down the back, only sideways onto the floor. And based on the blood patterns, there wasn't much of a struggle."

"Time of death?" Arnett asked.

"We got here at one forty-five. He's been dead no longer than an hour before that."

Jo checked her watch, then stepped to her left to see the entire figure. Michael Whorton was sprawled partially out of the desk's U, lying awkwardly on his stomach, hunched slightly toward the door. His black slacks and pale green shirt were well cut, and made from quality material. One blood-covered hand jutted out from under him, and the other lay palm-down on the floor. His eyes were open, gazing up toward the ceiling. The position and the face reminded her of something, but she couldn't remember what. She bent down to look more directly at the eyes, and the memory prodded her, but didn't come. "There's fear in his eyes, but something else, too. Can you see it?"

Arnett and Marzillo looked at his face, and Arnett nodded. "Like he was doing some sort of calculation."

"I think that might just be because he's looking up," Marzillo said.

"Fear and calculation, yes, but also something else." She shook her head and stood up. "Do we have time to do an interview before you're finished?"

"At least that, I'd say. I'll text you when we're done and walk you through the rest."

"Much appreciated." Jo turned to Arnett. "Rosanna Trenton first?"

CHAPTER FOUR

Rosanna Trenton didn't have much to tell them. She'd shown up for Michael Whorton's scheduled office hours at one p.m., and knocked to be sure he wasn't inside. She figured he was running late and settled in to wait, seated on the floor reading a textbook. When she looked up ten minutes later to check the time, she noticed something dark seeping out from the office threshold. Concerned, she called campus police. She claimed she had lunch with two friends in the dining commons next door, right before her appointment time. Her shock seemed real enough, and if her alibi held up, she'd have to be a very cool customer to risk killing him in a ten-minute window before the next student scheduled for office hours appeared.

Jo and Arnett told the officers she was free to go, then headed through the short corridor that separated the student services section of the departmental offices from the administrative section. This opened into a single, small alcove with security cameras perched above a second door at the opposite end. On the left, a large redwood desk ran almost the full-length of the room, and faced a row of four chairs on the right. The woman behind the desk wore her silver hair in a severe bob, and wore a cream button-down silk blouse over pristine black slacks. Her gold jewelry was deceptively simple, elegant, and timeless.

An image of a Siberian husky flashed through Jo's mind when the ice-blue eyes met hers.

"You're the detectives, I assume?" the woman asked.

"Detective Josette Fournier, and this is Detective Bob Arnett. We're here for Roger Latimer."

She glared at them. "Finally. He's been waiting for you since we got word, canceling appointments along the way. He needs this over as quickly as possible so he can keep the rest of his schedule." Translation: Dean Latimer was busy and important, they were not, and her job was to make certain they knew it.

A rare snarky response bubbled up in Jo, probably borne from the blunt, New England half of her upbringing. But the southern half, whose on-demand butter-doesn't-melt approach had finessed more mover-and-shaker egos than she could count, tamped it back down. She pasted on an apologetic smile. "We appreciate his cooperation. This shouldn't take much more of his time. Thank you   ?" She waited pointedly for the woman's name.

"Ruth Henderson, executive assistant to the dean."

"Thank you, Ruth."

Ruth picked up the phone, announced their arrival, and listened to a reply before hanging up. She typed something into the monitor in front of her, and the red light above the far door's handle turned green. "Go all the way to the back, then turn left. The dean's office will be in front of you."

Arnett stepped forward and pushed the door open, revealing a rectangular maze with six-foot high cubicles in the center and fancy offices lining both sides. Stares followed them as they strode past. Jo watched Arnett surreptitiously eye the nameplates, knowing he'd remember them with near-perfect precision should they become relevant.

They turned left when they hit the dead end, then crossed behind the final cubicles. Two closed offices flanked either side of an unattended open-air reception area.

Jo glanced back and forth between them, flummoxed. "Any guesses which is the dean's?"

"Flip a coin?" Arnett's jaw tensed.

Jo knocked on the closer of the two, and got no answer. She stepped over to the other door. It opened just as she raised her fist, revealing a tall, thin man with a long face, ditchwater hair and eyes, and a suit that hung a little too loosely. "I wondered where you'd got to," he grunted.

Jo made a quick decision. She didn't want to alienate the man, and knew all too well that the academic ego was a fiercely overinflated, fragile thing. But the power display had gone on long enough. "The doors back here have no nameplates. I'm surprised any visitors find you amid the labyrinth."

His eyes flashed to the door, then back up. "Yes, well. Security."

"From who? The students, or the professors?" Arnett asked.

Roger Latimer's eyes narrowed slightly, but he didn't respond. He turned back into the office, then sat behind his large mahogany desk, and gestured them into the two chairs facing it. "What happened to Dr. Whorton?"

"Our techs are still processing the scene. Tell me about him," Jo said.

"He was a biology professor who did neurobiology research on stem cells. Married, no children."

"I was hoping you'd go a little deeper."

"How so?"

"If you want answers, we need to know who might want to kill him. Was he a good teacher? Liked by his students? By his colleagues?"

"His teaching evaluations were standard for the department. I don't know that he's either liked or disliked generally by his students. But, there was an incident last semester, involving a student he failed. The student filed a discrimination claim against him."

"Racial discrimination? Sexual?" Jo asked.

Roger cleared his throat. "None of that. He just decided Michael had taken a dislike to him. The student"—he pulled an open folder on his desk closer—"Greg Crawley, says Dr. Whorton failed him without justification. Michael wasn't a fool, he kept copies of all relevant testing materials once Crawley started making trouble. Part of the coursework was graded on Scantron machines, so it's just not possible for anyone to manipulate that. His scores on those sections weren't failing, but they weren't excellent, either. Michael provided us with rubrics for the essays, and wrote justifications for the points taken off. The difficulty was, while Crawley's work was grammatically eloquent, the content was rambling and off-topic. That made assessing it difficult."

"So you're saying he deserved the grade he got?" Arnett asked.

Roger shifted in his chair. "I'm saying we didn't find any reason to override Michael's judgment. These issues can be subjective, and unless there's clear reason to believe there's bias, we're not going to override a trusted professor. The Scantron results alone shed doubt on his claim."

Jo was skeptical. Multiple-choice questions and essay questions were two different animals that required two different skill sets. Surely it was possible that a student could struggle with one and not the other? And, if he hadn't failed the Scantron sections, was it fair to use them to justify a failing grade on the rest?

"I'm guessing Crawley didn't agree with your assessment?" Arnett asked.

"No, he didn't."

Jo nodded. "And we're talking just about a single class?"

"Unfortunately for Crawley, his D in that class dropped his GPA under the acceptable minimum to keep his financial aid."

"Then he must have been flirting with the line to start with," Jo said.

Roger leaned back in his seat. "Academic excellence didn't come easy for him and he didn't take responsibility for that. In my experience, such people aren't likely to take responsibility for their other choices, either."

Jo eyed the shift in body language. "We'll need to speak with him. Any other problem students?"

"None that were brought to my attention. You can check with his current TA, but it's only the third week of the semester."

"Any other issues? Problems with colleagues or staff?" Jo asked.

"Four years ago a fellow professor filed a sexual harassment claim against him."

Jo's eyebrows shot up. "I'd say that's burying the lede, Dr. Latimer. Please, continue."

The dean pulled a second folder out from under the first, and opened it. "You understand, these reports are confidential, and anonymous."

Jo kept her eyes on his face. "You don't know who filed it?"

A very slight tinge of color touched his cheeks. "I'm saying nobody's *supposed* to know who filed it, including, technically, me. I'm asking for your discretion."

"We have no desire to make anyone's life more difficult than can be avoided. But we can't make any promises along those lines," she said.

"And I'm sure you'll get a warrant for the records regardless, so there's no point drawing this out. The complaint was filed by Dr. Terrence Shawnessy, on behalf of another professor, Beth Morlinski. She went to Terry upset about inappropriate advances and pressure from Michael Whorton."

"Is that common, for someone else to file the complaint?"

"It happens. We have a zero-tolerance policy against any sort of harassment, and a strict code of ethics. Once Dr. Morlinski told Dr. Shawnessy about the inappropriate conduct, he was required to report it. Had he failed to do so, he put himself at risk for liability."

"What exactly did she allege?"

"That Michael made unwanted sexual advances toward her, and when she refused him, he threatened her tenure."

"He had the power to do that?"

"No, but it's not quite as simple as that. He was one of only three full professors in the department, which meant he'd be on her P&T committee. And he was department chair."

"P&T committee?" Arnett asked.

"Privileges and Tenure."

The implication hit Jo in the abdomen. "Was there an investigation?"

"No, because Dr. Morlinski left shortly after."

Jo stared at him. "I don't understand. Whether Dr. Morlinski was here or not, you had a potential sexual predator among your faculty. Surely you weren't okay with that?"

Roger Latimer smiled condescendingly. "These situations are far more complex than you understand, Detective. As far as I knew, the entire incident was fabricated."

Jo opened her mouth to respond, but Arnett spoke over her. "Where's Dr. Morlinksi working now?" he asked, pencil hovering over his notepad.

Roger shifted in his chair. "I believe she went to teach at a liberal arts college, but I'm not certain where."

"So she left because of the harassment?" Jo didn't bother to keep the indignation out of her voice.

Roger gave a slight shake of his head. "She didn't confide her reasons to me."

"Pretty coincidental timing, don't you think?" Arnett asked.

"I find that sort of speculation dangerous."

I'm sure you do, Jo thought. "Four years ago. Any problems more recently?"

He broke eye contact. "Nothing serious that I'm aware of."

Jo smiled, and tapped a nail on the arm of her chair. "Sounds like you're hedging a bit."

His eyes flashed back to hers. "I suppose I am. Academic politics are complicated and continual, Detective. Someone's always annoyed at someone about something. I don't have time to keep track of all the leaks around the water cooler."

Jo leaned in, smile tight. "Your receptionist mentioned you have appointments you don't want to cancel, Dr. Latimer. Shall we chase the subject around the room for a while, or would you prefer to keep your next meeting?"

Roger's eyes narrowed again. Then, he seemed to make a decision. "Dr. Whorton had opinions about a direction for the biology department that weren't universally popular. But," he hurried to add when Jo's eyebrows went up, "that describes someone in just about every department I've ever been associated with, especially when they're in crucial growing phases."

"But they're not dead, and Michael Whorton is. As chair, I imagine his *opinions* had somewhat more sway than other people's did?"

"He's no longer chair, Arthur Kerland is. But yes, while he was chair, he had a fair amount of influence. And, frankly, he wasn't the most adept at dealing with people."

"He wasn't well liked?" Arnett asked.

Roger opened and closed one hand. "I'd call it a bimodal distribution. He has loyal friends. But he tends to use strong-arm tactics to get what he wants."

"Who has he strong-armed?" Jo's question was a bullet.

Roger sighed. "I'm not thinking of anyone in particular, I'm commenting generally, based on how he dealt with me and others during meetings and negotiations. But I suspect the list is long. He wasn't nuanced there, and I can't imagine he was *more* diplomatic when dealing with people over whom he wielded power."

Jo leaned back, satisfied. "Sounds like we'll need to talk with the other professors in the department, starting with Dr. Shawnessy."

"Dr. Shawnessy isn't here any longer, and I'm not sure where you can find him."

Jo paused for a beat. "When did he leave?"

"Officially, just over two years ago. But he found out a year before he left that he wouldn't receive tenure. When that happens, you're given a year to find another job."

Jo let an astonished laugh escape. "Let me verify the timeline. Terry Shawnessy filed a complaint against Dr. Whorton on behalf of Dr. Morlinski about four years ago. Dr. Morlinksi left shortly after that, and within the year, Shawnessy discovered he wouldn't get tenure."

"Correct."

"Let me guess. Dr. Whorton was involved in that tenure decision?" Arnett asked.

"Also correct."

Jo exchanged a glance with Arnett, who continued. "Did Whorton know who filed the complaint against him?"

Roger blinked, and shifted uneasily. "Complaints are confidential."

"Not what I asked."

He cleared his throat. "All I can tell you is, if Michael found out who filed the complaint, he didn't learn it from me."

Jo's phone buzzed. She checked it to find a text from Marzillo, telling them they'd finished processing the scene. "Where are the security cameras located in Dyer Hall?"

"There aren't any inside, just a webcam pointed at the front of the building. I suspect that will change after today."

"Any chance that's the only entrance?" Jo asked.

"No. There's another at the back of the building, and one that leads to an external stairwell at the east end of each floor. No camera on either."

Arnett snorted. "Two cameras for your administrative entry here, but in the busy areas, not even one for each entrance."

Before Roger could respond, Jo asked, "What's the point of putting up a security camera over only one entrance out of three?"

"The camera wasn't put up for security. We have ten webcams around campus that people can view online. That's one of them."

"Why on earth?" Jo asked.

The dean shook his head, with a genuine smile. "Something about online presence, attracting students, giving parents a way to see the campus. I'm not sure they record, but I'll get the footage for you if they do."

"We'd also appreciate it if you could put out a call for anyone who happened to take any pictures or video in or around the building between noon and one fifteen." Jo stood up, pulling a card out of her blazer pocket, and Arnett followed her lead. "How soon can you get us contact information for the student and professors in question?"

"I'll have it to you within the hour, along with supplementary information. Ruth's already putting it together." He closed the folders on his desk, and handed them to Jo. "This information may also be helpful to you."

She opened each and did a quick scan. "Is this everything related to the complaints?"

"Everything I have."

"Thank you, Dr. Latimer."

*

Roger Latimer closed the door behind the two detectives, then sat back down at the desk. He stared at his phone until, two minutes later, it rang.

"They're gone." Ruth's brisk, efficient voice had the slightest anxious edge to it.

He thanked her and hung up, then pulled open the lower-right drawer of his desk. He lifted out the bottle of Laphroaig 18, and poured a finger into his empty mug. He threw it back, hardly registering the warmth in the back of his throat as he glanced at the picture on the far corner of his desk. His wife, their son, and their two daughters on Waikiki.

He poured another drink. He'd walked the line as best he could. Had it been good enough?

He drank back the scotch, popped several Tic Tacs in his mouth, and let Ruth know he was ready for his next meeting.

CHAPTER FIVE

"Sounds like quite a guy," Arnett said as they tramped back to the biology building. "Any thoughts so far?"

"Definitely no shortage of leads to follow up, hopefully something in the scene will point us the right way. There's always the possibility of random violence, but I just don't see that being the case here. Either the killer got very lucky, or they knew Michael Whorton's schedule. At least his office hours."

"How hard is that information to get, when it's posted right on the door?"

"Good question. Anybody on campus could find it out if they wanted to. But, based on my time in college, I'd want to know more than that before I planned a murder that might get interrupted. Like if he had a class right before and would likely be trailing a line of students back to his office, or if he was perpetually late. So we need to find out how accessible all that information is."

Arnett nodded, and they rode the elevator up in silence. When they stepped out, he examined the area and said, "Office couldn't be better placed. Gotta be right on top of it before you can see what's happening in it. But that alcove at the end of the hall? Easy to monitor who's coming and going, then slip in, stab him, and be back in the elevator in a couple of minutes."

Jo's brows raised. "When you put it like that, there's minimal risk. Anybody could have a legitimate reason to hang out and study there, so you wouldn't draw attention unless you did something odd. So you could wait, and if the professor showed up with a student, you'd just hunker down behind a textbook and come back another day. If he came alone, you could slip in, kill him, and slip back out."

Arnett nodded.

Jo continued. "We'll need to check out how busy this floor normally is at the target time of day. If it's as slow as we've seen, the odds would be against anyone running into you."

"Who else is down the hall?"

As they walked past the caution tape, Jo held up one finger to let Marzillo know they'd be right back. "Copier room. Restroom. Two empty offices." The final door in the hall belonged to Professor Steve Parminder. She ran her finger down the blocked schedule taped to his door. "He's got a class during the time Whorton held his office hours. I can't see why this area would have much traffic this time of day."

"Marzillo said the earliest possible time of death was 12:45. Could Parminder have killed him on his way to class?" Arnett said with a half-smile.

"Nope. The class ran from twelve to two."

Once back at Michael Whorton's office, Jo and Arnett slipped into protective gear. The tech assisting Marzillo, a middle-aged blond man she called Pepper, stepped out so they'd fit more easily in the small office. Jo scanned the room to get a feel for the scene. "Fill us in."

Marzillo recapped the basics she'd given them earlier as Jo angled as best she could around the blood.

Arnett considered. "Suggests some degree of surprise. Either he was on the phone and the killer came in, or he had someone in the office, stopped to take a phone call, and the person attacked while his back was turned."

"Any sign of the weapon?" Jo asked.

"Yep, killer was nice enough to leave it right on the floor for us, there. Buck 119 hunting knife." She pointed first to the floor, then to an evidence bag.

Arnett picked it up for a closer look. "Gre-aat. You can buy one of these at just about any sporting goods store on the planet, not to mention the web. No help there."

Jo's eyes dropped to the blood smears on the carpet where Marzillo pointed. As her eyes swept an arc over the rest of the floor, she spotted an oversized card just visible behind the door. "What's that?"

"A tarot card. Since it's across the room and didn't seem to be important, we didn't bag it. Should we?"

"May I?"

Marzillo handed Jo a pair of tweezers and an evidence bag. Jo lifted the card and deposited it inside the bag. She sealed it, labeled it, then took a closer look. The back of the card was dark blue with yellow stars; the front had a skeleton riding a horse over a field of corpses, with the Roman numeral XIII at the top and the word *Death* at the bottom.

She groaned, and flashed the card to Arnett. "You have to be kidding me. Did we just step into a B-movie? Please tell me this is a coincidence, that he has a tarot deck sitting out somewhere."

The four did a thorough search. Ten minutes later, they'd pulled out every book on the shelves, dug into every drawer, and gone through the metal cabinets above the desk, but came up empty.

"Maybe a student dropped it?" Marzillo asked.

"Or our killer has a flair for the dramatic," Jo said.

Arnett took the evidence bag from Jo for a closer look, and shook his head. "Makes zero sense. You pull out a tarot death card, flash it, and then stab the guy? What's the point?"

"Maybe he or she left the card beforehand, to scare Whorton?" Marzillo asked.

Jo shook her head. "If so, they failed, since he either left his door open, or turned his back on his killer. From the position, I'd say he hadn't even noticed it."

"Or maybe Whorton worshipped Satan," Arnett said.

"I'm picking up a skeptical vibe from you, Bob." Jo laughed. "You're probably right to be skeptical, but it's so discordant, and I like all our nails to be pounded down. Maybe there'll be prints on it." Jo shrugged, then glanced around at the blood pool and the handprint on the desk. "Is this all the blood there is? Just pooling, no spatter?"

"Nope. There wouldn't be from this type of wound, inflicted on the ground. You have what looks like cast off from the knife here, and here, but very little." She pointed to the floor.

"So precise, controlled strikes?"

"From what I'm seeing here, yes. Calm and collected. Not reactive. No real struggle."

"So our killer could have walked out with little to no blood on them?"

Marzillo didn't hesitate. "Almost certainly, especially because they dumped the knife. From what I can see, the only way they'd get blood on them was if Whorton touched them with the bloody hand, or if they stepped in the blood. Maybe some on the stabbing hand, but not much."

"Enough that they could easily step into the restroom two doors down and wash their hands?"

"Excellent point. We'll process the restroom before we go," Marzillo said.

Arnett said, "Smart thing would have been to wear gloves. Keeps your prints off everything, and you can just pull them off if you need to."

Marzillo nodded. "We'll check all the garbage cans in and around the building."

Jo turned toward the desk and pointed to the drawers. "Let's box up any files and documents for a closer look at the station. I know we have his computer, do we have his cell phone?"

"In the briefcase."

"Any chance you can get me records for that, and the landline, as soon as possible?"

"I'll do what I can, but keep in mind the lab's backed up since I went on vacation."

"There's never a good time, is there? Anything else we should take a look at before we go?"

Marzillo's gaze swept the room. "Don't think so. As far as we can tell, nothing else was disturbed, nothing else out of the ordinary. Should we keep it taped off for now?"

"Yeah, I can't imagine there's a pressing need to get into the space. They can contact us if so."

CHAPTER SIX

I hurried back after the deed was done and pulled up the Dyer Hall webcam on an incognito browser tab. Morbid curiosity? Maybe. But predominantly so I could gather as much information as possible. No amount of forethought could eliminate all risk, or control all factors. And one of the factors I couldn't control was who the primary investigators on the case would be.

I needed to know what I was up against, and who to keep my eye on. Whether I should adjust my strategy. Every human has their strengths and their weaknesses, their particular point of view. All insight was helpful.

By the time I had the site up, someone had discovered the body, and had called the police. They'd put up caution tape, and a uniformed officer was restricting access to the building. Surely the detectives couldn't have arrived yet, so I settled in to watch for them.

The waiting made me antsy, far more anxious than I'd been when I committed the murder itself. The last of the adrenaline rush faded away, and the high I'd ridden after killing Whorton was gone, replaced by an insistent nausea as the weight of reality compounded with each moment that passed.

I'd killed a man. The chain of events had been set in motion. There was no going back.

And all of the months I'd spent planning everything out, working out every detail, trying to predict every eventuality?

There was no way of knowing how successful any of it would be. The killing appeared to go exactly as planned, but who knows what mistakes I'd made? Something as small as an errant fiber or a student snapping selfies could undermine it all.

I clicked on my Beethoven playlist, hoping the music would calm my nerves, and tried to shake off my miscalculation. Because I'd expected this moment, watching as the police set to work, to be a pleasant interlude. A time to relax and enjoy my triumph, akin to the feeling of finishing a difficult task. I was disconcerted that it hadn't turned out that way.

But, I was glad to see it impacted me, glad to see evidence of my humanity. Otherwise, I'd be no different from Whorton.

Finally, the easily recognized detectives in their polyester suits and earnest expressions arrived. And my stomach dropped further.

One of them was a woman. I'd known that was a possibility, but I'd taken solace in the knowledge that the odds were against it. That complicated things, added a point of view I hadn't factored in, and that could be inconvenient.

I took a screenshot of the pair, then shrank the webcam tab off my browser into the corner of my screen. I monitored it as I pulled up the police department's website and ran through the divisions there. There was no consolidated list of officers or detectives—they weren't going to make it that easy for me—and the only pictures were of the lieutenants for each area. But further delving revealed a smattering of articles about department happenings and accomplishments. I scrolled through them, comparing my screenshot to all the pictures of women I came across.

Ten minutes later, I found her: Detective Josette Fournier. The same article mentioned that her partner was Bob Arnett, and within minutes I verified he was the other detective in question.

I spent the next hour compiling as much information about them as the internet would give me. Arnett was solid; several articles praised him, and one reported an unusually high crimes-solved rate. But several sources noted that Fournier had more commendations during her time on the force than any other officer, even those who'd been there longer, and had the highest closure rate in the department. She'd even served as Lieutenant of the Criminal Investigations Bureau a few years before. I spent a good half hour trying to find out why she'd returned to detective—whether she'd been demoted or had some sort of black mark on her record, anything I might use to my advantage—but came away with nothing.

A few more searches provided their home addresses. (It's deeply disturbing what you can find on the internet if you have even half a brain and a little persistence. Or if you're willing to pay for a public records search.)

I maximized the webcam again when they exited the building, and watched them closely, considering

Was there anything I should change? A different approach, something else to cover my tracks? I tested out several scenarios in my head, trying to see them through different eyes, looking for superior options.

No, I finally decided. There was nothing I knew for sure, initially at least, and to make changes without good reason invited disaster. The only path was to wait.

And watch.

I pulled up Google street view. I clicked up and down her street, evaluating her property and her neighbor's property, but couldn't find anything that would work. I rotated the camera across the street from hers, and spotted a large birdhouse hanging from the branches of a majestic oak tree.

The perfect place to hide a camera.

CHAPTER SEVEN

By the time they finished talking to Marzillo, Dean Latimer had all the information they'd requested waiting for them, along with an SD card of the webcam footage. He also verified that Rosanna Trenton was a straight-A student who was well liked by her professors. "No motive, and a tight timeline. I can't see her being our killer," Arnett said. "So what's our plan of attack?"

"I don't believe for a hot minute Latimer doesn't know the ins and outs of every dispute in the School of Natural Sciences. There's something he's not telling us. I say we start with the colleagues."

But the other professors on the list were either in classes or had left for the day. Jo scanned the papers Dean Latimer left for them. "I'm not interested in playing hide-and-seek. I'll have Ruth set up interviews with the professors and TA tomorrow. In the meantime, I say we find the problem-child student."

They adjourned to the car to find a current address for him. "Looks like he's downtown now, on Euclid," Jo said.

Arnett looked at his watch. "I'm starving. Can we grab dinner before we head over there? Meatball subs?"

Jo's stomach growled. "On it." While Arnett eased the car into traffic, she selected the contact for Sal's and ordered the food. "Next up, a call to ADA Rockney. And if Garber just quit the lieutenant position, I'm sure he's gonna be in a *great* mood."

Rockney picked up on the third ring. "Fournier. What'd you find out about the professor?"

"Marzillo just finished the initial pass on the crime scene." She gave him a brief overview. "No clear leads, because everybody has a reason to hate this guy and we have a mountain of possibilities to sort through."

Rockney heaved a frustrated sigh. "Dammit. Did Arnett tell you about Garber?"

"He did." She fought back the urge to say more, grateful now that Arnett had kept her from being blindsided.

"Then you know I have my hands full, and I'll need someone to step up as interim."

She remained silent, nails digging into her own thigh with the stress of keeping quiet.

He sighed again. "Which means we'll all be strapped, and I can't give you a full team. Lucky for you, Lopez's partner is still out on medical leave, and she's been lending her tech skills to the lab since Renny retired. She can help."

That was a silver lining, at least. Christine Lopez had partnered with Arnett during Jo's brief tenure as lieutenant, and her tech savvy had been invaluable when the three of them needed to catch a serial killer hiding in cyberspace. She was bright, energetic, and professional. And since Marzillo had mentioned the lab was backed up as it was, Lopez's help would be a godsend.

"Great, I'll call her." Jo signed off quickly before he could change his mind, and dialed Lopez.

She picked up on the first ring. "Jo! How's it going?"

After initial pleasantries, Jo passed on Rockney's directive, and recapped the case for Lopez. "Our first priority is Michael Whorton's computer and his cell, so if you can check them for anything helpful, that would be great. Marzillo's got a few boxes of paperwork, too, but hopefully we'll be in shortly to look at that."

"Anything else?"

"I'll text over some names we need to look into. We have current info for most of them, except for a woman called Beth

Morlinksi. She used to be a professor at the university until about four years ago."

"On it."

As she disconnected with Lopez, Arnett pulled into Sal's. They collected their food from the counter and grabbed a red-and-white checked table in the back. Jo took a long inhale over the top of her sub, relishing the scent of warm Italian spices, tomato, and cheese before she dove in. Arnett finished a third of his sandwich in his first bite, and they both turned their attention to the files Roger Latimer had given them while they continued eating.

A few minutes later, Arnett let out a low whistle. "Take a look at this. E-mail from Crawley to Whorton."

Jo took the sheet from him and skipped past the headers.

Michael Whorton—

(Note I will no longer use the titles 'Doctor' or 'Professor' when I address you, because you clearly do not deserve the respect of either position.)

I have come to you twice now to discuss your ineffective teaching, in the hopes you'd have enough concern for your students to listen. I tried explaining that no matter how much I study, I cannot pass your exams, and I get unacceptable grades on my papers. I am extremely bright; I have a high IQ and exceptional writing capabilities. I have scoured my papers and exams for any justification of the failing grades you assigned me, and can only conclude the problem is yours, not mine. I'm not surprised you're unable to recognize intelligence and talent when it's sitting in front of you—you are incapable of recognizing anything that doesn't feed your ego. When I watch you banter with the sycophantic sub-par students in your class, I become violently ill. Of course you failed me, I refused to take the knee in front of your greatness! Uninterested in dealing with such a peon, you brushed me off to your TA, and I went, hoping that maybe, just maybe, she'd have enough integrity to see sense. But she proved to be another top-notch dotard unable to see past your ersatz patina of accomplishment. Like you, she tried to blame me for your deficiencies as a teacher, but in the process, did admit that you'd added up the score on my last exam incorrectly. I danced a jig of joy! How deliciously absurd it was to discover that a man so enamored with his own pretension cannot do simple math!

But I digress. This e-mail is a warning to you that I will no longer tolerate your clear bias against me. Should I fail your course, I want you to be certain that I will sue you, and the university. I do not run from bullies.

Most sincerely,

Greg Crawley

"Holy shit. Whether he deserved the grade he got or not, this guy wrote the textbook on grandiose and delusional," Jo said.

Arnett tapped the file in front of him. "Whorton reported the e-mail to the administration, worried that Crawley had some sort of mental illness. After that, Crawley *did* file a complaint when he failed the class, but it went nowhere, since the administration had already reviewed the grading on his exams and papers." He pushed the file toward her. "See for yourself."

Jo opened the bluebook and set it next to the associated answer key. As in the e-mail, Crawley's writing was fluid and advanced in terms of structure and vocabulary. As Roger Latimer had claimed, his answers were off topic and rambled, but he did touch on the answers indicated in the rubrics. Jo couldn't determine whether the deducted points were fully justified or not. She shook her head. "I can't tell if he's got a persecution complex too, or if he deserved to fail. Did the administration do anything when Whorton reported this e-mail?"

He flipped back a page. "Apparently they suggested to Crawley that he visit the counseling center and speak to one of the therapists there."

"Did he go?"

"Nothing says one way or the other."

"So, whether deserved or not, he didn't like his treatment in the class. He sent what can, at best, be considered an inappropriate e-mail to Whorton, and, at worst, a not-so-veiled threat. He partially follows through on that threat by filing a complaint against Whorton when he fails the class. I can't imagine he reacted well when they told him the grade stood as given."

Arnett answered as he chewed. "Question is, was he angry enough to kill?"

CHAPTER EIGHT

Twenty minutes later Jo rubbed at a spot of marinara on her blouse, as Arnett pulled up to Greg Crawley's apartment. Downtown Oakhurst was fairly well-to-do, but The Golden Horse Apartments were on the outskirts of the downtown area and showed a little more wear than most. Sparse landscaping framed the dingy beige paint, with raggedy bushes and bare sections in a lawn made up of weeds. Each unit had a separate landing on a zig-zagging external staircase, but while some residents spruced theirs up with potted flowers and plants, only a few third-floor residents were brave enough to put out chairs or tables. University regalia dotted the windows, and Imagine Dragons wafted up from the well-lit pool area along with the scent of marijuana. Jo glanced toward it, trying not to think about how much underage drinking they'd find if they moseyed through that gate.

Greg Crawley turned out to be a tall, muscular man in his thirties, far older than the typical OakhurstU undergraduates. A dark band of stubble ringed his pale head, and his brown eyes were set close together, under thick glasses that intensified the effect.

Jo identified herself and Arnett, and asked if they could come in.

His glare flicked between them. "We can talk just fine right here."

"Something you don't want us to see?" Arnett asked.

"I know my rights." Color rose up his neck.

Jo sighed mentally. She knew his type well, and guilty or innocent, dealing with him wouldn't be pleasant. She pulled out her notebook, and smiled. She and Arnett had agreed she should take the lead, on the off-chance he played better with women in authority than men. "No problem, we understand. Smart of you to protect yourself."

Greg looked her up and down, but remained silent.

"You know why we're here?" she asked.

"I can guess. It's all over the news that Michael Whorton was murdered in his office today. I'm surprised it didn't happen sooner. But it wasn't me. I was in another class at the time."

"Sounds like he wasn't very well liked."

The squint around his eyes relaxed slightly. "He was an asshole."

Jo laughed. "I had my share of those professors when I was in school. Which brand of asshole was he?"

"The horrible-teacher-with-a-huge-ego brand. If you didn't understand something, it couldn't possibly be his fault, it was because you were stupid. And if you called him on it, he failed you."

Jo's voice turned concerned. "He called you stupid?"

Heat flashed in his eyes. "No, he knew better than to say something like that outright. But he made sure you knew. In my case, he suggested I *avail myself of the additional resources at the student services center* since I was struggling." Greg framed the words in air quotes. "Also told me to get a tutor, or go to the TA office hours and talk with them about how to study the material. Like I'm illiterate."

"And the TA was no help?" I asked.

His scowl deepened. "She was useless. Just sat there nodding and saying 'uh-huh,' then suggested I go talk to someone in the counseling office. I told her the problem wasn't me, it was *him*. I'm not sure what I expected, of course she'd be in league with him."

"The counseling center, that seems like a leap. Did you go?" Jo asked.

Suspicion crossed his face, and he leaned back slightly. "No. I'm not going to buy into some label that I'm some sort of defective."

She noted the sore spot, but nodded. "And then he failed you?"

Greg's eyes flashed again, and one hand tightened into a fist. "Of course he failed me. I told them he would. I got a C on the first test, and a D on the second, *after* I tried to talk to him about the first. They just let him do it, they don't give a shit. Of course they sided with him when I filed the complaint. Way easier to label me trouble and get rid of me than roll over on one of their professors. That grade lost me my financial aid, and *that* made my parents cut me off."

"They cut you off? That seems drastic. Anybody can have a bad semester."

He opened his mouth to speak, then snapped it shut again before finally answering. "My mother said I'd broken her heart. And I can't blame her for being deeply disappointed, except it wasn't my fault. I didn't really fail. And now I'm trying to fit in double-shifts flipping burgers so I can stay in school. Which makes it pretty much impossible for me to study. And if I don't raise my GPA this semester, they'll throw me out of school."

Jo furrowed her brow sympathetically. "Can't you talk to someone else? They have an ombudsperson, right? Or maybe an attorney?"

His eyes narrowed slightly, and he paused again before responding. "No point. Nobody's going to do anything."

Jo shook her head. "More power to you. I'm not sure I could just let it go like that."

His face turned to stone. "I didn't say I let it go."

Arnett spoke up. "No? Got something planned?"

His eyes flashed to Arnett. "No need. Haven't you heard? Someone else took care of it for me."

CHAPTER NINE

"He's got balls, I'll give him that. Didn't even bother to pretend he was sorry to see Whorton dead," Arnett said when they reached the car.

"I can't decide if he killed Whorton, or just wishes he had," Jo replied. "And even if we get confirmation he was in the other class, what's to say he didn't duck out, dash over to the other building, and stab him?"

"I got no problem believing he'd walk right back into class and start taking notes again like nothing ever happened."

An hour later they'd dug up the phone number for the teacher's assistant in Greg's class. She confirmed that he'd been in class—she was hyper-aware of him because he was 'icky'—but couldn't say whether he'd stepped out during the lecture, since he always sat in the back.

"Where to now?" Arnett asked, as he pulled out into traffic.

Jo glanced at the time. "Doesn't Parminder have office hours now? I bet we can talk him into fitting us in."

Arnett changed lanes, and fifteen minutes later, Jo and Arnett were again walking past Michael Whorton's taped-off office, down the hall to Steve Parminder's office. The man who opened the door was stylishly dressed, something Jo wasn't accustomed to in a professor, with a perfectly ironed cerulean button-down tucked carefully into black slacks. His black hair was arranged in the sort of casually rakish spikes Jo knew took artful skill.

"Steve Parminder?"

"Yes. You're the detectives, I assume?"

Jo went through the initial introductions as Dr. Parminder motioned to an oak desk dotted with orderly stacks of papers. "Dean Latimer indicated there might be some behind-the-scenes politics relevant to Michael Whorton's death."

Dr. Parminder sat, leaned back in his chair, thought for a moment, then nodded. "I don't like speaking ill of the dead, but I also don't see how it helps anyone to prevaricate. Not many people cared for Michael, including me. Professionally, he and I were at odds. He had a very specific vision for the future of the biology department, and it conflicted with just about everyone else's."

"How so?"

"He wanted a focus on neurobiology."

Jo glanced down at her notes "I'm guessing your emphasis in biochemistry doesn't fit with that?"

"Not in his version, no."

"So he had the power to make those changes? At least when he was chair, I'm guessing?" she asked.

"His status as chair was a help, but wasn't crucial." Parminder glanced back and forth between them. "How much do you know about the structure of academic programs?"

"Not enough. I'd appreciate any insight you can give us."

"Large, established programs have the ability to build strength across a wide range of sub-specialties within a discipline. Meaning, their biology department can have a strong neurobiology faculty, a strong immunology and pathogenesis faculty, organismic biology faculty, et cetera. But when you have a small program like this one, you have to make choices. You can take one of two approaches. You can focus on one sub-specialty, say, neurobiology, and be very strong at it, or you can go the jack of all trades and master of none route. In that case you have one, maybe two, professors in as many sub-specialties as possible, so you'll be able to offer breadth for your teaching and your graduate students. There are pluses and minuses to both types, depending on what you're trying to do. In line with the university's previous mission statement, our program embraced the breadth approach." He paused and checked Jo's and Arnett's expressions.

"With you," Arnett confirmed.

"I'm not sure Michael was ever happy with that, but when we were allotted our share of the monies from the UniversalApps donation, everything changed regardless. Biology was given our own building, and the resources for top-notch labs—space, equipment, and new billets."

"Billets?" Jo asked.

"Sorry, academia loves jargon. That's what we call professor hires."

"Got it."

"So, suddenly we had to make decisions about how to expand. Some wanted to continue with breadth. Whorton did not."

"But he's only one man," Jo said.

"Two, actually. He and Arthur Kerland were united on this issue. Which adds up to two of the three tenured professors here."

Jo's eyebrows raised. "And you're the third."

"Correct. They initially spun a tale that included biochemistry, to lure me to their side. I didn't go along, but it didn't matter. They had the numbers."

Jo looked down at the sheet again. "There were three junior faculty at that time, too. They had no say?"

"They get a vote on hiring decisions, yes. But it's not as simple as that."

"Why not?"

Parminder shifted in his seat, and glanced toward the door. "Only tenured professors sit on P&T cases."

Jo held up her hand. "So what you're saying is, if people didn't play along, their futures were in danger? But surely there's some sort of protection against that?"

"Of course there is, in theory."

"What's the reality?" Arnett asked.

"There's a sad truth in academia. If people want to work with you, they'll find a way to get you tenure. If not, they'll make sure you don't. Tenure evaluations are highly subjective. You're evaluated on three main areas: research, teaching, and administrative duties. In theory, all three have equal weight. But in reality, at a research university, research is the end-all-be-all. You have to publish, in the right journals, and show potential impact on your field. Even then, there are no hard and fast rules about what constitutes 'right' or 'enough' on any of those levels. Add to that the fact that one researcher's paradigm may take two to three times as long to yield results as another's, so they might only get out a third as many journal articles in the same time. Someone who has personal issues with that researcher can use the relative paucity of publications to deny them tenure, while someone who likes them can point to the value of their difficult paradigm to argue for promoting them. Same researcher, same research, manipulated based on personal agenda. The other two prongs are similar, although they count for far less."

"So, even if someone has great teaching evaluations, that isn't enough?"

"At a research university, you can be the best teacher that ever walked the earth, and not get tenure. And, being the worst won't prevent you from getting it. Administrative duties are somewhere in the middle, but are just as subjective as research evaluations. And proving bias is nearly impossible unless you have hard evidence of discrimination predating your evaluation."

Jo's head swam. She'd had a hard enough time dealing with politics on the force, but this sounded like a breeding ground for Machiavellian evil.

"So Michael Whorton wanted to take the department in a more focused direction, and that meant some of the existing professors were going to have to go bye-bye?" Arnett asked.

"Correct."

Jo scanned the list of professors, current and previous. "And the three junior professors at that time? What did they research?"

"Geraldine Mapa is a neurobiologist, so she fit with their plans. Beth Morlinski was our evolutionary biologist, and Terry Shawnessy's specialty was in immunology and pathogenesis. Not commensurate with their plans."

"Morlinski's departure must have been convenient for him, then. And Terry Shawnessy didn't get tenure, which I'm guessing isn't a coincidence?" Jo asked.

Steve glanced toward the door again. "I'd say *convenient* is a generous way of describing what happened. I think it's safe to say Beth realized her prospects were better elsewhere. Whether there was any sort of active pressure, I can't say for certain, but I'd guess there was. As for Terry, all I can say is his tenure committee's decision wasn't unanimous. I voted for promotion."

"That must have put a target on your back," Arnett said.

"There's already a target on my back. Not much reason to keep from doing what's right."

"If they're coming after you too, why don't you leave?" Arnett watched Parminder carefully.

Parminder shrugged. "I've considered it. But I have two daughters who have an established life here they don't want to be ripped away from, and my wife's family is here. Relocating us all, even if I found a job within Massachusetts, would be difficult. I'm high enough up on that ladder that I'm not easy to get rid of, and I don't particularly care who likes me."

Jo hid her smile; she liked Steve Parminder. "We've covered the professors who clashed with Michael. Was there anybody else?"

Parminder gave a genuine laugh. "How much time do you have? Administrators, because he was the very antithesis of a team player, didn't care for rules, and would stab you in the back as soon as look at you. Students, because he didn't care about teaching, and they knew it. And—" He stopped short.

"And?" Jo held his gaze.

Parminder's face tensed, and his eyes closed. "And a long line of women, including his wife, because—well—the best way to put it is he didn't comport himself as a gentleman."

"Cheated at cards?" Arnett shot, blank faced.

Parminder's glance was sharp. "The cheating part is right."

Jo nodded. "Can you give us names?"

Parminder sighed. "I try to avoid that sort of gossip as much as possible. I just know it was a long-running joke. More like a warning, really. And the strain in his marriage was palpable."

Arnett rifled the pages of his notebook with his thumbnail, usually a sign he'd thought of something important, and always a sign he was ready to go. Jo stood. "Thank you so much for your help, Dr. Parminder, your candor is much appreciated. Please let us know if you remember anything else."

✦

"What's on your mind?" Jo asked as she pulled away from the university.

"Nothing, exactly. Just that everybody we talk to, except Crawley, claims they didn't want him dead, but adds in another layer of people who did. Students, professors, now wives and potential lovers. All of which makes me more antsy that I can't talk to the most likely suspect."

Jo glanced at the car's clock. "Nine thirty on a Tuesday night. Whorton's wife may or may not be in a car driving home, but either way, time to give her another try." Jo pulled out her phone, entered Camilla Whorton's number, and was startled when she picked up on the second ring. Jo identified herself, and her purpose. "We'd like to speak to you as soon as possible."

"I'm leaving in the morning, it should take me about four hours. Barring unforeseen traffic, I should be home and available by about twelve thirty. But I have an appointment I can't miss at two."

"We'll make sure to be there at twelve thirty on the dot."

"Very well," she said, and hung up.

Jo stared at the phone and recapped the brief conversation for Arnett. "Expediency. That's a version of grief I haven't encountered before from a vic's spouse."

Arnett shook his head.

Jo looked down at the manila envelope Ruth Henderson had left for them. "I can't see us having any more luck with interviews tonight." She paused. She wanted to dig further into the mass of information waiting for them back at the station, but didn't feel right about keeping Arnett away from home. "It's late, I'm sure you want to get home to Laura."

Arnett shot her a look and smiled. "I know you better than that. We should at least take a look at the camera footage tonight, even though it's almost certainly a waste of time. Anything to help us narrow down this suspect field."

Jo made a U-turn and drove to the station. "Sounds like a plan."

They grabbed coffee from the break room, then plugged the SD card into Jo's desktop and clicked on the video. The time stamp started at eleven forty-five, an hour before the earliest plausible time of death, and ran for an hour and a half. The camera pointed down the side of the building, capturing the entrance as well as the main doors to Dyer Hall. They settled in to watch as a trickle of students ran into the hall, late for their noon class.

Jo sipped the coffee gingerly to make sure it wasn't a slop of sediment, since any coffee left out this close to shift change was hit-or-miss. Tonight was miss—more toxic sludge than coffee. She winced, and thanked goodness she'd added extra milk. "No idea how you drink this stuff black."

"Still better than the herbal tea Laura makes me drink at home."

Jo pondered the horror of life without caffeine as they stared at the screen in front of them. Leaves blew in a circle between the lecture hall and the building doors, and a student plopped onto one of the benches and pulled out a sketchpad. Students entered and exited in ones and twos, just enough to keep Arnett from being able to fast-forward much.

"Are those kids really college-aged? They look about fourteen to me," Jo said.

"You're one to talk. You even have any gray hairs yet?"

"That's between me and my stylist, and she knows I carry a gun."

They slipped back into a companionable silence, taking stills of everybody who entered or exited, while keeping a special eye out for any student who looked like Crawley, or for any older adults who entered the building. Three did, all angled so their backs were to the camera, and Jo marked the time so they could return to the locations as needed. A flood of students poured out of the lecture hall at one, then stood around in small groups discussing some paper or exam they'd received back, most likely comparing answers and points docked.

The trickle of students turned back into a stream entering for the next class, then died down again shortly after. Then nothing of interest until two campus police strode through the doors, followed fifteen minutes later by the city police.

"Can't say I expected more. Who knows, maybe one of these is our killer," he motioned to the computer, "but I doubt it. Anybody with half a brain would use the back entrance."

"Agreed."

Arnett yawned. "I'm done for the night. Back here bright and early to head over for those interviews?"

"Sounds good."

Jo jotted notes on a legal pad while he grabbed his coat and headed to the door. Then, she picked up her phone and sent a text.

You up?

CHAPTER TEN

Jo propped herself up on her elbows and took a long, languorous look at Eric's chest, appreciating the smattering of brown curls that covered the sizable pectorals, and his hint of six-pack. "I'm so glad you don't shave your chest. I like a man who looks like a man."

Eric laughed, and pulled her up his side. "These kids today." He kissed the nape of her neck and worked his way up to her mouth. "Nice surprise, hearing from you tonight."

Jo inhaled his earthy musk, wondered if it were his natural scent or cologne, and pushed down the small tinge of guilt that whizzed through her. "Sorry about the lack of notice. We had a homicide this afternoon, and it went later than I would have liked."

He tugged at her lip with his teeth. "So I'm your stress relief?"

"Yoga and meditation are for suckers." She slipped her finger into the curls. "I'd kill for a pizza. Are you hungry?"

"Your wish is my command. Pizza My Mind?"

"I much prefer Sal's…" She kissed his chest.

"They're closed. Combo?"

"Mmm." She watched his profile as he ordered the pizza. She'd never had a type, exactly, but couldn't deny a soft spot for dark hair and soulful brown eyes. And while she usually found dimples a bit too sweet on men, his took the edge off his rugged park-ranger looks—well-tanned skin, chiseled chin, thick brows—and kept him from looking like a weathered mountaineer.

As he finished the call and set the phone down, she checked the time, and sighed. He had at least another ten minutes left on his refractory period. She'd have to find a way to fill the time. "So tell me about your day."

He wound a strand of her hair around his finger. "Same old. Had to clean up a couple of dead fisher cats. And the coyote population has skyrocketed this year. They're talking about opening the deer hunt to include coyote too, but I'm not sure how possible that is."

A vivid image of a fisher cat corpse flashed before her eyes, and she bit back a quip about how they both spent the day with death. Experience had taught her that no matter how tough an exterior men put forward, they didn't like that kind of humor on their dates. "The coyotes are getting dangerous?"

He shook his head in a back-and-forth maybe. "There've been more pets reported missing around the outskirts. When they don't have enough to eat, they get more desperate."

Jo's stomach grumbled, and she looked down at it. "I know how they feel."

He laughed. "Tomorrow I'm on field-trip duty, I get to take a few classes on tours. That's always a fun day."

She traced his smile with her fingertip. "That's very sweet."

"You gotta get 'em into preservation while they're young. Teach them about respecting nature, and how to put out those campfires. Besides, kids are good for your soul."

She thought about her best friend Eva's kids and her nieces, the closest she was likely to get to having her own. Adorable, but wild and filled with non-stop energy, she enjoyed spending time with them, but was glad to be able to hand them back to Eva or Sophie when she'd reached her limit.

She shifted mental gears, did a time check, and let a wicked grin spread over her face. "You know what else is good for your soul?"

He matched her grin with one of his own. "Show me."

They finished up with just enough time to throw on their clothes before the pizza arrived.

*

At five the next morning, Jo slipped out of Eric's warm bed and pulled on her clothes. She let herself out, taking care to close the door quietly behind her so she wouldn't wake him. She raced home and hurried through her shower, already regretting the only-four hours of sleep she'd managed to get. She threw a black suit over a blue blouse, then put on her thirty-second face—a swipe of mascara and a dab of berry lipstick to play off the blue blouse. Every morning she was tempted to skip even that, but as much as she hated to admit her mother was right, people responded better to someone at least somewhat put together. She glanced at the time, and swore under her breath. Thank God it was Arnett's day to pick up the coffee.

When she grabbed her phone again, it vibrated a notification. Her mother had left a voicemail while she was in the shower. "Josette, I need you to call me back as soon as you get this, it's urgent. I'm not kidding."

The edge in her mother's voice worried her. Admittedly, her mother lived in a different sort of reality, where a missing recipe book was *urgent* and not hearing from her daughter at least every few days constituted an *emergency*. But this was something else, something more intense. She tapped the screen to call her back.

"Oh, thank goodness, I wasn't sure when you'd call."

Her mother's tone canceled the annoyance hovering in Jo's periphery. "What's wrong?"

"Your father called last night to tell me he's been diagnosed with prostate cancer."

Jo's entire body went numb. "Cancer? But why did he call *you*?"

"You know how he is, Josie. He's not going to call you or Sophie directly. He said he didn't want to bother you, so he left it to me."

Jo groaned inwardly at the mention of her sister. They'd never gotten along even as children, so much so they'd gone on separate trips to visit their father in New Orleans. But adulthood had magnified the complexity of their relationship, such that for over a decade, Jo had limited contact with her sister as much as possible. Her mother complained about it periodically, but Jo firmly believed their ability to keep up a civil front at holiday dinners depended on that critical space. She didn't want to call her sister for any reason, let alone one as explosive as this.

"Does Sophie know yet?"

"I just got off the phone with her."

Jo tried not to audibly sigh with relief. "How serious is the cancer?"

"Serious enough that he actually went to see a doctor. And serious enough that he'd call."

Jo nodded to the empty room. For years, whenever she reminded her father to get a checkup, his only response was to glare at her like she'd suggested he wear a bra. And she couldn't remember the last time he'd willingly updated anyone about his life; he kept those details close to his chest like an alligator drowning its prey. Whatever led to the doctor visit wasn't pretty, and whatever the doctor had said was uglier still. "I'll call him, right now."

"Please let me know what you find out. You know your pépé on that side died of cancer."

"Don't worry, Ma. Prostate cancer is very treatable. I'm sure he's going to be fine."

"From your lips," her voice quivered. She hung up.

Jo pulled up her father's contact and hit send, but the call went straight to voicemail. "Dad, call me back as soon as you get this."

She snatched up her keys and her badge, and bolted toward the door, cursing how very typical it was for her father to drop a bomb and then disappear into a foxhole.

CHAPTER ELEVEN

I woke the next morning far more apprehensive about the second kill than I'd been about the first. I knew I wasn't likely to enjoy the second kill any more than I enjoyed killing Whorton, and this time I wouldn't even get to see the realization on her face. But I didn't anticipate how very nervous I'd be.

I reminded myself that anxiety had a useful side-benefit— it ensured I didn't rest on my laurels. The key to success is never, ever taking for granted that everything will go according to plan. And to allow myself to sleep at night, I'd created not just a plan A and B, but also a C and D.

The time had come. And my window was small.

The only part of her routine that never changed was her weekday morning run. When it came to her fitness, if nothing else, she was disciplined—the only days she missed were when she was out of town.

So in the wee hours, I ignored my nausea and purchased an Egg McMuffin with coffee so I'd have an excuse to linger in a parking lot near the jogging trail, then pulled out the phone to watch her via the camera I hid near her apartment. As soon as she left home I'd head out, which would give me plenty of time to beat her to the trail and position myself.

Her start time varied somewhat each day—I assumed some days it was harder to get out of bed and face herself in the mirror than others—but never by more than fifteen minutes. So when she was twenty minutes late, I started to worry. I ran my mind over everything I'd seen her do in the last forty-eight hours. I hadn't seen any sign she wasn't feeling well, and even so, her religious morning runs had never been preempted by illness, even when she caught a nasty cold. There had been no midweek event the night before to give her an unexpected hangover, and, in fact, the light in her window had gone out half an hour earlier than it typically did.

When there was still no sign of her after half an hour, my anxiety skyrocketed, and the McMuffin flopped in my stomach like a dying fish.

I pushed down the nausea and forced myself to stay calm. And logical. This wasn't a problem—I had my backup plans. I could try again the following day, although that would mean racing back from the Berkshires in the early hours. If that failed for some reason, I could make another attempt on Friday morning. The odds were astronomical she'd miss three mornings in a row. But if she did, I had a far more expedient, if less elegant, plan D in my metaphorical back pocket. Stashed right next to my very literal Beretta pistol.

I crumpled my wrapper and my cup, and started the car. As I drove back home, I fine-tuned the timing for that night's plan, slotting in the additional task I now had for the following morning.

CHAPTER TWELVE

"You look like something the cat puked up." Arnett handed Jo a large Starbucks mocha.

"I got a call from my father. Or, my mother did, actually."

Arnett's head snapped up. "He called your mother?"

She sipped her coffee, and stared straight ahead. "He told her he has prostate cancer."

"Shit. Did they catch it early?"

"I don't know. I haven't been able to reach him."

He put a hand on Jo's shoulder. "I'm sure it's fine."

She waved her free hand in a dismissive gesture. "I don't want to think about it. I'll just drive myself crazy when I don't even know what's going on."

He examined her face for a long moment, but then looked away. "Gotcha. Back to Whorton, then. Next on the list is Shawnessy, unless our priorities have changed."

Terry Shawnessy's apartment was in the most depressed part of town, and his complex, a boxy cement tenement building, was in desperate need of paint. The interior stairwell reeked of cheap air freshener failing to mask urine.

Terry opened the door almost as soon as Arnett knocked, wearing faded brown slacks and a blue button-down shirt. After they introduced themselves, he stepped back and allowed them in. Jo initially placed him around forty-five, but reconsidered when she stepped past him and got a closer look at the strain pinching his face.

The tiny one-bedroom apartment was nearly as spartan inside as the outside was shabby. While the furniture was of higher quality than the surroundings, Terry had no artwork and nothing homey, except a few pictures of a woman and a young man.

"Can I offer you coffee? Tea?" he asked, and motioned to the gray couch against the wall.

Jo shook her head. "No, thanks. We'll just get started, if you don't mind?"

Terry nodded. "Yes, let's get down to it. I'm sure the first thing you want to know is where I was when Michael Whorton was murdered. Unfortunately for me, I don't have much of an alibi. I was out running errands, and I already checked—no convenient receipts timestamped on or around the reported time of death."

"How is that possible if you were running errands?" Arnett asked.

"Because I spent a large chunk of that time at a coin-operated laundromat."

"Your complex doesn't have laundry facilities?"

"Two washers, and they're both broken."

"Most laundromats these days have cameras, hopefully we can clear you that way. Address?" Arnett's pen hovered over his pad.

Terry gave the cross streets, and listed the other establishments he'd visited that day, then continued. "And to save everybody time, I'm going to put my cards on the table—if you're here, you're already aware I had plenty of reason to dislike Michael."

Jo kept her face passive. "We'd like to hear your side of the story."

"Sure. The short version is, Michael destroyed my career."

Cards on the table indeed. Was everyone going to admit to wanting Michael Whorton dead? "How did that go down?"

"It's a long story, but the straw that broke the camel's back was most likely the complaint I filed against him. A colleague came to me desperately upset because he came on to her, and when she rebuffed him, he told her she'd better rethink her answer if she valued her job."

"Beth Morlinski."

His jaw tightened. "Are you aware that you shouldn't even know that name? That the entire complaint was supposed to be anonymous? I actually believed that, and believed I'd be protected as a whistleblower." He smiled wanly. "Didn't take long to learn how ridiculously naive that was."

Jo shook her head in sympathy. "What sort of overture did he make toward her?"

"Trapped her in a corner and tried to kiss her, grabbed her breast. Nothing at all open to interpretation."

"That must have been a difficult position to be in, deciding to file that complaint," Arnett said.

He leaned forward slightly. "Not nearly as difficult as having a senior colleague who'll decide your tenure demand sexual favors from you."

"Agreed. But at least she got out of there. Was she able to find a job after she left?" Jo asked.

"I don't know, we didn't keep in touch. I think she wanted to cut ties with anything to do with the university, and I can't say I blame her for that."

"That must have left you high and dry after you stuck your neck out for her," Arnett said.

He met Arnett's gaze. "Not at all, I was just glad she found a solution. And I wouldn't have been able to live with myself if I hadn't. But, to be honest, I'm not sure it mattered. Michael was going to get rid of me one way or the other, although I didn't know that at the time."

"How so?"

"I didn't fit into his ambitions for the department. Around the same time I found out about the harassment, the department was in the process of reviewing potential hires for an open billet. When it came time to vote, I voted for a different candidate than Michael favored. His reaction was ugly. From that point on, he took every opportunity to make life as difficult for me as possible."

She shook her head, and tried not to sound like Columbo. "Help me out. You're just one person. He had the numbers to outvote you, didn't he?"

His smile took on an ironic edge. "He did, but the dean and the provost, along with the committees that approve the hires, don't like to see split votes. It signals discord. In a small department like ours, even one dissenting vote raises a flag, and I would have been required to write a minority opinion explaining why I wasn't in favor of the hire." He leaned forward again. "And the problem with that is, I wasn't voting out of political interest. I truly didn't believe the candidate was qualified for the job. The committee would have taken that seriously, would have looked into my points, and would have rejected the hire. Michael couldn't risk they'd look too closely at the split agendas for the department, and realize two assistant professor's futures were in danger. Also, it would have given me documentation that the later decision to deny me tenure was retaliatory. So, they abandoned the hire."

Machiavelli again flashed through Jo's mind. "So, you believe he torpedoed your tenure case because of it?"

A red flush tinged his cheeks. "There's no doubt about it. Michael made it clear. And he made my life a living hell in the interim, probably hoping I'd leave before my time was up."

"Why not sue?"

His laugh was dry. "What you know and what you can prove are two different things. Especially when facing an administration whose standard of proof is *avoid-trouble-at-all-costs*. I suspect that's why Beth left, too. She wasn't going to get justice."

Jo nodded, as did Arnett. Internal regulations, even federal laws, were only as effective as those who had the power to enforce them. "Where did you go when you left the university?"

"I'll let you know when I get there."

"What do you mean?"

His voice flattened, and he looked out the window. "There were no academic openings in my specialty at any nearby universities, so I applied for several industry positions in Boston and Western Mass. Capwell Laboratories, Hawthorne Therapeutics, Parkland Tech, a few others. But news of my demise preceded me."

"The industry is that small?" Arnett asked.

Terry paused a moment before he replied. "I had a reference from Steve Parminder, and another from Beth. But apparently that wasn't enough."

Jo read between the lines. "You think Whorton was tanking you?"

"Somebody was." He shrugged, and rubbed a hand over his knee.

"How have you been paying the bills?" Jo asked.

He laughed a dry laugh. "I haven't been. I qualified for unemployment, but that only lasted thirty weeks, and it wasn't even half my normal salary. When that ran out and it became clear I wouldn't be finding a job *commensurate with my experience*, an old friend pulled some strings for me, and I've been substitute teaching part-time whenever they need me. Occasionally I manage some consulting work, but that's few and far between."

"And your wife doesn't work?" Arnett asked.

Terry glanced down at his hands. "She was a homemaker."

Jo felt the pain in his voice. "Was?"

"She died a year ago. Breast cancer. Deeply ironic since my research dealt with regulatory T-cells and their role in cancer treatment."

Jo found herself at a loss for words, mind spinning, as pain sheared through her. To have your spouse die from the very disease you'd been prevented from researching? Irony didn't seem to quite cover it.

"I'm sorry for your loss," Arnett said.

Jo realized Arnett was staring at her, and finally managed to speak. "My father was just diagnosed with prostate cancer."

Terry met her eyes like he was seeing her for the first time. "I'm so sorry." He leaned toward her, and jabbed a finger on the coffee table. "Make sure he gets the very best care out there, no matter what they say. Even if it bankrupts you."

Anger burst through Jo as the shabby lodgings took on new significance. She forced herself to push it back down. "I am truly, truly sorry."

Terry met her eyes again for a moment, then nodded.

*

"What a son of a bitch." Jo shook her head ten minutes later as Arnett steered the car away from the curb.

"Shawnessy?" Arnett asked.

"Funny." She shot him a glare. "The more I hear about Whorton, the more I agree with Crawley. I'm surprised this didn't happen sooner."

Arnett pulled up to a light, and turned for a quick glance at her face. "He's not gonna win Miss Congeniality anytime soon, no."

"Crawley. Morlinski. Shawnessy. And from what Parminder said, Whorton's own wife. I'm losing count of how many people he screwed over." She ticked off her fingers as she spoke.

Arnett gave a yes-and-no wag of the head. "Hang on. He was an asshole, no question. But Crawley's perception of reality may be warped, it's possible he really did deserve that grade. Unlikely, I know. And Shawnessy isn't the first world casualty to office politics."

Her eyes flicked to his. "This isn't a simple case of office politics. Michael Whorton wanted Terry gone, that's one thing. But then to blackball him from getting another job, prevent him from being able to support his family? That's another thing entirely."

The light turned green, and Arnett turned back to the road. "We don't know for certain Whorton blackballed him. He might not have gotten those jobs for legitimate reasons."

Jo threw him a *come-on-now* look.

"Fine, I wouldn't place a bet against it. But I doubt Whorton thought any further into it than his own agenda."

Jo studied the people walking through the downtown streets, some strolling along with friends, some steaming toward an appointment or errand. Each had a life, including people they loved and obligations they needed to fulfill. "That's why you don't just screw people over, because you never know. Actions have consequences. But Whorton just didn't care about the consequences, or who they impacted."

Arnett nodded. "I agree. He did despicable things, and maybe he even deserved to die. But does that mean someone gets to take the law into their own hands, stab him in the kidneys and the back of the neck?"

"No, of course not."

"Then what are you saying? You're normally ride or die when it comes to justice. You latch on like a lamprey and you don't let go. Hell, you couldn't put the lid on the Hammond case because we didn't know exactly *why* the killer died, *that's* how important it was for you to get justice for his victims."

She frowned. What *was* she saying? She shook her head to clear it. "I don't know. You're right. I'm not sure where this is coming from."

He was silent for a moment. "You want my opinion?"

Jo's chest tightened. "What?"

"The cancer. It hit a nerve for you. You just heard about your father, and as soon as you heard the word 'cancer,' your father connected with Shawnessy's wife in your head."

A pang tugged at her heart. Terry's story resonated, she couldn't deny that. Her father's condition brought home Terry's pain in a way she wouldn't have felt yesterday. But, empathy had always been one of her strengths, and a tool she used to her advantage. The ability to put herself in a suspect's shoes, or in the victim's shoes, to identify and find something relatable, all of that helped her solve her cases. So surely understanding Terry's pain wasn't a bad thing?

Except, she realized, this was different. This had triggered an instinct to protect someone she loved, an emotional response that ran far deeper than any involving herself.

And one equally as powerful as the need for justice triggered by her failures to protect Marc and Jack, the two men she'd loved and lost.

CHAPTER THIRTEEN

Twenty minutes later, they rounded a corner of Dyer Hall, toward the graduate student offices. The relevant door was ajar. A woman in her late twenties sat at one of three desks pushed against the wall, and looked up at the sound of their approach. Her flat-ironed hair was blonde from her brown roots to her shoulders, and she wore a pink twinset with a low neckline over a brown A-line skirt. Heavy layers of shimmery make-up accented the woman's brown eyes, foundation caked around her nose and eyes, and her lips were painted the same color as her skin. Jo's mind flashed to a reanimated corpse in a late-night thriller.

She held her face blank. "Britney Ratliffe?"

Britney nodded, and started to rise.

Jo stepped to one of the empty desks. "Please, don't get up. I'm Detective Josette Fournier and this is Detective Bob Arnett. Thank you for talking with us."

Tears sprung into Britney's eyes. "I can't believe anyone would do something so horrible, especially to Michael."

Jo exchanged a look with Arnett. Someone who actually missed Michael Whorton? That was new. "You're his teaching assistant, correct? Did you work closely with him?"

"I did. I'm actually his graduate student, too, have been for four years, so we knew each other well." A tear overflowed one eye, and she pushed it up and away from her lashes, careful to keep her make-up from smearing.

Still nonplussed, Jo put her hand on Britney's arm for a brief moment. "I'm sorry for your loss. We won't keep you long, we just have a few quick issues we're hoping you can help us with."

She nodded as she dealt with a tear flooding the other eye. "Okay. Anything I can do to help."

"First off, the dean mentioned there were problems with a student Dr. Whorton failed last semester, who claimed Whorton was biased against him?"

Her eyes widened, and her posture straightened. "Yeah, Greg Crawley. Man, that guy is something else."

"How so?"

"Okay, so, he comes to my office hours, right? He tells me he's struggling with the material, that he can't get his mind around it. So, I do what I normally do, ask him about specific areas where he's struggling. He starts talking and talking, about his personal life, not anything that's actually part of the class. So, I pull out the textbook and start asking him about specific topics we recently covered, trying to zone in, and he'd start to answer my question, but then veer off to something else." She leaned forward. "He kept talking about how he'd been severely depressed over his grade, and how he struggled from PTSD because he used to be in the military for a year or something, but when I asked him if he saw action he looked at me like *of-course-not-idiot*, so I'm not even sure what the problem was there. I finally had to cut him off because my office hours were over and I was late for class. So, I told him he'd have to come back, and that he should bring something specific he wanted to focus on and we could do that. So, he came again, and brought a paper he got a D on, and I started going over why we took off points, but he just went off about his depression again. So, I figured, if that's the problem, he should go to the counseling office because they could help with that better than I could."

"How did he respond to that?" Jo asked when she finally paused, wondering if Crawley'd had a small crush on her, and had been trying to connect with her in his own awkward way.

"He sort of shined me on, nodded when I said it, but didn't agree and just kept on talking until he ran me out of time again. Then he came back a third time, only that time he signed up for my early slot, and I had another student waiting, so I had to be firm with him, and told him more firmly that he should talk to the counseling office. He didn't like that, *at all.*"

"What did he do?"

"He got angry with me, said he'd thought I was nice and I'd actually listen to him, but I was just a minion who'd never admit Michael wasn't being fair to him, and that I was trying to pass him off to someone else. Then he called me a bitch and stormed out. One of my office mates, Serina Blake, was here that day working on her research, and after I finished with the other students, I told her how freaked out I was, and she said I should talk to Michael about it."

"Smart girl," Arnett said.

"So, I told him. He said he'd received a special accommodations request from the disabled students office for Greg, asking for extra time and a separate testing location. He put two and two together and called the disabled students office to find out what was going on."

"Was that unusual?"

"I mean, it doesn't happen every semester, but I wouldn't say *unusual.* There are a lot of reasons why students request specific accommodations, especially for testing. Dyslexia's pretty common, but the requests come from lots of things, even stuff like anxiety disorders. So, with Greg's threats, Michael decided it was time to talk to someone about it all."

"Don't they have to keep all that confidential?"

"I'm not sure exactly how that works, but if there's a request for an accommodation, they usually give the professors and TAs the basics about the situation so we can help as much as possible. But we can't tell anyone, and if we do, we can be kicked out of the program. But you're the police, and after what happened to Michael, I don't care if they do." More tears sprung into her eyes.

"Don't worry, they'll need to disclose it to us anyway. What did they tell you?"

Her voice went up an octave. "Basically, that he's nuts. He has a history of severe bipolar disorder, and he's schizophrenic."

Jo tensed. Issues of mental health were tricky, requiring a delicate balance between protecting the rights of students who struggled with mental illness without stigmatizing them, and protecting other people if there was a possibility of instability. This was most likely why Greg had decided Michael Whorton was biased against him—he would have known the disabilities office contacted Whorton about his accommodations, and assumed they divulged his medical history. And as far as she could tell, he might have been right. Britney's rush to label Crawley "nuts" suggested she and Michael Whorton were biased to some degree against him, and that may well have leaked out into the grading process.

"They were able to be that specific?"

"They said something about because of his behavior, we had a right to know. I told them right then and there that I didn't feel safe and there was no way I was going to be alone with him again."

"How did you work that? You were the only TA, right?" Jo asked.

"I made sure I always had someone else with me in office hours. Serina was fine with it. But luckily, he never came back. I never heard anything about him again until he challenged his grade."

That brought up a memory. "Dr. Whorton had you grade his final exam, right?"

"The TAs always do the grading. Mostly, anyway. Some professors want to have a hand in it so they can get a sense of how the students are responding. But yeah, Michael had a feeling Greg was going to come after him and make some sort of claim like that, so he stayed hands-off."

"Classy," Arnett mumbled.

Jo silently agreed. "And you were okay with that? After making sure not to be alone with him? I'm not sure I would have been willing to take the risk."

Britney's eyes flashed between the two of them, and she bristled. "Michael always produced very specific rubrics to help his TAs grade, and obviously it's better if the person who creates the rubric is not the same person who grades the exams. You know, for bias. And, Greg didn't know who did the grading."

If it were that obvious, Jo was too ignorant of teaching procedures to see why. Wasn't the purpose of the rubric itself to eliminate bias, because the correct information was either present, or it wasn't? And was Britney really naive enough to think that when push came to shove, the students couldn't figure out who did the grading? She studied Britney's face. "Ah, so that was standard procedure."

Her eyes flicked away. "Of course."

Jo decided not to press. "Did you know about the e-mail Crawley sent to Whorton?"

Confusion flashed across Britney's face. "Which e-mail? He e-mailed Michael several times."

"Were there any other problem students that you're aware of? Maybe this semester?" Jo asked.

"Not that I'm aware of, and I TA for him every semester." Britney shrugged, and shook her head.

"Were Dr. Whorton's office hours the same this semester as last?" Arnett asked.

"Office hours are listed on the website, and he also had a sign-in sheet on his door, so it's not like it's hard to figure out. But yes, they were at the same time as last semester. Michael kept as regular a schedule as he could manage, including his class times."

Jo nodded, and took back over. "Did he ever make appointments with students outside of office hours?"

She shook her head. "Maybe twice the whole time I've worked for him. Otherwise students take advantage. And there's no way he'd have done it for Greg without an administrator being present, because he wasn't stupid."

"Who else might have had reason to dislike Whorton?" Arnett asked.

Her faced scrunched, and Jo couldn't tell if she was concentrating or trying not to cry again. "Nobody. I mean, not enough to kill him. He was a great guy. But I guess some of the other professors were jealous of his success."

A flicker of suspicion flared brighter as Jo noted Britney's spin on the situation. "Tell me about that."

"I know there's some tension with Dr. Parminder. And Dr. Shawnessy, he left when he couldn't get his way about the department's new direction. I actually came in as his graduate student, and switched to Michael when he left. But that turned out to be far better for me."

Jo gave a sympathetic nod. "What do you think of the changes to the department?"

"I know we got Professor Mashtel out of it all, I hope to collaborate with him if I can, the more publications the better. And I know our lab has exploded in the past few years, tons of new equipment we've needed, research opportunities, everything. I just can't see how that's bad. But there are haters everywhere." Her hand flipped in a "stop" gesture, dismissing any criticism, real or imagined.

"So Dr. Parminder or Dr. Shawnessy. You don't think they'd do this?" Arnett asked.

Her eyes widened. "I guess you never know, but that seems farfetched. Steve does his own thing, and Terry's been gone for years."

Jo watched Britney's face carefully. "Can you think of anyone else, for any reason, that might have had an issue with him?"

She took a moment too long to respond. "No."

Jo glanced at Arnett, who shook his head. She stood, and held out a card. "If you think of anybody or anything else, please let us know."

Arnett and Britney also stood, and Britney reached to take the card. "I will, thank you."

Jo's grip tightened on the card at the sight of Britney's now-exposed wrist—an armored skeleton riding a horse peeped out from her cuff. "Interesting tattoo."

"Oh, thank you!" She pushed up her sleeve to reveal a stylized version of the tarot card they'd found in Michael Whorton's office. "It's a tarot card. All of the women in my family are tarot readers. Not very scientific, I know. I don't believe in the fortune-telling stuff, but the symbols keep me grounded in another world."

"I wouldn't have taken you for a skeletons-and-death sort of girl." Jo kept her expression pleasant.

She rolled her eyes and gave a half laugh. "Right? Everyone says that. I wish I'd put it on my hip or something. People see the whole cliché, the gypsy pulling out the death card for someone who's about to die. But it's not really about that, it's about change. Transformation. The death is metaphorical, death to an old way of being. Sometimes change is unpleasant, but you always come out better for it. That's why I chose it, to remind me that whatever I'm going through in life is temporary and for the best." She faltered on the last few words, and tears filled her eyes again.

Jo laid her hand on Britney's again. "I know it doesn't feel like it right now, but that's true. This pain will pass, and your life will be better for it."

Britney looked up and searched her eyes a long moment. "Thank you."

Jo forced a smile. "You said you don't believe in the fortune-telling, so you don't have an actual deck?"

Britney's face brightened. "Oh, I do! Like I said, I think there's wisdom in the symbols. I use them like daily affirmations."

Jo feigned happy surprise. "Here, in the office?"

"Yes, why?"

"I have an aunt who reads tarot cards, and the death card I remember is a little different. Can I see yours?"

Britney shrugged, and dug into her backpack. "Sure, I guess." She pulled out an oversized deck and rifled through it. When she found the death card, she pulled it out and held it up, next to the tattoo on her arm. "Here. My tattoo doesn't have all the detail because I wanted it smaller. So I simplified."

Jo made a show of comparing the card and the tattoo. "Yep, that's more like what I remember. The bodies and the Pope and all."

Britney followed her gaze. "You know, I probably should have just gotten the flag. Then the skeleton wouldn't freak everybody out."

"I don't know," Jo said, thinking. "Dramatic images are far more effective at eliciting powerful reactions."

As soon as the elevator doors closed behind them, Arnett turned to Jo. "Okay, I was wrong. The one person who actually misses Whorton has the damned tarot card tattooed on her wrist. That can't be a coincidence."

Jo tapped her leg. "No, I don't imagine it is."

"She's either innocent, or a pathological liar," Arnett said. "Place your bets."

The corner of Jo's mouth curled up absently. "You've been spending too much time with Marzillo. My hope was Britney had dropped the card the last time she was in his office, and we'd be able to put that whole element to bed. Because if we're placing bets, I'd bet every dollar in my bank account she had nothing to do with Michael Whorton's death. Her loss was too real, and she didn't react at all when we saw the tattoo."

"She had to know we'd see it," Arnett said.

"And her emotions? You don't think they were genuine?"

Arnett took a deep breath. "She was convincing. I just think there's something she's not telling us."

"Of course there is. First and foremost, that she was sleeping with Michael Whorton."

Arnett's head jerked around. "She has feelings for him, I agree. But an affair is a big leap."

"I could be wrong. But she was far more broken up than she should be. And she was terrified of Crawley—exactly the sort of thing that could lead to biased grading, by the way—but graded his paper when Whorton asked, then rushed to defend his selfish choice. That feels like more than hero worship to me."

The elevator doors opened, and Arnett waited until they cleared the building to continue. "Maybe Whorton just took advantage of her feelings."

Jo shrugged. "Maybe. I wouldn't put it past him to exploit any advantage he had over anyone. But, when we pushed her about who else had a problem with him, I got the sense she was hiding something inappropriate."

"Could have been hiding his affair with someone else, protecting his reputation."

Jo laughed. "No way. Had it been with anyone but her, she'd have been crazy jealous, and she'd have fallen all over herself to tell us. And her expression when she talked about transformation and going through hard times in life? I know that look, I've seen it more than once. That was far more personal than losing an admired mentor."

Arnett considered. "You think the wife knew?"

"From Britney's reaction when I asked who else might want him dead, my guess is yes." Jo thought for a moment, fingering her necklace. "I'd like you to take the lead when we interview her, if you don't mind. I want to try something, so hold off on mentioning Britney's potential affair until I do."

Arnett twisted an imaginary key next to his lips as they opened the doors to the Crown Vic. "My stomach's growling, and we just have time to grab some lunch before we head out for our chat with Camilla Whorton—"

Jo's phone vibrated in her pocket, and she pulled it out to check the number. She held up her hand to Arnett as she answered. "Dad."

Arnett turned to watch her.

"Josette. Guess your mom called you," her father said.

"Of course she did, you knew she would. This is your *life*."

"No it isn't, it's hardly anything, but I knew you'd throw a fit if I didn't call you about it. It's just a little trouble with my prostate, is all."

She gritted her teeth against her frustration. "I see. Just a little prostate trouble."

"You know how doctors are, always make more out of something than it really is."

"And this doctor's just trying to make it into cancer? What stage, Dad?"

"Stage three, he thinks. But he doesn't like my test scores."

Her knees turned to rubber, and she reached to steady herself against the car. She searched her memory for information about cancer. Didn't stage three mean it was starting to spread? "Test *results*, Dad."

"Don't correct me, baby girl. He kept talkin' 'bout a Gleason *score*."

"Fine. The point is, they can treat it, right?"

"He said something about chemotherapy, and he wants me to take some sort of hormones."

She pushed down a vision of her father, hair falling out, his tall, sturdy, frame reduced to a frail wisp. "Tell me you said yes."

"I'm not stupid."

"No, you're not, just stubborn as a mule on a summer's day."
She glanced at her wrist for a watch she hadn't worn in a decade,
then looked around absently. "When do you start the treatment?"

"Depends. He said I should have someone with me for the
first few sessions, 'cause I might not react well. I say that's crazy,
but he pushed the issue. I told him you and your sister have lives,
you don't have time for this nonsense. I don't want you changing
anything around."

But of course he did, or he wouldn't have called, and he wouldn't
have started with their mother. "I'll talk to Sophie. One of us will
find a way to get down there. Set up the next appointment you
can. How are you feeling?"

"Don't you worry about me, I'm fine. Tired is all. Damn doctors
are a pain in the ass, and the last thing I need is all this fuss. Call
me back after you talk to your sister." He hung up.

Jo slipped the phone back into her pocket. Arnett's arm, which
she hadn't noticed take her elbow, steadied her as she bent into
the car. "He's gonna be fine, Jo. Seven years it's been since my
brother was diagnosed, and he's still going strong. The treatments
are highly effective."

She waited as he circled the car, and got in the driver's side.
"They caught his early."

He nodded. "But the survival rates are high no matter what."

She stared forward. "I hope you're right."

CHAPTER FOURTEEN

Arnett didn't mention lunch again, which frightened Jo almost as much as the conversation with her father had. She needed to get the focus back on work, for both their sakes. "We still have time to grab something at Dunkin'. I could use a refill, anyway." She lifted her empty from the cup holder, and gave it a shake.

Twenty minutes later they'd gone through the drive-through, and were en route to the Whorton residence. Arnett pounded three jelly donuts, while Jo forced herself to eat several bites of oatmeal for the show of it, silently berating herself for forgetting how much she hated oatmeal.

They turned the corner onto Hopkins Drive, and Arnett choked. "How the hell much do professors make?"

Jo took in the Tudor house in front of them. Mansion, more like, with red brick covering most of the first story, topped with faux exposed brown beams. "Did you know, back in the day, the number of gables on your house was a measure of your social stature?"

"I didn't. But I bet *they* do." He pointed his chin toward the house.

Jo bobbed her head in acknowledgment. "Maybe his wife comes from money?"

"Guess we'll find out."

They parked at the top of the arching driveway, then strode up a stone walkway that wound between bushes and now-empty flower beds toward the front door. A melody chimed when they hit the doorbell, and, after a pause, the click of heels made their way to the door.

"Camilla Whorton?" Arnett asked when she opened the door.

"Yes. Come in, Detectives."

She led them through the large, Italianate foyer to an open living area. Her belted teal sheath dress fit like a glove, not a wrinkle along the cotton, and her hair was styled in gentle, perfect waves. When she turned back around to gesture them toward the twin beige couches, Jo noted that the full-face of make-up was flattering and subtle.

Camilla sat on the edge of an armchair and reached toward a tray in front of her. "Tea?"

Jo matched her careful posture, automatically crossing her legs at the ankle as she'd been trained to do in semi-formal settings. Then she mentally shook herself—what was it about Camilla Whorton that took her right back to her southern etiquette lessons?

Arnett, who didn't suffer any such compulsions, plopped firmly into the other couch. "No, thank you. But I would like to extend our sympathies for your loss," he said.

She nodded, but her face remained unchanged.

Jo watched her expression closely as Arnett gave her a stripped-down explanation of what had happened to her husband.

"He didn't deserve that," she said when he'd finished, with a look of genuine, if distanced, regret on her face.

"I'm sure you'll understand, we need to know where you were yesterday, and why."

"I was in Portland, on business. I drove back this morning."

"In my experience, most wives don't wait until morning to come back when their husband has been killed." Arnett kept his eyes on her face.

She met his eye with an icy stare. "Would it have helped him if I'd hurried back through icy roads in the middle of the night?"

Jo watched Arnett battle to keep his face passive. "What sort of business are you in?"

"I'm co-owner of Vestments, a chain of clothing boutiques throughout New England. I stopped to do some reconnaissance on two comparable stores in the area, then met afterward with my store manager there." She rattled off the woman's name and contact information.

"Your stores must be doing well to afford a home like this, in this part of town," Arnett said.

"On the contrary. The government keeps telling us the recession's over, but you'd never know it from my sales totals. We're in the black, but barely. I made more as a summer intern when I was a graduate student."

"You're telling me a professor's salary pays for this?" Arnett gestured a circle around his head.

She laughed. "Of course not. Michael had been with the university long enough to be on a fairly high salary rung, but that doesn't count for much when the rung is on a stepladder. His industry work paid for this."

Jo and Arnett were silent for a moment. "Industry work."

Her expression was scornful. "Of course. Research he does on the side for pharmaceutical companies."

"The dean didn't mention anything about outside work. Aren't universities strict about intellectual property?"

"They are. Any profit that comes from research done on university premises or funded by university-related money must go directly back to the university. But anyone with a halfway-decent IQ knows how to keep their pans on different burners. I'm not sure how much of it the dean was even aware of." She waved the problem away like an insignificant gnat.

"Where was he conducting this industry work?" Arnett asked.

She pulled a silver cigarette case from a drawer in the end table. "I didn't concern myself with that sort of thing. But I can pull out his records if you feel it's relevant."

Jo swallowed a smile as Arnett's jaw tensed. Despite having quit several years ago, he still struggled to keep away from cigarettes, and having to watch her smoke would only take his temper from bad to worse.

"The thing is, Mrs. Whorton, *we'd* actually like to know who killed your husband, so yeah, I do feel it's relevant." Arnett leaned forward. "And I gotta be honest. I don't get a sense you're *concerned* with any of this."

She lit the cigarette she'd extracted without a blink. "I'm not. At least not in the way you mean." She took a long draw.

"What do I mean?"

"You mean I'm not broken up over it, not wailing or gnashing my teeth, desperate for revenge. I'm sure you think I'm a cold bitch, and maybe I am, but if so, that's what being married to a serial cheater will do for you."

Arnett glanced at Jo. She shook her head ever so slightly to let him know she still wasn't ready to deploy her bomb.

He continued. "Why didn't you leave him, then? Unless I'm wrong, you don't have children, and you have your own career?"

She leaned back in her chair, and crossed her legs. "I like my life, Detective. I like living in a large house in an exclusive part of town. Driving a Lexus. Carrying designer bags. And I believe I've already mentioned my business isn't all that lucrative—yet."

"So you're in a holding pattern?"

"I suppose you could put it like that. And, before you ask, yes, I was angry about his infidelity. There were days I could barely stand to look at him. But I wasn't angry enough to kill him."

"Did he know you knew?" Jo asked.

Camilla considered Jo with an expression close to admiration. "He did not—at least, he wasn't certain. *That* would have brought the situation to a head."

Jo nodded, and Arnett took over again. "So you didn't want him dead. Who do you think did?"

She laughed again, and flicked the ash from her cigarette into what Jo had previously taken to be an objet d'art. "Any number of people. My husband was ambitious. Co-workers. Administrators. Students. Jilted lovers." She elaborated on the first three, without adding anything they didn't already know.

"How about the ex-lovers? Can you give us any names?"

She stared out the picture window, and her chin quivered, so briefly Jo wasn't sure she'd seen it. "I tried my best to find out as little as possible. The only one I know for certain is the one I discovered. A chemistry professor, Linda Gutierrez. We were at a barbeque thrown by the dean for all of natural sciences, and he was making an ass out of himself with her. Some other professor I don't know saw me watching them, and said something to him. I left the room as they were talking, so I'm not sure how Michael reacted, but he went out of his way to avoid Gutierrez for the rest of the night. I hired a private investigator to follow them. He got me evidence so I could confront him if I ever wanted to." She stabbed out her cigarette, and her eyes shifted back to Arnett's. "I should have left it at that, but I didn't. I made it my business to know everything about her, really reveled in my misery for a few months. Went to the cafes she went to. Joined the gym she belonged to, and made sure to be there when she worked out. Stalked her on social media." She held up her hand. "Yes, I know what that sounds like. One day I caught myself looking up all the men on her Facebook page, considering contacting their wives to warn them about her. That's when something in my brain clicked, like I'd caught a glimpse of myself in a psychological mirror, and it nauseated me. I stopped all of it right then and there. Ironically, about a week later, the PI reported that they'd stopped seeing each other, and that he was now seeing someone else. I told him I didn't want any details, and terminated him."

"I'm sorry you had to go through that nightmare," Arnett said, face blank.

Camilla turned to him. "I don't recommend it, no. But the point is, I don't have names for you. I tried my best to focus on building Vestments. But I have suspicions, and I've heard rumors. He was far too friendly with the female assistant professor they hired a while back, Morlinski, I think? She's gone now, regardless. And a graduate student called me a few weeks ago, wanting to meet for coffee. I deleted the voicemail and never called her back, but I remember her name, because it was so disgustingly lurid. *Britney*." She lit another cigarette.

Arnett followed the cigarette with his eyes. "Be careful with those. You just got your freedom, don't want to find yourself in a cancer ward." He winced, and shot a quick glance at Jo, who looked down at the phone she'd pulled from her pocket.

Camilla's gaze flitted between them before she spoke. "Yes, well. Freedom isn't free." She drew herself up. "Is there anything else I can help you with?"

Arnett glanced at his notebook. "One other thing we hadn't heard before. You mentioned a problem with an administrator?"

"Right." She took a draw on the cigarette, brows creased in concentration. "A few months ago I think, maybe more? I remember it was a cold day but I didn't have my winter jacket in the front hall anymore, so no more than six. He was arguing with someone, loudly. He said something along the lines of 'maybe if you weren't one of the most ineffectual administrators in the university's history, I wouldn't be reduced to such measures to get funding,' which is how I know it was an administrator. But I don't know who, or what the conflict was about."

"What made it worth noting?"

"Michael could be unpleasant in many ways, but he didn't yell or make scenes. *If* he confronted you directly, it was from a position of strength. He was deliberate and careful, and you often didn't realize exactly what had been implied until after the fact." She shook her head and stood up. "Screaming insults wasn't his style. Someone had wrong-footed him, and it was about something important."

"You weren't curious?"

"My curiosity over anything related to him died the day I realized I'd allowed him to reduce me to a desperate, pathetic, scorned woman."

"One last question," Jo asked. "Was your husband a hunter?"

Camilla looked confused. "No."

"So you never saw anything like this among his belongings?" Jo held out her phone, displaying the hunting knife she'd googled as they spoke.

"Not that I'm aware of. Why—" Her face paled as realization hit her. "Oh, God."

"Thank you," Jo said, and they took their leave.

*

"You're developing quite a flair for the dramatic."

"She ruined my other ambush, what was I supposed to do? And she didn't recognize that knife, although after pretending she didn't care about her husband's infidelity all these years, her acting skills may be finely honed. Regardless, I wouldn't want to run into her in a dark alley."

"Truth. Good catch on the affair with Britney. Not that I ever doubted your reading-people superpower."

"Thanks." She put her hands on her hips in a seated attempt at a Wonder Woman stance.

Arnett signaled a lane change, then took the next turn. "So, Britney called Camilla to have a little chat. You think Britney's worried Camilla killed Michael on account of the affair?"

Jo nodded. "That would fit Britney's brand of evasion. But on the other hand, a call like that is what you do when you're trying to get your married lover to leave his spouse, and he refuses.

Maybe when she realized Camilla wasn't going to step in, she confronted him."

"And maybe he put his foot down, and she killed him."

"When he turned around to take a call, and she grabbed the hunting knife she had conveniently stashed in her pocket?" Jo laughed.

"Hey, I bought both of my daughters a taser to carry in their purse."

Jo slapped her hand over her eyes. "Please tell me you had a training session with them."

"Tcha. Of course." He steered into a turn. "What was your take on Camilla?"

"Ah, she's a tough one. Reminds me of my friend Eva's cousin, who was also married to a serial cheater. He used his obsession with golfing as cover for his affairs. Over the years she built up this incredible veneer of impenetrability, and overcompensated by putting a nuclear level of energy into her mothering. Then, out of nowhere one day, she lost it. Took his golf clubs and used them to beat his beloved Ferrari into a crumpled mound, then threw his golf clothes in and set the whole deal on fire."

"Nice." Arnett smiled.

"So my question is, did Camilla reach that same point, maybe brought on by Britney's call? I'd hazard it's very likely."

"Good point. So we have Britney, who may have killed Whorton if he refused to leave his wife. Camilla, who might have reached her breaking point, and killed him over the affair with Britney."

"Greg Crawley, who lost his financial aid and his parents' support over his D in Whorton's class. Terry Shawnessy, who lost his job because of Whorton. And Beth Morlinsky, who he was allegedly harassing. Which reminds me, I need to check in with Lopez about her location."

Arnett nodded. "And Whorton had issues with some administrator, but we have no idea who. If it happened while Whorton was still chair, that would put Roger Latimer directly over him in the hierarchy, and if more recently, Arthur Kerland would have been, as chair of the department."

"And while Latimer certainly didn't go an inch out of his way to elucidate the political situation for us, his alibi is iron-clad. Well-attended meetings all morning up until the murder."

"And Kerland was Whorton's partner in crime, so that doesn't make sense, since we have no reason to believe that relationship soured."

"Right. So, given that, I think we need to nail down whose alibis hold up and whose don't." Jo picked up her phone and called Lopez. "Any chance you've located Beth Morlinski?" she asked after initial greetings.

"I have. She lives in Beverly. Single, at least not officially married, and has no sort of record to speak of. She teaches at Beverly College. I haven't had a chance to dig into the other names yet, I've been concentrating on the phone records. I'll e-mail it."

"Perfect. Thanks," Jo said, and once they'd ended the call, pulled up the e mail. She first called Morlinski's office number, and got her voicemail. She called the home number Lopez had listed, and got voicemail there too. This time she left a message identifying herself and why she'd called, and asked for a return call as soon as possible.

They spent the rest of the afternoon verifying alibis. The manager at the Portland Vestments verified she'd met with Camilla Whorton at four p.m. the day Michael Whorton had been killed, and the manager at the local Holiday Inn verified she'd checked in that night at seven p.m., and checked out the following morning. Neither the laundromat nor the other errands Shawnessy had identified provided him with an alibi. Only one of the locations, the grocery store he'd claimed to visit, had security cameras, and the footage had already been recorded over. And, none of the few employees they managed to track down who'd been on shift could remember seeing him.

"That's not good news for Terry Shawnessy," Jo said as they left the grocery store. "I was hoping we'd find something to confirm. But, he's got one of those faces that blend. Just because they can't remember him doesn't mean he wasn't there."

Arnett flashed her a look, but moved on. "As for Camilla Whorton, I just did the math. We only have her word she stopped off to check out comparable stores. If she killed her husband and then left right after, it would have been close, but she could have made it to her Portland meeting on time."

"I'll call her and get the names of the stores she stopped at. One of them must have surveillance cameras, and hopefully they don't rerecord every twenty-four hours like GroceryMart." Jo put through the call as they pulled up to the station, and left a message requesting the information as they stepped out of the vehicle. Jo started toward the building.

Arnett stopped. "Six o'clock. I'm not sure what more we can do tonight, and it'd be nice to sneak in a hot dinner with Laura. Rockney's been in a mood about overtime, regardless."

"Right, that makes sense. I need to talk to my sister anyway, and I have no idea how long that's gonna take." Jo said. *Or how it's gonna go.*

Arnett took off, and Jo glanced toward the building. She'd just received another batch of information on the most recent Golden Gate Bridge suicides, but she could look those over at home. She did an about-face toward her car, climbed in, and pulled out her phone.

She sat staring at her sister's number for several minutes, trying to come up with some way to avoid the call. She took a deep breath, and said aloud, "I will not let her get to me," and then tapped the call icon.

CHAPTER FIFTEEN

Five years separated Jo from her little sister Sophie, and those years had turned out to be important ones. Sophie had few memories of their time in New Orleans, and not many more of their father as anything but a long-distance parent. Most likely because of that, Sophie viewed their mother as a long-suffering saint and her father as a devil that had destroyed the relationship, while Jo was stuck with the inconvenient memories of a truth that was far more complex. Always one to stand up for those who weren't able to stand up for themselves, she became her father's defender. As a result of it all, Sophie had a much closer bond to their mother than Jo did. If life had been fair, Jo would have been closer to her father than Sophie was, but that hadn't happened either. Neither of them lived up to her father's expectations, but he let her know that Sophie at least made an effort. And so Jo had been left feeling like a resentful outsider for much of her life.

But none of that was the reason why she and Sophie didn't get along. If you asked Sophie why, she'd claim it was because she took after their mother, and Jo took after their father. But Jo knew they both took after her father—stubborn and independent—but expressed that in different ways. Jo pointed it toward her career, while Sophie pointed it toward being the dutiful daughter who never failed to be everything both parents wanted her to be. She'd married a handsome, affable man, had three children she stayed at home to care for, and earned herself pocket change by selling some sort of exercise-wear at parties.

But rather than be happy with the path that she'd chosen, she consistently blamed Jo for not doing enough for her parents, and thus not lifting the burden off Sophie's shoulders. So Jo's resentment and Sophie's martyrdom sat between the sisters like a graffiti-littered cement wall.

Just as she thought she'd have to leave a message, her sister's voice broke over the line. "Josie. I wondered how long it would take you to call."

Jo's entire body clenched. "Great to talk to you, too, Sophie. I only just got Dad on the phone, so I'm not sure how I could have called any faster."

Her sister ignored her tone. "Let's cut to the chase. You're on some big case and there's no possible way you can get free any time soon. So, I've already made arrangements. I'm going down Sunday night to take Dad to his therapy next week. He'll actually start it on Friday, but there's no way I can get there that soon. They aren't sure how long he'll need the treatments, but this way he'll at least have someone with him when the side effects hit."

Damn it. Jo hadn't had time to research the treatments and side effects, but there was no way she was going to let Sophie know that. "What about the kids?"

"They'll stay with Mom during the day, and David will take care of them in the evenings."

"Mom's knees have been bothering her."

"I'm sorry, do you really think I don't know that? What other option is there?"

"That's why I called, Sophie, so we could figure something out. But it sounds like you've already settled everything." She just managed to hold back a snarky comment about Sophie's fast train to martyrdom. Why did she become eleven years old again whenever she had to deal with her sister?

Sophie took in a deep breath and let it out in a controlled *I'm-dealing-with-a-child* sigh. "What do you suggest?"

Jo's face screwed up into a ball as she willed herself to come up with something. "If you're going next week, I'll talk to my boss and see if I can go for a few days at least the week after."

"Sooner would actually be better, if possible. David was supposed to go to a conference next weekend, and he's really pissed that he won't be able to go."

"That doesn't sound like David."

"Yeah, well, my job is to take care of the kids and the house. That was the agreement, right?"

The frustration in her voice set off Jo's alarm bells. It wasn't like her sister to admit to anything short of perfection in any aspect of her life. "Soph, are you okay? Is everything alright?"

Sophie paused before answering. "Yeah, I'm fine. Everything's good. All marriages have their issues, you wouldn't..."

"Understand?" Jo finished for her.

"I didn't say that."

An uncomfortable silence grew as Jo struggled with her own stubborn nature. Her father needed their help, and further conflict between them would only make things worse. And, at least her sister had stopped herself this time before saying it.

"I'll see what I can do." She squeezed her eyes shut, and forced out the next words. "Thank you for stepping up so quickly."

"Great, I appreciate that." Someone shrieked in the background. "Shit, Emily hurt herself. I have to go." She hung up without waiting for a response.

Jo leaned over and banged her head repeatedly on the steering wheel. There was no way she'd be able to get time off in the middle of the case, and it would take a miracle to sort out the massive field of suspects within the next few hours. All she'd done with her promise was delay the inevitable because she was too proud to admit to Sophie that she'd been right.

Her phone dinged. She rubbed her neck and picked it up to find a text from Eric.

Hey babe. You busy? I can order another pizza…

She smiled. Truth be told, she'd love to lose herself in some mindless sex, and Eric was hot enough to make a great distraction. But two nights in a row would send the wrong message, and, more importantly, her heart just wasn't in it.

Too much work. Later this week?

Five minutes passed before the response came.

I'll look forward to it.

For the first time in her life, she saw the appeal of emojis, and considered sending one that would assuage his hurt ego. She scrolled through them for several minutes looking for a magic bullet.

She gave up, pulled a number out of her contacts, and dialed it.

"Hey, what's up?" Eva Richards, her best friend, said.

"I need a drink. Can you get away for an hour?"

*

Half an hour later, Eva sat across from her in a red-white-and-green swag-decorated booth at Fernando's, ignoring the light mariachi music playing over the speakers and waiting for their margaritas to arrive. Jo gave her the news about her father.

Eva reached over and squeezed her hand. "I'm so sorry, Jo."

Jo gave a sad laugh. "No assurances that he'll be fine? That was the first thing Bob said. I figured for sure you'd remind me about your mother."

Eva's gaze remained steady, but she leaned back and tucked her auburn curls behind her ears. "Nope. Doesn't matter what the statistics are when it's you or yours, does it? All you can see is the bad. Hell, I'm still worried her cancer will come back, even with the mastectomy."

The waiter dropped off their drinks. Jo pulled hers close, and took a long draw. "It's so strange, Eva. He drives me crazy. Whenever I visit him, I spend the whole time feeling like he doesn't really want me there and I can feel his disapproval of me like one of those lead blankets they use during X-rays. But I don't know what I'd do if he died."

Eva nodded and remained silent.

"And I know, I know, it's my own fault I don't go back more. But my work is what it is, and since he's the exact same way, I don't understand why he doesn't understand that. It's not like he'd ever come out here for a visit, even now that he's retired."

Eva nodded. "The whole *your-extended-family-is-out-here* thing."

"Exactly." Jo reported the conversation with Sophie. "So I have to hope I can get Rockney to let me go. Make the case that Arnett can handle it himself, especially with Lopez's help. We've done that before, for lots of reasons. But..."

"But?"

"But this case has a strange hold on me."

"How so?"

"The best way to put it is, everyone wanted this vic dead, and for good reason. I certainly can't say his death was tragic, and I can't say I'm desperate to get him justice."

The waiters brought a plate of nachos, and took their order for a second round of drinks.

Eva's brow pursed. "That's not like you. You've investigated the murders of some nasty scumbags that the world's far better without, in my opinion. That never clouded your perspective."

"Bob said pretty much the same thing. And that it's the cancer that's clouding my judgment."

Eva swallowed the sip she'd just taken. "I'd be surprised if it wasn't. For months after my mom's diagnosis, I burst into tears at the strangest times for the strangest reasons, and I know I took it out on Tony. Maybe for you it's making it hard for you to be emotionally invested in other people's bullshit."

Jo shook her head and stabbed a chip in her direction. "No, see, that's just it. It's not that I'm not emotionally invested, it's that I'm invested in the wrong way." She gave a brief description of the case. "I'm angrier about what Whorton did to Shawnessy than I am about Whorton's murder. Bob said it's because of Shawnessy's wife, that now his wife and my father are fused together in my brain because of the cancer. And I think he's right. So I'm in a catch-22 where I want to go back and be with my dad, but I also don't want to turn my back on this case, because either way, I'm failing my father."

Eva shook her head. "I worry about you sometimes."

Jo was nonplussed. "What do you mean?"

Eva paused, and wiped the remaining salt from the rim of her drink. "You entangle yourself in situations you can't win. There are two parts of you that are diametrically opposed to one another. Usually it's not a big deal, because the side that's focused on career is far larger than the other. It wins the vast majority of the time, and that's fine. But the part you try to pretend doesn't exist, the one that wants home and family and meaningful connection with another human being, it's always going to tug at you. So you're always going to be a bit unhappy, like your own personal limbo."

Jo shook her head, annoyed. "I have a house that I love, I have plenty of family, and I have meaningful connection with lots of human beings. Well, one or two, at least. You, for example."

Eva gave her a cut-the-shit glare. "You know what I mean. I'm talking about a man."

Jo leaned back, and grabbed her drink. "See, that's disappointing. You of all people know how I feel about that."

"I sure do. Because, in case you've forgotten, I was in your life when Jack died. I was in your life before *he* was in it. I know how happy he made you, and how different you were. That part of you didn't die just because he did. What I don't know is whether that connection really isn't *that* important to you anymore, because people do change, or if you've just stuffed it down into some mental shoebox so you can pretend. Either way, the need is still there, and the two parts haven't found a way to be okay with each other."

"Low blow, bringing up Jack." Jo pushed the memory down before too much of it flooded back. "And I've found balance just fine."

"I'm sorry, I know you don't like to think about him. But maybe you need to, because if you had found balance just fine, you'd have peace with it all." She dipped another chip, and continued. "Look, I'm not trying to play therapist here, Lord knows I have enough underlying bullshit of my own to fertilize Iowa. And I'm not saying you need to find a husband, I'm not talking about only that kind of connection. I just know what I see in front of me, and I think Arnett's right. Of course your dad's cancer has you spooked—he's *the* important man in your life, and whether he lives or dies is out of your control."

A chill instantly invaded Jo. Of course she didn't want her father to die, and of course she was terrified and angry that there wasn't anything she could do about it. But was the rest true? Her relationship with her father was complicated, she'd never argue that. She'd always assumed her problems with men stemmed from her issues with him, but maybe her issues with him were complicated by her history with men, as well. Had she put him up on some sort of shelf because of it?

She didn't know. And it was very possible she was too late to do anything about it.

CHAPTER SIXTEEN

Jo bolted out of her sleep at three a.m., gasping. She sat for a moment trying to get her breathing back under control. When she failed, she got up, hurried to the kitchen, and chugged down a can of ginger ale.

She hadn't had the dream in years. It only came under very specific circumstances, usually when she was working shootings that were headed for cold storage. But nothing like that had crossed her desk in a while.

She clutched the diamond at her neck. Why did Eva have to bring up Jack?

Jo met him when she was twenty and studying criminal justice at Boston University. When her roommate Sallie suggested Jo meet her medical-student older brother, Jo had hesitated. She hadn't dated much after Marc, her long-distance boyfriend in New Orleans, was killed in a gang shooting when she was sixteen—only a few times here and there, and nothing had lasted for long.

But, of course, Sallie invited her brother over for a visit. And the moment he'd walked into their apartment, the chemistry was immediate and undeniable. He was five years her senior, with jet-black hair, warm azure eyes, and the sexiest smile she'd ever laid eyes on. Where she was outgoing and had a natural affinity with people, he was introverted and cautious. But somehow their combination worked. She brought him out of himself, and he slowed her pace. He made her laugh and he made her feel safe—something she hadn't felt in years. Knowing he loved and wanted her wrapped her in a cocoon of warmth and acceptance that made her feel she could face anything, fend off any blow, triumph over any obstacle. They were engaged within a year.

The night he died, they'd gone out to dinner, then decided to try out a new comedy club in Mission Hill. They'd had to park a fair way away from the restaurant, and the stroll from the restaurant to the club took them still farther from Jack's car. The temperature dropped by the time the show was over, and given the cold, they decided to take a shorter route to get back to the car. But halfway back, the well-lit sidewalks populated with a smattering of other students vanished, replaced by a dark, empty street with alleys and doorways that popped out from nowhere.

"I'm pretty sure I've seen horror films that start out this way," Jo joked as they turned down a second, still darker, street.

"Psh, I've seen worse," Jack replied. But he picked up the pace.

They were almost to safety, within sight of a street they knew, when a figure stepped out of one of the dark doorways and pointed a gun at Jack. "Gimme ya wallet."

Jo's heart pounded, and the world seemed to slow. She tried to control her breathing and keep focused—since deciding she wanted to become a detective, she'd begun training herself to notice significant details. She studied the man, who was out of reach but close enough to see in broad strokes.

Young, possibly not old enough to drink legally.

Dirty, with clumped hair and a garbage-like stench radiating around him.

Caucasian, just under six feet. Jacket and trousers too large for him, torn in several places.

Skin with a too-pale sheen around cracked lips. And shaking hands.

Jack raised both arms. "Okay, no problem. I'm just going to reach for it, okay?"

"Don't do anything stupid. I *will* shoot you." He jabbed the gun toward them.

A vision of Marc, her high-school boyfriend, flashed before her eyes. His death replayed in her head—she watched him fall, shot by the drug-dealing banger, and the panic that had taken her over back then rose in her chest again. She couldn't let it happen a second time, couldn't let another man she loved die. She'd allowed Marc to just walk into danger, then stood by and watched from afar while he was murdered. She wouldn't cower like a passive child. She had to do something, she had to act, before it was too late.

Jack carefully pulled out his wallet, and she forced herself to concentrate. What did she know about this guy? He wasn't a drug dealer, nothing like that, he'd never risk a penny-ante robbery if so. No way any backup would appear out of one of the buildings to help him. He was just a scared kid, most likely a crack addict. Probably detoxing, and looking for a way to get his next bump. Most likely he'd run as soon as he had the money.

The man snatched the wallet out of Jack's hands, and rifled through it.

"Okay, you've got the money—" Jo reached for Jack's arm with a protective gesture like a mother holding back a child.

The man jumped back at the motion, and the gun in his hand wobbled between them. "Control ya bitch!"

"Josie," Jack said, his voice calm.

"It's okay," Jo said to the man, and fanned her hands in front of her, palms down, to show she was no threat.

The crackhead followed her gesture. "Nice rings. Give 'em here."

Shit. Her stomach plummeted. She only wore two rings: her engagement ring, and her grandmother's emerald wedding ring. All she had left of her grandmother, presented to her by her father after her grandmother's funeral service the year before.

She forced herself to think—a cop would know how to handle this. "I-I can't get them off, they're too small—" she sputtered, hoping he'd give up and run.

"Josie, give him the rings, don't be stupid," Jack said, the calm in his voice straining.

The panic swelled up again—she was losing control of the situation. There had to be a way to turn this around, to de-escalate, isn't that what the police did? How could she de-escalate the situation? She needed something, now, time was running out—

Jack reached over to grab her hand.

The man, startled by the quick motion, pulled the trigger.

Jack fell to the ground, blood gushing from the hole in his temple.

Jo dove for Jack, amid fuzzy footsteps disappearing in the distance and the gunshot still ringing in her head. Oh, God, he wasn't moving, and there was so much blood—she threw herself next to him and felt for a pulse. Nothing. She bent over him and started chest compressions, counting automatically until it was time to breathe into him, then pounded his chest again. Press. Breathe. *Please, Jack, please, oh God please stay with me.*

She didn't remember doing it, but she must have called out, because three college-aged men appeared around the corner and ran to her. Someone pulled her off him. She kicked and tore at the arms that held her back, the rush of blood in her ears dulling the agitated voice spouting details to a nine-one-one operator, the thumps of a stranger pounding on her fiancé's chest, and her own screams.

An ambulance blared around the corner, followed by a second. Paramedics flew out of both, one pair surrounding Jack, another racing to her side, cutting off her view of him.

She fought against the new arms grabbing at her. "Get off, I'm not hurt—"

"Miss, you're covered in blood, we need to examine you," a woman's voice said.

Jo looked down at herself. Her blouse was stained red, and her jeans were dark. When she lifted her head back up, the mobile gurney elevated, and paramedics pushed Jack toward the ambulance.

"Jack—" she screamed, and pushed toward him.

The woman's arm hooked around her shoulders, and dragged her toward the second vehicle. "They need to get him to the hospital as fast as possible. We'll take you in our ambulance."

The words took a moment to penetrate her fog. "Yes. Right. Okay. Let's go, now." She bolted forward and climbed in.

As the ambulance screamed toward the hospital, the paramedic checked her for injuries and treated her for shock. When they arrived, they lowered her stretcher out of the vehicle and wheeled her into the ER.

She struggled to make sense of the words flying around her in the frantic triage room—she was feeling fuzzy, had they put something in her IV?—what was happening to Jack?

A tight voice called out. "DOA. There's nothing we can do but call it. Time of death, twenty-three forty-seven."

She flew upright, knocking the paramedic off her and onto the floor.

Six feet in front of her, Jack's head lolled to the side of his pillow, covered in blood. The doctor standing next to him shook her head as she pulled off her latex gloves.

Jo screamed, and all the medical professionals ran to her. One called for a medication she didn't recognize, and she felt a sting in her upper arm. The next thing she remembered was waking in a hospital bed, with her mother holding her hand.

She didn't have to ask. The confirmation was clear on her mother's face.

Jack was dead. Murdered, just like Marc, again because of what she had failed to do.

She turned away and pressed her head into her pillow, trying to muffle her wrenching sobs. Her mother rubbed her back, waiting for them to subside, but they continued, relentless, until her mother called the nurse. She gave Jo another, less powerful, sedative, then returned with a prescription for Xanax and the number of a grief counselor. Then she discharged Jo to make room for the victims of a multi-car pile-up.

Jo refused to take even a single pill, but still spent the next months shambling through her life like a zombie. She stopped eating and sleeping almost completely, and sat in the grief counselor's office in crushing silence until her sessions ended. Her professors offered to allow her to make up her coursework after the end of term, when she'd had time to process the death. She declined. She missed only one day of class—the day of Jack's funeral—and handed in every paper and exam on time. She worked every scheduled shift at her library job, checking every student backpack with her blank, dazed expression.

And, she showed up at the police station every day.

They searched for the junkie, or at least, they claimed they did. They humored her as long as possible, probably longer than they should have, she knew now. They'd most likely abandoned the search quickly, not out of neglect, but because random crimes were nearly impossible to solve. After having her sort through endless mug shots and bringing her in for two line-ups, there wasn't much they could do. The information she gave could fit hundreds, even thousands, of junkies in the city, and if the suspect had any sense at all, he'd been on his way out of Boston before the police finished processing the scene. And after telling her every day for three months they had nothing new, they began turning her away at the door, telling her they'd be in contact.

That's when her obsessive-compulsive disorder returned.

Once her hands began to crack and bleed from the handwashing and she'd lost so much weight none of her clothes fit, her mother begged her to see the therapist she'd gone to after Marc was killed. Over the next six months she mustered enough strength to limit her compulsions and put on an act that allowed her mother peace of mind. But even if she no longer looked like a zombie to the rest of the world, she had no illusions about what stared back at her from the mirror—the warm, loving cocoon that Jack spun around her had been ripped away, and left a gaping void in its place.

Eighteen months passed before her mother finally convinced her to stop wearing the engagement ring. And even then, she hadn't, not really. Instead, she set the diamond into a necklace so she could wear it without anyone knowing, so she no longer had to deal with the sideways glances and the constant pleading that it was time to *move on.*

Jo stared into the darkness of her kitchen, crumpled the ginger-ale can, then tossed it into the recycling. She pulled down the calvados from her cabinet and drank off a healthy gulp directly from the bottle. Then she climbed back into bed and stared at the ceiling, hoping the warmth from the brandy would cancel out the chill radiating from the void at her core.

CHAPTER SEVENTEEN

Britney Ratliffe woke at five a.m. and hit snooze on her phone's alarm with a groan.

After a second night of tossing, turning, and crying her eyes out, the last thing she wanted to do was get up and run. But she'd already allowed herself one day off, and it didn't look like she was going to be any less emotional anytime soon. Besides, running always helped her process emotions—and if she didn't find a way to get out from under them soon, she'd go crazy.

She whipped back the covers before she could talk herself out of it, then pulled on leggings, a Lycra top, and a hoodie. She grabbed her headphones, her water, and her keys, then stopped. She thought a moment, grabbed the pepper spray she purchased during the situation with Crawley last semester, then headed out the door.

Ten minutes later, she pulled into the trail parking lot. She switched off the ignition, but sagged against the steering wheel. As the cold seeped in through the door, her body turned to lead. All she had to do was turn the key again, and drive back home. She could dive back under the covers and hide from the world.

But she forced herself out. She selected her most energizing playlist, hoping the music would fuel her, and worked quickly through her stretches. Then she started down the trail, first at a walk, then a slow jog.

She eased into her stride and tried to focus on the smell of the crisp fall air and the pine trees that surrounded her. Normally they brought her peace, but her mind was immune today. Her thoughts repeated through the same circles they'd been racing since she heard about Michael.

Had she done the right thing with the police? Maybe she should have been honest with them about everything. But she couldn't risk putting herself on the line like that. What would the point be? It wouldn't bring him back, it would just make him, and her, look bad. Surely that wasn't the way to honor someone's memory? No, it didn't make any sense. None of it was related, Greg Crawley was the murderer, and bringing up anything else would only confuse the issue.

She shook her head and picked up her pace as the trail wove through the dark trees.

Tears filled her eyes and blurred her vision. Why did things like this always have to happen to her? She'd been so close to happiness, he would have been forced to leave his wife soon. But now the man she loved was dead, murdered, and she was alone again. Back to square one. At this point she'd be thirty before she had her first child, even if she met someone else tomorrow. And who would help launch her career? She didn't have time to start over with a new advisor.

To her right, a flurry of leaves rustled. She reached up to wipe the tears away with one gloved hand, and clutched her pepper spray with the other.

It rolled away, useless, when something smashed against the back of her skull.

CHAPTER EIGHTEEN

A stack of boxes, courtesy of Camilla Whorton, awaited Jo and Arnett that morning when they arrived at headquarters. They brewed a fresh pot of coffee, rolled up their sleeves, and dove in.

"I've got a stack of term papers," Jo said as she opened the first box.

"I raise you several binders of department and university bylaws."

"Looks like we're in for a scintillating morning."

They worked steadily, checking every page to be sure there were no important notes scribbled in corners or items folded and shoved within others, interrupted only by a call from Beth Morlinski. Jo scheduled an appointment for the following day and returned to sorting.

"Ah, now we're getting to it. Looks like I have some invoices here," Arnett said.

Jo wheeled her chair over to Arnett's desk to take a look. "Lab equipment?"

"Looks like. For now I'm just sorting them out. I think we need to compare with the files from Whorton's office in order to get a full picture of anything."

"And any tracking software he has on his computer," she added.

They finished up Camilla's boxes, then headed in to grab the other records from Lopez.

She greeted them enthusiastically. "Hey guys, you beat me to the punch. In about half an hour, I'd have been calling for you.

Marzillo's got some news for you, too." She grabbed several stacks of paper off her desk and gestured for them to follow.

Marzillo was concentrating so intently on her computer, she didn't hear them come in. "Ahem," Lopez said, with a laugh.

"Oh, hey, sorry. Pull up a couple of chairs. I have a few things to show you."

As they settled in, Marzillo pulled up a picture on the large screen in front of her. "My speculation on site was generally correct with respect to time of death and method. ME confirms Whorton was stabbed first in the side, then in the neck. We can now add that the first stab was targeted and skilled—he knew what he was doing, and Whorton would likely have bled out before help arrived, even after that first stab."

"Could he have been lucky with the hit?"

She looked skeptical. "Maybe, the same way monkeys with word processors might be lucky enough to type out Hamlet."

Jo tapped her pen onto her notepad. "Would it take any particular strength to stab from the side like that?"

"Not really, he'd just have to know what he was doing."

"We keep saying 'he.' Is there reason to believe a man rather than a woman did it?" Jo asked.

Marzillo tilted her head to consider. "No, not that I can see. I'm just using 'he' for expedience. A woman of even average strength could have done it with a sharp blade like this. And we can't really estimate height from the angle of the wound, because the attacker might have hunched over, or might have come straight up. The best I can tell you is he, or she, wasn't notably tall or notably short."

"Gotcha." Jo's pen flipped back and forth.

Marzillo continued. "We processed the restroom, plenty of prints in there, but no blood we could find. We also didn't find any handy-dandy gloves covered in blood in any of the building's garbage cans. That's always a good time, by the way, searching through garbage. Anytime you guys wanna help with that part, just ask."

Jo laughed. "Far be it from me to get in the way of your fun. I *will* bring you a latte next time we drop by to say thanks, however."

Marzillo laughed. "I'm not proud. I'll take it."

"My turn," Lopez said, and slid a stack of papers over to each of them. She paused while they scanned the information on the top page.

"Phone records. The call Whorton was on when he was stabbed was an incoming call, from a number that turned out to be a burner phone. I tracked it down to a mom-and-pop in Springfield. They checked their records and the phone was purchased with cash, about two months ago. They don't have surveillance tapes going that far back, they have one memory card for each day of the week, so nothing lasts longer than seven days. So, dead end there. But." Lopez paused, eyes gleaming. "That was the only call ever made from the phone."

The implication settled on Jo. "So either the killer happened to have an unused burner phone laying around, or he's been planning this for a while."

"Correct. So the next thing I did was access all of Whorton's phone records, from the office, from his lab number, from home, and from his cell." She pulled out the next four paper-clipped set of papers from her own stack, set them on the desk in front of her, then pointed to each in turn. "Office, lab, home, cell. I checked into the names you said were suspects. Of course there are calls from his wife, those are always on the cell, and from Britney Ratliffe, also mostly on the cell, but one to the home number. Some from Arthur Kerland, also on his cell. Nothing from Crawley or Shawnessy. But now look at the yellow highlights."

Jo and Arnett peered at the numbers, and Lopez's neat handwriting next to them. "Dean Latimer's office and cell. That's not surprising."

"Nope. Now look at these, on his cell phone."

"Latimer's home and—wait—*Nicole Latimer*. He was calling Latimer's wife? Why am I not surprised?" Jo said.

Lopez shook her head, and jabbed her finger at the name. "Not his wife. His daughter."

*

Five minutes later, Jo pulled the car out of the HQ lot and headed toward the university.

"I can't tell you how much I'm gonna love nailing Latimer for lying to us. No way he didn't know about this." Arnett scoured the pages he'd snatched up as they left.

"I'm positive he knew about it. Explains the way his secretary treated us, and his reluctance all around. And why he was so fast to pull up confidential files implicating other suspects," Jo said.

"I knew Whorton was a cheating slimeball, but this is beyond," Arnett said, as Jo read him the text exchanges between Whorton and Nicole Latimer that Lopez had printed out for them. "She's practically a child."

Jo tried to keep the wry smile off her face. "Looks like we've hit *your* nerve, now."

Arnett glared at her. "Yeah, I guess borderline statutory rape is nothing to get worked up over, right?"

"I didn't say that. And, she's twenty. She's been legal for four years according to the Commonwealth of Massachusetts."

"But what really gets me is that he must have known her when she was younger, both he and Latimer have worked at the university for years. Disgusting. Yeah, that pisses me off."

"Hey, I'm right there with you. But let's not forget what you told me yesterday." Jo's phone rang. "Lopez. Do you have more news?"

Lopez's voice vibrated with energy. "I do. I just got Greg Crawley's school records. Turns out, his stability wasn't just questionable, it was non-existent. He has a definite and disturbing history of both mental illness and violence. His file with the disabilities services office notes he's been diagnosed as a paranoid schizophrenic with post-traumatic stress disorder. He suffers from depression and anxiety, and has a history of self-medicating."

"They released his psych records without a warrant?" Jo asked.

"These aren't his psych records. He had to allow his psychiatrist to report his issues to the office in order to qualify for accommodations, so it's a bit easier to get access to the records. But get this. Not only did they know all of that, they also have two violent incidents in his report, both where he attacked another student. In both cases, after a meeting with the administration, the students in question didn't file charges. My guess is the university talked them out of it, why I don't know, but it fits with the sweep-it-under-the-rug theme we've seen so far."

Arnett growled, "They kept that quiet even when a professor and a graduate student were worried about their safety? Nice."

"Right? Anyway, that got me wondering, so I did some digging and got access to his military records. He was in the army from 2013 to 2014, and excelled at his training. Which, of course, includes weapons and outdoor training, among other skills. However, he quickly showed signs of instability that worried his superiors, so they sent him for evaluation. And here's the kicker—what finally got him kicked out was an attack on a fellow soldier, *with a knife*. Luckily the guy was pretty proficient in hand-to-hand combat and Crawley only managed a flesh wound on his arm."

"Holy shit," Arnett said.

"Yep. And in addition to his flimsy alibi for the time of Whorton's death…" Lopez said.

"Right. Looks like we need to pay him another visit," Jo said. They wrapped up the call, and she disconnected. "Before or after Latimer, do you think?"

Arnett considered. "Before. Rockney's gonna want a name from us any second now, and while Latimer may know more than he's saying, he couldn't have killed Whorton. But Crawley's looking more and more likely."

Jo's phone rang again. "Speak of the devil and he shall appear." She tapped the screen. "Fournier. We were just about—"

Rockney barreled over her. "Get over to Mount Misty, now. Britney Ratliffe was found stabbed just off the jogging trail."

CHAPTER NINETEEN

Mount Misty was a small wooded area on the north-most section of the OakhurstU campus, and the moniker was tongue-in-cheek. While the woods were centered around a hill, it was so small it took no more than half an hour to climb to the top. The relatively flat trail that skirted the hill was a favorite spot for student joggers, as well as some non-student residents in the area. Jo off-roaded the car as close as possible to the section where Britney's body had been found, then she and Arnett hiked the remaining short distance.

Marzillo spotted them as they approached the yellow crime-scene tape. She straightened, and, careful to avoid contact with her glove-covered hand, wiped her forearm across her brow. "Suit up and follow me," she greeted them, and disappeared around a ten-foot-tall rock that edged the trail.

Jo and Arnett put on their gear, then ducked under the tape and surveyed the area in front of them. A rough swath of disturbed leaves and dirt cut across the ground in an arc from the trail around to the back of the rock. They picked their steps carefully to the back of the rock, where Marzillo stood waiting. Next to her, Britney sprawled face down in the dirt at the end of the swath, arms near her head and legs askew, as though she'd collapsed forward. Dirt and leaves caked what they could see of the front of her black leggings and red hoodie, but the backs were relatively clean. "Looks like she was dragged back here from the trail," Jo said.

Arnett bent to point at the gash on the back of her neck. "That the cause of death?"

"Possibly. She was also bashed on the head, most likely with that." Marzillo pointed back toward a large stone nearby. "You can't see it from here, but there's blood and hair on it. We'll check for a match of course, but I'm fairly certain it caused the nasty contusion I found on the back of her head. So nasty, she may have already been dead by the time he stabbed her."

Jo bent. "Looks like the same sort of laceration we found on Whorton's neck."

"And the knife we found next to the body is identical to the one that killed Whorton."

"Not much doubt this is the same killer," Arnett said.

"And if there were, this would finish it." Marzillo bent and lifted Britney's chest slightly off the ground, exposing an object underneath.

"You gotta be kidding me," Arnett said.

Jo's pulse quickened. "Another tarot card."

Marzillo nodded. "You want to bag it?"

Jo took the forceps and an evidence bag. She carefully removed the card, closed it into the bag, then flipped it over. On the front, a devious-looking man was making off with five swords while casting a furtive glance back over his shoulder toward two that remained on the ground. "That closes the door on the possibility the tarot card was left there by accident," Jo said.

Marzillo handed a second bag to Jo. "So it's a good thing I brought the tarot card found at the Whorton scene to compare. They're both from the same deck, a very common one called the Windym-Taylor deck. This card is called the Seven of Swords, for obvious reasons."

Jo examined the card through the plastic. "I don't suppose we know they're from the self-same deck?"

"That I can't tell for sure."

Jo frowned. "Sure seems like someone's sending a message."

Arnett grimaced. "The whole thing is just a little too precious, if you ask me."

Jo nodded. "It has an odd feel, I agree. But nobody does something like this without a reason. And, it's pretty safe to say they weren't sent to scare the victims beforehand."

"So some sort of signature." Arnett shrugged.

Jo remained silent, unconvinced, frustration mounting and without a better theory to offer. She glanced back up at Marzillo. "Any estimate of the time of death?"

"Approximately between 5:30 and 6:30 this morning."

"While it was still dark out." Jo tapped her leg. "Who found her?"

"Jogger with a Yorkie who ran behind the rock and didn't want to come back out."

Jo gazed back and forth between the rock and the path. "Not sure how much good it will do with the darkness, but we need to put out a call for anyone who was in the area between 5:30 and 6:30. Do you know if the parking lots have security cameras?"

Janet shook her head. "They don't, but even if they did, it doesn't matter. I jog here all the time, and there are a hundred ways you can enter the trail without going near a parking lot. The killer'd have to be an idiot to risk being seen in one."

"Great," Arnett said. "Any other wounds, or sexual violation?"

"Not that I can tell, but the ME will need to take a closer look."

Jo glanced down. "Nice soft leaves everywhere, no way we're going to find a footprint. I don't suppose there are any cigarette butts brimming with DNA nearby?"

Janet shook her head. "My team has been radiating out, and they're to the point where anything they find would most likely be unrelated. All we can hope is she managed to fight back somehow and got some of her killer's DNA under her nails. But since she has no defensive wounds that I can see, my guess is our killer knocked her unconscious before she knew what was happening."

Jo nodded her understanding. "So, recap. Most likely he hit her near the path, and she fell to the ground unconscious. Then he dragged her over here, and stabbed her in the neck. Minimized the risk to her fighting back, and made sure she wouldn't be discovered right away."

Marzillo nodded. "That's what I'm seeing."

"And I'm guessing from Rockney's call that nobody has notified a next of kin yet?"

"Not that I'm aware of."

Arnett winced. "I hate this part."

*

After touching base with Lopez about the new victim, Jo and Arnett spent the next two hours notifying Britney's parents and her roommate, Jennifer Koske, of her death. Jennifer confirmed for them that Britney jogged on the trail every weekday like clockwork, first thing in the morning, and usually alone. She couldn't confirm exactly when Britney left because she hadn't been awake yet, and no, Britney hadn't exhibited any strange behavior recently. Moreover, she and Britney weren't close. They hadn't lived together long, and although she knew Britney was seeing someone, she never met the guy. Jennifer was a linguistics student, so knew nothing about the inner workings of the biology department. She did, however, remember Britney mentioning Greg Crawley, in excruciating detail.

They did a quick, careful search of her belongings, but found nothing of interest. They taped off her room and told Jennifer nobody was allowed to enter without official state police detective unit permission. Then Ruth Henderson allowed them into Britney's graduate student office on campus, where they found her desk empty, aside for a small array of pencils, pens, and Post-it notes.

After Arnett called his wife to let her know he'd again be home late, they drove to Sal's for a quick dinner break.

"Laura ticked off?" Jo asked while they waited for their Sal's Supreme.

He wagged his head yes-and-no. "She's not overjoyed. Tonight was date night."

"You don't look broken up over it," she said.

"Painting," he said.

"Painting?"

"Painting. You get a bottle of wine and they show you a prototype and you get to recreate it." His eyes remained firmly on his coffee cup.

Jo nodded, and sipped from her Coke. Several years back, Laura had cheated on Bob. When the dust settled, the couple had decided the infidelity flagged an underlying problem with the relationship, that Laura felt abandoned by Bob. As a result, they'd agreed to find ways to spend time together. This painting excursion was the most recent in a string of activities, most of which drove Bob insane. But Jo smiled at the exasperated expression on his face. The truth was he loved Laura dearly and would paint a million such pictures if that's what it took to keep a firm grip on her heart.

She cleared her throat. "So. Rockney's expecting a call from us, pretty much now. I'm thinking we'll need to check out the key alibis tonight, and see if we can give him a preliminary name until the evidence starts coming back?"

Arnett nodded. "Sounds about right. At the very least, this should narrow things down for us. We assumed Greg Crawley didn't know Britney had graded his test, but like you say, students pick up on these things."

"And, he was almost as angry at Britney as Whorton for ignoring him and pushing him off on the counseling office."

Arnett leaned back from the table as the waitress slid their pizza onto the table and confirmed they didn't need anything else.

Jo grabbed a slice of pizza and set it on her plate to cool. "Then there's Camilla Whorton. If she lost it after Britney called her, she may have decided to kill them both, although it's pretty stupid to mention to us that Britney had called her if so."

Arnett also grabbed a slice. "Nah. She's smart enough to know the call will show up as soon as we check the records. Smarter to get out ahead of it." He folded the corners of the slice together, and angled the point into his mouth.

"And of all the explanations for the tarot cards, a scorned woman visiting the fires of revenge on her cheating husband and his mistress seems to fit better psychologically to me than the others. And it would have a poetic justice to it, using the symbol on his lover's wrist when she kills him." She jotted a note down. "Which reminds me, we need to figure out what the Seven of Swords means."

"Assuming she knew Britney had it on her wrist. But they supposedly had all those mixers with graduate students and professors, so probably not too far-fetched," Arnett said. "Next is Terry Shawnessy. No reason to want Britney dead that I can see. No contact with her according to the phone records."

Jo shrugged. "Not that we know of yet. But it's a small department, and every time we turn around we find out something more disturbing. If something illegal is going on financially with Whorton's industry work, the same may have been true for Kerland, and Britney Ratliffe might have found out about it. Or even be involved in it."

"And that would be a possible motive for Kerland, if Whorton and Ratliffe both knew something that threatened him, or if they'd betrayed him." Arnett reached for another slice of pizza.

"Good point. That just leaves Beth Morlinski, but she has zero reason to want Britney dead. She never worked with Britney, and wasn't involved in any of the industry dealings we've found so far," Jo said.

"We're meeting with her tomorrow, right? I'd be interested to see if she knew anything about the industry work they all were doing, or about Whorton's affair with Britney."

Jo nodded. "But she was gone before Shawnessy, so was Britney even working with Whorton then?"

Arnett shook his head. "Still, you never know, the affair may have predated all that. It's worth asking."

Jo nodded, and shoved her plate away. "So. The first thing we need to do is check out the alibis, and hope that narrows us down to one."

CHAPTER TWENTY

Nancy Kerland slipped into her kitchen and clicked the back door into place behind her, then thought better of it. The house was a bit too warm, which would only make her feel worse. She propped the door back open so the cool autumn air could circulate, then set down her keys and the mail she'd picked up from town, and sank down into the nearest kitchen chair. She closed her eyes, then took herself through a full-body relaxation paired with deep breathing.

It hadn't been a good day. Or week, or even month, for that matter. The bad patch she'd been going through wouldn't seem to end, and the doctor today hadn't been any help. Not his fault—multiple sclerosis and advanced heart disease were just like that. So she did the best she could do, walked every day and ate a healthy diet. Meditated and tried to get enough sleep, although a full night's rest was a unicorn she'd given up on finding.

But the fatigue and constant aches of this flare-up were making it harder and harder for her to stave off the depression lapping at her psyche, so she'd been counting the days until she could get out here to the Berkshires. She smiled to herself, and took in a deep breath of the fresh forest air. The quiet here instantly relaxed her, and the air cleansed her.

She opened her eyes again and reached for the mail. She was surprised how much junk mail came even to a vacation home in the woods, but what a lovely surprise, there was also a card from her niece. She opened it and smiled—kittens in human clothes were very much Tasha's style. She propped it up open on the table and worked through the rest of the pile.

When she reached the final envelope, she frowned. It was too light, as though it were empty. She ripped back the flap and looked inside. Some sort of playing card—she pulled it out and flipped it over, and her hard-earned peace disappeared.

The oversized card featured a happy couple gesturing toward a rainbow marked with chalices, surrounded by playing children. An X, the Roman numeral for ten, rode the rainbow's crest.

She double-checked the envelope. Addressed to *The Kerland Residence*, it had no postmark or stamp, or return address. How had it been delivered? And why would someone send something like this? Was it some sort of message? Oakhurst circles were small, and the politics Arthur dealt with at the university were toxic. Had he done something to upset someone? For her part, she couldn't imagine whose nose she might have put out of joint, since she kept mostly to herself these days.

She slipped the card back into the envelope and shook her head. She was being paranoid. This was probably just some sick idiot's idea of a bad joke. But it was the sort of thing her mind couldn't let go of, so she picked up her phone. She'd call Arthur, and he'd laugh it off and tell her it was nothing, and that would put her mind at ease.

She placed the call, but he didn't answer. She checked the time, and winced—he was right in the middle of a lecture. Hopefully his phone had been off. He got so angry when she didn't remember his schedule and disturbed him in class. She slipped the card back into the envelope.

On a positive note, she was feeling a bit better physically. She brought the groceries in from the car, then made another trip for her small travel suitcase. She paused and considered whether she was still feeling good enough to bring up a few fall decorations.

Yes, she decided. She'd give at least the kitchen a little seasonal color, then make an early dinner.

As she headed down to the basement, a strange sound stopped her short.

She waited, but it didn't repeat. Was something wrong with the furnace? It was certainly working, perhaps too well. Arthur would have to check it when he arrived, and he'd be none too happy about it. She sighed, and swung open the door at the bottom of the stairs.

Something between a snarl and a howl ripped through the air. Huge golden eyes surrounded by white fangs leaped for her head. She screamed and ducked as the beast barreled into her, knocking her to the floor.

Then it flew past her, up the stairs.

She sat up, heart pounding, trying to catch her breath. What was that? She tried to keep hold of logical thought as her mind tried to convince her a huge, rabid, mythical beast had just attacked her. No, she told herself, it just looked fierce and menacing because of the dark, and the shock. But she couldn't seem to quiet her gasping.

She closed her eyes and told herself to be calm. *This is only a panic attack. You've had dozens before. You just need to focus.*

But her body screamed for oxygen, as though she were submerged underwater, and she involuntarily gasped. Shallow, rasping, ineffective gasps, because her lungs refused to expand. The harder she tried to take a long, deep breath, the more her chest contracted.

Then her heart skipped.

She tried to stand, to get to the aspirin in her pocketbook. Her legs wobbled and buckled out from under her. She reached out her arms, trying to climb the stairs on her hands and knees, but she could only manage a slow crawl. She needed her phone—

She was halfway up when pain shot down her arms, and her chest caught fire.

CHAPTER TWENTY-ONE

Jo and Arnett spent the next two hours back at HQ checking the alibis of the suspects they could reach for the time of Britney Ratliffe's murder. Which turned out to be very short work, because Greg Crawley, Camilla Whorton, and Terry Shawnessy all claimed they'd been in bed, sleeping. Not unreasonable given the time of day, but also not useful for narrowing down suspects.

Next, Jo researched the Seven of Swords card. "All the sites seem to agree the card boils down to deception and betrayal," Jo said.

"Pretty intuitive match for the picture, then." Arnett leaned back in his chair.

"Yep. And I can see that applying both to Crawley, who believed Michael and Britney were taking his test scores, and to Camilla Whorton, if she was angry about the affair."

"But Michael's the one that deceived and betrayed her, not Britney. I was angry with Laura when she cheated, not with the man she met up with."

"That's because you are an exceptional person, my friend. But I promise you, most people see it differently. Think of all the assault cases you've seen where someone attacks their partner's lover."

"When you put it like that, I see it." He laughed. "And if there was something illegal going on with Whorton and Kerland's industry work and Ratliffe got caught in it, I could see the card applying there too."

Jo leaned forward and picked up her phone. "Very true. So I might as well call Kerland again and see if he'll finally set up an appointment with—" Her phone rang. "Okay, this is getting creepy. It's him." She answered. "Detective Josette Fournier."

A frantic voice crackled over the phone. "Detective Fournier, Roger Latimer informed me you're one of the detectives investigating Michael Whorton's and Britney Ratliffe's murders?"

"That's correct. We've been trying to reach—"

"My wife's dead, and I can't get these morons to listen to me. I'm absolutely positive this is related to their deaths. This was intended for me—someone is trying to kill *me*."

CHAPTER TWENTY-TWO

Jo and Arnett pulled up next to a floodlit tent outside the Kerlands' rustic wood-timbered two-story Berkshires country home. Arnett studied the house, and whistled. "I'm telling you, I missed my calling."

Jo narrowed her eyes as she scanned the building and the surrounding property, which sat five minutes down a dirt road from the nearest sign of human habitation. "Yeah. One might be a coincidence. But two professors with assets they shouldn't be able to afford is a little much."

A thirty-something man with dark hair and eyes strode out to their car. "Arnett? Fournier? I'm David Perdue, Berkshire County SPDU. Your ADA called mine and told me you were on the way."

Jo reached out for his hand. "We don't mean to intrude on your crime scene, but Arthur Kerland insists there's a connection with a pair of murders we're investigating. What happened here?"

"I don't see how, we're not even convinced it's a crime scene. His wife had a heart attack is all."

"He said something about an animal attack?"

A shaggy blond-splotched-with-white head popped out of a Mercedes E 400 pulled off the side of the dirt road. When the rest of him emerged, he turned out to be well over six feet tall, wearing a polo shirt and khakis both too tight around his waist. He hurried over to them. "What's he telling you?"

Perdue glared at the man, then back at Jo. "Mr. Kerland here became alarmed—"

"*Dr.,*" Arthur Kerland said.

Perdue's jaw twitched. "*Dr.* Kerland became alarmed when he wasn't able to reach his wife either by cell phone or landline. He drove out here to check—"

Arthur pointed at Perdue. "Don't make it sound like I'm overreacting. She has multiple sclerosis and a heart condition!"

Perdue's eyes stayed on Jo. "When he arrived he found his wife just below the top of the basement stairs. He found no pulse, and called nine-one-one. Paramedics report she was deceased when they arrived, of an apparent heart attack. We found no forced entry, nothing missing, no bruises or other evidence that she was attacked. We're open to all possibilities, and of course the ME will examine her. But for the moment, best we can tell, she overexerted herself climbing up the stairs and had a heart attack."

"The back door was wide open, and the—"

Arnett took a step toward Arthur, but Jo laid a hand on his arm. She interrupted Arthur, her tone firm but kind. "Dr. Kerland, please. We want to help you, but we can't unless you let us all do our jobs."

A series of thoughts danced across his face, then his shoulders drooped and he nodded.

She turned back to Perdue. "Dr. Kerland told us there was some sort of break-in? That the back door was open and the mesh ripped out of the screen door?"

Perdue's eyes flicked between her and Arnett. "Dr. Kerland tells us his wife was often in the habit of leaving the back door open, and there's no way of knowing how long the screen had been like that. The house had been vacant for two weeks since their last visit, so that could have been caused by a tree branch from the last storm, or a foraging animal. We're dusting for prints, but I'm not confident we'll find anything useful."

"And he mentioned you found animal feces in the basement?"

"If I had a dime for every time someone found animal feces in a basement out here, I'd be a rich man."

Arthur reanimated. "These weren't rat droppings, you imbecile. They're large, from something at least the size of a dog."

Perdue's face flushed, and Jo's hand flew up before he could reply. She needed to de-escalate this before Perdue arrested Arthur Kerland just to get him out of the way. "Would you mind if we take a look at the crime scene, whenever it's convenient for your team?" she asked.

"I don't have any objection." He pointed to a tall man dusting the screen for fingerprints, his speech clipped. "Talk to him. Keenan Mayfair. He'll get you suited up and make sure you don't get in the way."

"We appreciate it. Dr. Kerland, we'll come talk to you after we take a look." She pointed back to the Mercedes. Arthur opened his mouth to speak but thought better of it, then spun on his heel and headed for the car.

Arnett turned his back to hide his smile from Arthur. "Nice Jedi mind trick," he said.

She checked over her shoulder to be sure Arthur was out of earshot, and laughed. "The moment I saw him, all I could think of was my uncle Roland. He was one of those guys who always had something to prove, and would flip if another man invaded his space, literally or metaphorically. But as soon as my mémé or one of his older sisters said something, he'd deflate like a chastised child."

"Some sort of mother complex?"

She shrugged. "Whatever it is, I'll take it."

They introduced themselves to Keenan Mayfair, who gave them protective gear. Jo leaned forward to inspect the torn screen. The edge had almost completely separated from the left side and half of the bottom, and the sheet was slightly rounded outward. "Fair amount of damage, but from the wrong direction. If a branch hit it or an animal was pawing at it, you wouldn't see an even curve like that. Something would have to push through it from the inside to get that."

Arnett pressed the release and the door swung open with a hydraulic whoosh from the spring mechanism. "Opens easily enough. You can lock it, here. Was it locked when you arrived?"

"Nope," Mayfair answered.

Jo snapped several pictures with her phone, then straightened up. "Can we see the victim?"

"Over here." Mayfair led them to the basement stairs, which were a few feet away from the back door, on the right side of the room. He pointed. "We found her in that position."

Jo had seen hundreds, possibly thousands, of dead bodies in her time on the police force, and had long since developed a thick professional distance for viewing them. But every so often, one wriggled under her protective coating, and this was one of those times. Nancy's brown eyes, so dark they were almost black, stared up toward the top of the staircase, past her outstretched hand, expression twisted as if caught in a scream. Her other hand clutched her blouse. Her knees were tucked partly under her, braced on a lower step. "She looks terrified."

"Heart attacks are painful. And with her history, she likely knew what was happening to her."

Jo nodded, considering. "How long has she been dead?"

"Coroner's estimated time of death is between two and two-thirty this afternoon."

Arnett didn't need to check his watch. "So about five hours ago. Can we go downstairs? The husband said something about animal feces."

Mayfair led them carefully down to the basement. "The scat is over there, and there, although I'm not sure what it has to do with anything. We got wild animals all over the place out here. The problem is, city folk come out here because they think the woods are quaint, but they have no idea how to handle themselves. A couple of months ago we got a call because a lady came downstairs in the middle of the night to find an adolescent bear in her kitchen. That's what happens when you leave a damned coffeecake out on your table and your window open so anything and its brother can smell the damned thing. Bear climbed right in."

Arnett raised his eyebrows at Jo behind Mayfair's back, and she pushed down a smile. They stepped over and inspected the two piles. "Arthur's right, definitely not small. Too big for a cat or a raccoon."

"'Course it is. It's from a coyote."

Their heads snapped up. "You sure?" Arnett asked.

"Pretty damned sure. I've lived and hunted in these woods my whole life. And I'm an eagle scout."

"Could it be from a dog?" Jo asked.

"Not likely. See that one especially? All the fur in it, and how it's all twisted? That's because coyotes eat other animals. If your dog drops something like that, get him to a vet."

"Does *that* happen a lot around here, too? Coyotes in the basement?" Arnett asked.

Mayfair's eyes narrowed at the sarcasm, then he pointed at shreds of plastic by a metal shelving unit. "Food has been scarce this year, we've seen plenty of them starved to death. My guess is he was looking for food."

They followed his gesture and bent down to examine the shards. A memory of Eric mentioning something similar about the coyote population stirred in Jo's mind.

"Looks like a bag of beef jerky. Can we get this bagged up as evidence?" Arnett said.

Mayfair shrugged, somehow infusing the gesture with scorn. "Sure, if you want."

Jo squatted next to the piles of scat. "This one looks older than the other."

The men leaned over. "Huh, it sure does," Mayfair said.

Jo straightened up, considering Mayfair's change in tone. She'd dealt with people like Mayfair before, in fact, half her family in Louisiana were exactly this type of people. Excellent at their jobs, but they could come off as rigid and unreasonable because they didn't put much stock in strangers, and because they didn't appreciate being treated like hicks. The more she and Arnett, let alone Arthur Kerland, insisted he was wrong, the more he'd dig in.

She adjusted her response. "Here's our problem. We have a man upstairs who's certain this indicates some sort of foul play. I need to explain to him how this happened so he'll understand and get off all of our backs, but I have to admit, I don't fully understand it myself. Help me out."

Mayfair gestured around the room. "Not hard to explain at all. His wife had the back door open, then had a heart attack. A hungry coyote looking for food found his way in, then couldn't get back out. Maybe knocked the door closed when he was nosing behind there for food. Then he'd be stuck."

He was right. To get to the metal shelves, the coyote would have had to nose the door out of the way. Jo tested the door—it swung easily, and clicked into place, revealing deep grooves scratched along the bottom and two feet up the side. She snapped several pictures.

"So, then, how did he get back out of the basement?"

Mayfair scratched his chin. "Maybe something was wedged in the door, and he was finally able to paw it open."

"Like what?" Jo searched around the floor.

Mayfair's expression started to shut down again. "Could be anything. A piece of that plastic from the jerky, even."

Jo decided not to press the sketchy logic, and nodded. "Can we look through the rest of the house?"

"Sure thing." He led them carefully back upstairs, then took them through the tidy house room by room. Other than a small suitcase waiting in the master suite to be unpacked, the only room that showed anything out of place was the kitchen. "Groceries never made it into the refrigerator. Heart attack must have happened right after she got home," Arnett said.

A young woman with a blond ponytail called in from the porch. "Keenan, I need you to come sign off on these photos."

"I can trust you guys not to touch anything?" he asked, looking at Jo.

"Of course," she answered, and waited for him to leave. Then she turned to Arnett. "What's your take?"

"I'm not a big fan of coincidences, but if it weren't for the timing, I'd see no reason to consider this a homicide."

"Agreed. It feels off, but if it looks like a duck, and quacks like a duck, it's most likely a duck, right? Sometimes strange things just happen. And who knows, with the murders on campus, Nancy's anxiety may have been higher than normal." Jo scanned the room again while she spoke. "Quick recap, then put it to rest?"

He nodded, and scanned the room. "She comes home, brings her suitcase upstairs and her groceries in from the car."

Jo also scanned the room, and noticed something on the kitchen table. "And brought in the mail."

Arnett followed her finger. "Nice catch."

They crossed to the large pile of letters and magazines splayed across the Formica. "Looks like she'd gone through it, or at least most of it."

Jo called to Mayfair, and waited impatiently until he returned. "Has your team gone through this yet?"

He cleared his throat. "We didn't think it was relevant."

Jo pushed down the urge to snap at him. "It may not be. Would you mind if we do it now?"

He shrugged, and called in the woman with the ponytail to photograph the pile. Jo began with the greeting card propped up against the wall, and checked the matching envelope. Then she slipped her gloved hand into the next item on the pile, a plain, letter-sized envelope with no return address.

She pulled out a tarot card.

"So much for our duck," Arnett said.

*

After a loud conversation with his lieutenant about the tarot cards, Perdue was more than willing to turn jurisdiction of the scene over to Jo and Arnett. As they waited for Marzillo and her team to arrive and get up to speed, they waved Arthur Kerland out of his car.

"You okay with me handling him?" Jo asked.

"Nothing would please me more," Arnett replied.

"What did you find?" Arthur asked as soon as he was in range.

"Dr. Kerland, you mentioned on the phone that you believe this attack was meant for you, and not your wife. Why?"

"My wife didn't have enemies. She was a gentle soul, and everybody loved her. Someone came for me, and was thrown off when they encountered her instead. And whatever happened frightened her literally to death." His throat seized at the end of the sentence.

"Were you supposed to come out here today?"

"No, I wasn't supposed to come out until Friday morning. I never come out during the week, but she does. The air quality is better out here, and the surroundings calm her. Someone must have seen the car and assumed it was me."

"Who knew you were coming to stay this weekend?"

"Almost everybody. I hold my office hours and any other meetings I need to take via Skype when we come out here, and I post notices on the course website. So, students, TAs, colleagues, friends. Anybody who checks the website."

"So they would know *you* were coming, but not that your wife was."

"Yes. No, that's not true. Everybody knows about her condition, and that she's the reason I come out here as often as I do."

"Even your students?"

"As I say, they know that's why I have to hold certain office hours off campus."

"In that case, we need to know why you're so sure this is related to Dr. Whorton's murder."

Arthur shifted his weight from leg to leg, and paused before answering. "I already explained that to you. The timing."

Jo studied his face. A couple of hours ago, Arthur Kerland had been begging them to come investigate the scene. Now he'd turned oddly cagey. "Dr. Kerland, if the timing of the deaths is the only reason you feel there's a connection, that's fine. But if there's some other reason you think someone wants you dead as well as Michael Whorton and Britney Ratliffe, now's the time to tell us about it."

Arthur's face went pale. "People in positions of power have enemies. I'm the chair of the department and Michael was chair before me. And Britney works closely with him. I'm sure we've angered more than a few people, especially people who'd rather blame others than take responsibility for their failures."

"Who in particular?"

He paused, expression like a trapped animal, then spat out his words. "Start with Roger Latimer and Terry Shawnessy. There's also Steve Parminder. And I'm sure more than a few students would love to see us dead."

"And their motives?" she asked.

Anger flashed in Arthur Kerland's eyes. "Terry blamed us for his failure to get tenure. Steve Parminder is one of those idealistic idiots who can't see past the nose on his face. Our plans for growth were a burr in his side. And Roger Latimer would do anything to keep the status quo in the school of natural sciences. He—" Kerland stopped, and cleared his throat.

"He what?" Arnett asked.

Kerland's gaze slid back toward the house. "He doesn't like the direction we're taking the department."

Jo was sure he'd been about to say something else, and was fairly certain Roger Latimer didn't give a rat's ass which direction the department took. "Not liking the direction of the department doesn't sound like a good reason to murder one person, let alone three. And I'm not sure how Britney would be relevant."

Kerland's gaze shifted again. "You tell me. I'm a biologist, not a psychologist. But I'll tell you this—you'd be surprised how invested people get in academic politics."

Jo blinked. "I'm beginning to see that. Tell us about your relationship with Michael Whorton. Were you friends outside of work?"

His weight shifted again. "Friend*ly*, yes."

"What does that mean, exactly?" Arnett asked.

"Occasionally we'd have dinner together. Not much more than that."

Jo glanced back at the large house, but kept her skepticism to herself. "And your relationship with Britney Ratliffe?"

He met her eyes full on. "I don't have a relationship with her. She's taken several of my classes, of course, just like all the other graduate students, but nothing more. But she's Michael's right hand. She's his senior graduate student and she runs his lab. She is—was—involved in everything he does."

Jo decided she was unlikely to get more, and circled back. "You mentioned students. Any in particular?"

"Almost anyone who's failed my class would have motive, and there are several every term. I can have my lab manager pull up my rosters and grades from the past few years."

"That would be helpful. The student would have to be angry at both you and Dr. Whorton, and so be someone who would have taken classes from both of you. Is there any way of separating those out?"

"Any student majoring in biology would have. He and I both taught required upper-division classes."

Jo mentally rubbed her face at the thought of how many students that involved. "Does the name Greg Crawley ring a bell?"

Arthur's flushed faced drained of blood. "Oh, God. Crawley. Complete nightmare. I had him three semesters ago. How he's still allowed to set foot on campus, I'll never understand. Michael told them he was dangerous, but they refused to do anything about it. Something about a disability." He scoured the surrounding forest, and the pitch of his voice rose. "Oh, God. I said it then—I said, what happens if he shows up with a gun? I said that very thing!"

Jo reached out and laid a hand on his arm. "Dr. Kerland, I need you to stay calm. Is there any way he'd know where this house is located?"

Kerland stared at her blankly for a moment. "Several of the faculty have houses in the general area, and between us we have at least one gathering each summer and winter for the faculty and graduate students. I have a weekend retreat out here at the end of the year as a thank you to all my research assistants. So yes, a number of undergraduates know where the house is." His eyes swept the darkness again. "He could be out there right now, watching us."

Jo forced herself not to turn. "If he did this, he's too smart to be nearby. I need you to focus for just one more question. Did your wife read tarot cards?"

He looked at her like she'd lost her mind. "Tarot cards? No. She didn't believe in anything like that. Why?"

"So she didn't visit psychics, anything like that?"

Scorn fought with the fear on his face. "Not a chance." He looked back out toward the woods. "What if he comes back for me?"

"Don't worry, Dr. Kerland. We'll find the person who did this. And in the meantime, we'll get you into a hotel, and have an officer stay with you."

*

Two hours later, Marzillo and her team had taken over the forensics tent and had gone over enough of the evidence to have an initial conversation with Jo and Arnett.

"Three murders in three days isn't rage, it's a to-do list. Whoever this asshole is, he's not even giving us a chance to catch our breath," Marzillo said.

"I suspect that may be the point," Jo said, frustrated. "Sorry again to pull you so far from home so late, but we wanted the same eyes on all the scenes."

Marzillo shrugged, her expression still grim. "I was over at my in-laws. Dinner was done, and since that was the only pleasant thing about the evening, I couldn't have been happier to leave. Apologize to Lopez over there, she had some sort of video-game convention."

Lopez shook her head without looking up from the evidence she was logging. "Convention? Really? It was an Overwatch tournament. But my sister took over for me, thank God. Otherwise I could kiss my rep goodbye."

"Honey, I don't even know what Overwatch is." Marzillo threw up a hand in a *stop* gesture. "And before you take up brain cells I need for other things by explaining it to me, just don't."

"Another Luddite," Lopez said.

"Everyone's a Luddite when they stand next to you," Arnett said.

"Says the man who has no idea how to forward a text," Lopez shot back, eyes still on the table in front of her.

Arnett glared at Jo, who'd had to show him how to do just that a few days before. She threw up both hands. "Don't look at me, I didn't say a word."

Marzillo waved them to one of the tables. "Back to the matter at hand, so we can get to bed before the sun rises. I can't find fault with Mayfair's team's conclusions. They didn't overlook anything else in the house that I can see, and cardiac arrest at fifty-two isn't unheard of, certainly not with her health complications. Yes, the screen, the animal feces, those are unusual, but if it weren't for the tarot card, I'd argue for a very strange accident."

"Since we have reason to believe something nefarious happened here, is there anything that gives a hint as to who the intended victim was, Nancy or Arthur Kerland? Arthur feels certain they were after him, not his wife."

"In terms of hard evidence, no. Not unless something unexpected comes back from her autopsy."

"Everything hinges on that card." Jo tapped a pen against her leg. "The Ten of Cups. It's been a while, but if I remember correctly, cups are about emotions, and this card is about domestic happiness."

Lopez's eyes widened and sparkled. "Please tell me you know how to read tarot cards."

"No. But I have an aunt that does. And while the other two cards are appropriately ominous, this is just confusing. What's it supposed to be telling us, and who sent it? There's an important key here we're missing, and with our abundance of suspects, this might be crucial to helping us narrow down the field."

"An attempt on Kerland or his wife doesn't narrow it down?" Lopez asked.

"Not as much as you'd think. Kerland and Whorton were allies, so most of the people on our list had reason to hate them both. Although, I suppose this knocks out the theory that his infidelities are the motive," Arnett said.

Lopez tilted her head to the side. "You said Whorton was a slut, right? Maybe he was doing Kerland's wife."

The tent fell silent.

She continued. "I mean, faculty wives hang out, right? Imagine if she was friends with Camilla Whorton. That particular betrayal might have been too close to home."

"And imagine if Camilla found out about Nancy and Britney at about the same time. That might have pushed her right over the edge." Jo tapped her finger on her thigh.

"Good point," Arnett said. "In that case, Nancy might have been the intended victim. Shit. Could this get any more complicated?"

Marzillo laughed. "Sure. If Kerland found out about the affair, and he's the one that killed them both."

"He taught two classes today and had office hours in between. About a hundred students put him firmly in Oakhurst all afternoon," Jo said.

Lopez leaned forward in her chair. "Yeah, well, the strength of that depends on what we think happened here. If you think someone was physically here, followed her to the house or was lying in wait, then yes, that leaves him out. But..."

Jo's instincts buzzed. Lopez's out-of-the-box thinking had helped crack more than one case. "But what?"

"Okay, I know this sounds weird. But. We have evidence that a coyote was in the basement. He got in somehow, chowed down on some beef jerky, then left behind a commensurate deposit plus a bonus. Mayfair's team argued that the coyote got in *after* Nancy Kerland had her heart attack. But, there's no good explanation for how he got back out of the basement. And, based on years of experience picking up after my dog, I'd say the one deposit is at least eight hours older than the second, which means the coyote would have had to be inside the house *before* she died. I'd have to do some tests to verify, but I'm pretty sure."

"Right, that's what we thought happened at first. Coyote traps itself inside and she stumbles on it, accidentally scares herself to death. But that doesn't explain the tarot card," Arnett said.

"Or, and here's where it gets weird—what if the killer stashed a coyote in the basement on purpose? It fits the evidence, and Arthur said her heart condition is common knowledge. And if that's the case, the killer could have left the coyote behind as early as Wednesday. And that means Kerland *could* have done it. All this insistence that he was the intended victim may be him trying to throw you off."

Arnett paced across the small tent. "Oh, come on. Who would choose a coyote as a way to kill someone? There are a thousand things that could go wrong with bringing a coyote to a home without being detected."

Jo shook her head. "There's nothing for miles out here, the actual town of Granton is fifteen minutes away, and the closest house is at least ten. It wouldn't be hard to avoid detection at all, especially under cover of darkness. And our killer knows his way around a hunting knife—any good hunter could tag a coyote with a tranquilizer gun."

Lopez jotted down a note. "Aren't drugs like that controlled? That would narrow things down quickly."

Jo shook her head. "Two-thirds of the people involved in this case have careers that involve a reasonable knowledge of chemistry, or are studying it secondarily for their biology degrees. I'm guessing it wouldn't be hard to come up with something."

Marzillo nodded. "I could put something together for you no problem if you gave me a few days. Maybe even a few hours."

Jo stared at her. "And here I was thinking Lopez was the scary one."

"Doesn't have to be one or the other," Arnett muttered under his breath.

"So it's possible, and maybe not even that hard. But I admit, he'd have to have balls of steel. He couldn't guarantee the shock would be enough to kill her," Lopez said.

"Exactly. Why go to all that risk rather than just killing her himself?" Arnett asked.

Jo wagged her head. "The more I play devil's advocate, the less sure I am that it's the riskier choice. Let's say the killer is Camilla. It might have surprised Nancy to find Camilla waiting in her house, but would it be enough of a shock to trigger a heart attack? I doubt it. Camilla would have had to physically lay hands on her. And any confrontation would leave behind evidence."

"Fine. But no matter what, why leave the damned tarot card?" Arnett asked. "I doubt Whorton even saw the one in his office, and Britney certainly never saw hers. We haven't released any information about the card, so why would the killer expect it to mean anything to the Kerlands?"

"Maybe he's just a sick fuck who thinks he's the Angel of God or something, and this is his calling card to mark his job well done," Lopez said.

Jo shook her head to clear it. "I think we're just going in circles now. Back to the evidence. Is there anything else you can tell us, Marzillo?"

"Not yet. We'll process the envelope and card for prints, maybe he made a mistake this time. We'll run what we find along with the prints from the house tomorrow, and also do the autopsy. Mayfair's guys already did a quick search of the perimeter, but we'll wait until the sun's up and do another, see if we can find any evidence of anyone being out here that shouldn't have been."

"Sounds good." Jo checked her watch, and turned to Arnett. "So, *our* to-do list. No way we can talk to anyone this late. But, before we grab a few hours' sleep, we need to put out an alert that anyone who receives or finds one of these cards needs to contact us immediately. Lopez, can you do that, and arrange to have all our suspects come in to give us their fingerprints? We also need to check out Nancy's phone, e-mail, all that."

"And compare all those financial records as soon as possible," Arnett said.

"Right. In the morning I'll ask Granton PD to do a canvas of the actual town, see if anyone saw anything out of the ordinary the last few days. From the size of it, it shouldn't take long, so I don't think they'll mind too much. Kerland is already having the records for all the students he failed pulled, and we'll need to have that cross-checked with Whorton's students. We'll need to check alibis *again* tomorrow, although since we're not sure what exactly happened when, I'm not sure how much that's going to do for us."

Arnett smiled wanly. "Who knows, maybe we'll get lucky and everybody but one will have an ironclad alibi. And we have our visit to Beth Morlinski tomorrow, maybe she'll remember something strange with Kerland's finances or seeing Camilla Whorton in a murderous rage."

CHAPTER TWENTY-THREE

I'm not a fool, I know the coyote was a gamble that could have gone very wrong. I had a backup plan in place, as well. I doctored the daily vitamins in her cabinet—if the coyote hadn't killed her, the potassium chloride would have. But that sort of death wouldn't have sent the message I needed to send. That would have been lazy and cheap—so much would have been lost.

And I desperately needed the serenity I found in the woods when I caught the coyote. Killing Whorton set so much into irrevocable motion, and after my first attempt at killing Britney went wrong, I'd barely been able to sleep. So many potential problems kept running through my head, and there was so much at stake. When I was able to sleep, I dreamed repeatedly of a high-speed train derailed by a small pebble on its tracks, lurching off its trajectory at two hundred miles an hour, directly toward where I stood rooted, unable to move.

So that morning fed my soul, at least at first. When I was a child, my father used to take me camping. He taught me to hunt, but I hated it, and eventually persuaded him to replace it with birdwatching. We'd go into the woods early in the morning and sit, as still as possible, and wait. I'd forgotten how calming it is to wrap yourself into a thick woolen coat against the frigid air, completely still inside your own cocoon. Ten minutes pass. Then fifteen, twenty. Finally, the animals and birds forget you're there, and the forest resumes its rhythm again, embracing you as one of its own. Gentle whispers and rustles fill your mind like a mantra, and time begins to stand still. It's a form of meditation, really, slipping back into the wild ecosystem civilization strives to overcome—and it happens faster and more fully than any of us would like to believe possible.

Until I heard the snap. The adrenaline pounded through me, and I fought the urge to leap up and out into the filtered light.

I'd refused early on to shoot at living targets, and I'd never shot a tranquilizer gun. The same principles apply as with target shooting, of course, but I was nearly paralyzed with fear that my aim would be off and I'd kill or maim him, or balk and give away my position. I paused, took a deep breath, and raised my arms with slow precision.

He was beautiful, and strong. I double-checked my aim, and as steadily as I could, took my shot. He howled, but the tranquilizer was fast acting, and he passed out almost immediately.

Almost as soon as I'd left him in the basement and the card on the kitchen table, the anxious paranoia came flooding back. What if Nancy Kerland decided to delay her trip to the Berkshires? Even a day's delay could mean the difference between life or death for the coyote. I needed him hungry and desperate, but couldn't bear the thought of him starving or dying of thirst, or pacing, terrified, any longer than absolutely necessary.

The drive back to Oakhurst was interminable, and the wait in the McDonald's parking lot for Britney to leave her house drove me nearly to distraction. But once she appeared my fears stilled, and once she was dead, a good portion of the peace returned.

Still, I couldn't sleep until I knew the coyote was okay. So I spent every moment I could that morning and afternoon glued to the screen, watching the Kerland house. You can imagine the relief I felt when I saw him burst through the screen door, and disappear back into the woods where he belonged.

Then, thankfully, I managed a long nap before I spent my evening with a bottle of wine, watching my very own episode of CSI: Berkshires.

CHAPTER TWENTY-FOUR

Jo dragged herself out of bed the next morning, the first warning signs of a migraine hovering behind her eyes. She checked her messages then left one for her father, asking him to call her once he'd finished his first chemo treatment later that day. She turned several shots of espresso into lattes in two travel mugs, then downed an Excedrin Migraine, gambling on the fifty-fifty shot it would short-circuit the headache. Ten minutes later she leaned against her parked car at HQ, waiting for Arnett to pull up.

"Not up for going inside today? You must have woken up to the same angry phone message I did," he said when he arrived.

She handed him a travel mug. "Home brew. And, yep I don't need to risk running into Rockney when he's on the warpath."

Arnett sipped his latte as they both crossed to an unmarked Chevy Cruze. "Not sure what he wants from us, the scene isn't even fully processed yet. And I only got about an hour's sleep last night as is."

"Same. I left a message for Latimer, but haven't heard back yet." Jo fell back to the passenger side of the car. "Do you mind driving? I'd like to look up the Ten of Cups on the way. The tarot cards keep pulling at me."

"As long as you talk me through it while you do it." He climbed into the driver's side, then plugged in Beth Morlinski's work address and started to drive. "Two hours to kill on the way to Beverly."

Jo took a long draw of her latte as he pulled out into traffic, then started her search. She read over several sites that explained the meaning of the Ten of Cups, summarizing for Arnett as she went.

"So, contentment, stability, happiness, especially in the realm of home. Good fortune, fulfillment. So why send a happy, positive card to someone you're going to kill?"

"You mentioned several times something about reversed meanings. What's that, exactly?" he asked.

"During a reading, when cards appear upside down, that can change what they signify. Make it the opposite, or indicate with a card like this that a phase of domestic bliss is ending. But how would the killer have communicated that was the intention? There's no way you could ensure someone would take a tarot card out of an envelope the way you intend them to."

"Maybe you're being too picky. Maybe it was enough that *he* knew he intended the reversed meaning. The victims didn't have much time to think about the cards, regardless. At least, Whorton and Ratliffe didn't. Or, here's another theory: whoever killed Nancy destroyed Arthur Kerland's happy family. Maybe it's as simple as that."

Jo's eyes scanned the image of the card. "Or, if our infidelity theory is right, maybe the card was more of a commentary, like 'your family isn't what you think it is' kind of thing, or an accusation to a homewrecker."

"Which sends us right back where we started, with a motive for everyone."

Jo sighed. "But, without a perfect motive for anyone. The case for Greg Crawley and Camilla Whorton fit the best, but still have huge holes. In Greg's case, the motive is revenge on Michael Whorton for failing him, and on Britney Ratliffe for assisting in that. We still need evidence that he has a grudge against Arthur Kerland. But if he did, based on what we know of his history and his impulsive behavior, I'm not sure he even cared whether he killed Arthur or Nancy—either would probably have done just fine in his mind."

"The family connection could be that his parents disowned him, because they'd had enough," Arnett said.

"Right. And as for Camilla Whorton, her motive would be she'd finally had enough of Michael's philandering, possibly because she discovered he was sleeping with a friend, Nancy, or because one of these women contacted her and made it so she couldn't ignore the situation any longer. So she kills her husband and Britney, and in this scenario, Nancy Kerland was the intended target. Her alibi for her husband's death also has wiggle room."

Arnett nodded. "Next, Arthur Kerland. He might have discovered an affair between his wife and Michael Whorton, but I'm not sure I see why he'd want Britney dead. Maybe she knew something? Or maybe the slippery financial situation was to blame. And who knows, maybe his wife found out about some illegal activity, or had had enough, and was going to turn him in."

Jo wrinkled her nose skeptically. "Feels like we're going out on a limb there."

Arnett's eyes stayed on the traffic changing lanes around him, and he cleared his throat. "And, you're not going to like this, but, if we're talking about destroyed domestic bliss, we have to talk about Shawnessy, too. He could have killed Nancy to avenge his wife's death."

Jo pushed down the ember of defensiveness that flared up in her. "Now you've gone beyond reaching. Shawnessy's pissed at Whorton and Kerland over his career, so he just decides to kill Kerland's wife since he lost his own to cancer? That's beyond crazy."

"We've both seen psychopaths who are far more random than that."

She flicked a wrist at him. "Psychopaths, yes. Serials who have no connection to their victims. Not killers who have vendettas they're acting on. Cases like that involve causal motivations. And, regardless, I can't stretch far enough to find a reason why he'd want Britney dead. I mean, she went to work with Michael Whorton after he left, but what choice did she have?"

Arnett took a draw from his mug. "Agreed. I can't see a motive there."

They lapsed into frustrated silence.

Jo burst out. "Here's what's really messing with me. Marzillo nailed it. Three murders in three days isn't just murder, it's a to-do list. There's planning involved here, and clear premeditation. There has to be sense underlying it, but we can't make a clear case for anyone. We don't even have enough evidence to get a search warrant on anybody. If we arrest Greg Crawley now, any defense attorney in the world will have him back on the street before we can take a mug shot, and if we did get it to court, they'd point a very credible finger back at Camilla Whorton, or Terry Shawnessy. Same problem if we arrested either of them. And then there's the whole tarot card issue. I keep chasing it around in my head, and I can't shake the feeling that someone's playing a game with us. And that *really* pisses me off. And we can only dodge Rockney so long before he's going to want to know who we're bringing in for this. The minute we set foot inside HQ, he's going to be all over us like the fires of hell."

Arnett shook his head. "I hear you. All we can do is wait for Marzillo and Lopez to do their thing, and keep digging. Maybe Beth Morlinski will have something useful, she's been away long enough her different perspective might make something pop out."

"Let's hope." Jo's jaw clenched. "No, forget hope. It's time for prayer."

*

An hour and a half later, Arnett turned onto College Way in Beverly. "What are we looking for now?"

"Quaker Hall."

The GPS deposited them in the parking lot behind a three-story federal-style red-brick building, half-covered with ivy and lined with plentiful windows. They followed the path out of the lot, but discovered it zigzagged to the center of a quad facing the building.

"Here." Arnett pointed to a well-worn stripe in the grass that led to the building's steps.

Jo scanned the grounds. "I read once about a landscape architect who was hired to design the grounds of a college. Other than bushes and trees, he planted grass everywhere, didn't put a single path in between anything. He waited several months, then laid down the paths where the students had worn down the grass."

"Genius," Arnett said. "I wish more people thought that way."

"My, you are grumpy today, aren't you?"

Arnett growled. "Keep it up. Just give me a reason to pull out a cigarette."

They pushed through the door and found a directory on the wall in front of them, then rode the elevator to the third floor. Morlinski's office was the second door facing them, and the door was open.

A tall, slender woman with auburn hair and large green eyes stood as soon as she spotted them. "Come in, please," she said.

They sat in the two chairs she'd readied across from her small wooden desk, filling the postage-stamp office to capacity. Jo watched her expression while Arnett made the introductions.

"We mentioned originally that we needed to talk to you about Michael Whorton's death. Unfortunately, Arthur Kerland's wife, Nancy, and a graduate student named Britney Ratliffe have now also been killed as well."

Sadness crossed her face. "I saw that on the news. I'm truly sorry. Nancy was a lovely woman."

"You're not sorry to hear about Ratliffe's and Whorton's deaths?" Arnett asked.

Beth met his eyes without aggression. "I didn't know Britney Ratliffe, although I'm sorry to hear of any senseless death. My feelings about Michael Whorton's death are complicated. I'm sorry for what his loved ones are going through, but I can't claim to believe the world is worse off without him. But I suspect you know that, or you wouldn't be here."

"The sexual harassment claim," Jo said.

"Right. But not just that. Some people go through life leaving a wake of destruction in their path, whether they intend to or not. He was that sort of person."

"Do you think he intended to?" Arnett asked.

"I don't honestly know. I hope he was just oblivious. Myopic, focused only on his desires to the detriment of others."

"But unfortunately you got caught up in that wake," Jo said.

Her eyebrows bounced up, and she drew in a deep breath. "Luckily, no. He inadvertently did me a favor. When I left, I did some soul-searching. My research program was extremely time consuming to do correctly, and I would have spent my career fighting a never-ending battle doing twice as much work as my peers to get half as many publications. I worked non-stop, and still didn't have time to support my students. Here, I can focus on them, since BC is a liberal arts college."

"Which means what, exactly?" Arnett asked.

"It means the primary emphasis is on teaching. Most professors don't even have research programs, at least not the sort you find at research universities. We don't have graduate students either, none of that."

"So you work fewer hours now, have less stress?"

She shook her head. "Not so much *less* as *different*. But when you can breathe and enjoy your work, and are surrounded by supportive colleagues, it doesn't feel like work, if you know what I mean."

Both Jo and Arnett nodded their heads.

"Still, what he did must have been a nightmare for you, along with having it reported by Terry Shawnessy," Arnett said.

An emotion Jo couldn't place crossed her face, then disappeared again. "Yes, well. I put Terry in an awkward position. I knew the policy, and that he was obligated to report it." She took a deep, resigned breath. "It was stupid of me, but I didn't have anyone else to talk to, so I rolled the dice. And I have zero doubt he truly believed he could help me that way."

"You didn't believe that?" Arnett asked.

"No." She turned to Jo. "You must understand, as a woman in a male-dominated field? There's no good solution once you're put in that situation. If you don't report it, you're forced to be in the same room and work with someone who is harassing you every day, and he'll certainly retaliate. If you report him, even if you document everything and show retaliation, you're a troublemaker. The administration wants you gone so they don't have to deal with you. You become a pariah, and that reputation will follow you. There's really only one choice, and that's to leave quietly and hope you can find another job somewhere outside of your harasser's influence. Which, in academia, is not an easy trick, since it's a tiny, incestuous world. All because of somebody else's bad behavior."

Jo shook her head, disgusted. "I do understand. I'm sorry you had to go through that."

Beth continued. "And, of course, I knew the whole situation would become instant gossip fodder the moment Terry filed the claim, no matter how much they promise confidentiality. Even the graduate students knew about it."

"Did Michael Whorton interfere with your ability to get another research job? Is that part of why you came to a teaching university?" Arnett asked.

Morlinski's eyes flashed to Arnett, despite his gentle tone. "No. But I suspect my decision to do so made things easier for me."

"I ask because we have reason to believe he actively interfered with Terry Shawnessy's ability to get another job," he said.

"Terry left OakhurstU?"

"He didn't get tenure. He left about a year after you did. The scuttlebutt is that Michael Whorton and Arthur Kerland tanked his tenure case."

She shook her head and rubbed one hand with the other, as if it were cold. "That sounds exactly like something Michael would do. And it fits." She gave a description of the departmental situation that mapped on to what Jo already knew.

"So you weren't aware Terry left?"

She shook her head again. "I'm not in contact with anyone from the university anymore. I put that chapter of my life behind me when I left." She met Jo's eyes again. "I just want to move forward, I don't want to think about any of that. Brooding about the past isn't healthy. You'll just turn bitter, and expend energy better used elsewhere. All you can do is learn what lessons you can, and rebuild."

Jo nodded. "I apologize that we have to stir it all up for you. We just have a few more questions. Was Arthur Kerland involved at all in the harassment?"

Beth shook her head. "Not directly. He never said or did anything inappropriate physically. But when word started to get around about it all, he was fast to support Michael."

"How so?"

"He treated me differently, and told anyone who'd listen that I was making up lies. And he attacked my character."

"To your face?"

"Of course not. In academia, character assassination is most often whispered behind closed doors."

Jo nodded. During her time as lieutenant, she'd seen enough of the ugly side of office politics to last her a lifetime. She made a show of glancing down at her notepad, and switched gears again. "You mentioned you were sorry to hear that Nancy Kerland had been killed. Were you close with her while you were there?"

"Not close, no, but I knew her from faculty functions. She was a gentle soul, quiet and kind. When I knew her, she was going through a very bad phase of her illness, so she didn't come to all the department events."

"And Camilla Whorton?" Arnett asked.

"About the same, but for different reasons. She also avoided functions when she was able to, and she was suspicious of all Michael's female colleagues. I can't say I blame her. I'd heard rumors about his infidelity, although I dismissed them until he came after me."

Jo watched her face carefully as she asked the next question. "How likely do you think it is that Nancy Kerland was having an affair with Michael Whorton?"

A flash of confused surprise crossed her face, but disappeared into a blank expression. "I really couldn't say. I didn't know her well enough to make a judgment on that. But yes, I suppose it's possible."

"What was Arthur and Nancy's relationship like?"

She considered, and shrugged. "It's hard to say. I'd hate to cast aspersions when I don't know, because people who aren't feeling well often don't come across as happy. And the strain of that can lead to bickering. That doesn't mean there's anything wrong with their relationship."

Beth's response took Jo by surprise, and she wasn't quite sure why. "They bickered?"

She waved a hand. "Wait now, I don't want to make it sound like something it wasn't. There were times when I sensed some tension, but I wouldn't call it an abnormal level of tension. It didn't make me think there was a problem at the time. I don't want to taint that by looking back in light of current events."

"Fair enough." Jo pretended to consult her notebook again. "When you were at OakhurstU, did you know of professors who did industry work in addition to their university responsibilities?"

She shrugged. "Of course. Many."

"Any hints of impropriety that you were aware of around that?"

Again she looked genuinely surprised. "Nothing that I'm aware of. But if you're asking if Michael or Arthur might have been involved in something shady, I'd have to say it was possible."

Jo smiled. "Got it. One last question. We have to do our due diligence and confirm where you've been this week."

"That's no problem, my schedule is packed this quarter. I teach four classes, two Monday-Wednesday-Friday classes, one mid-morning and one mid-afternoon, and two Tuesday-Thursday classes in the same time slots. Add in office hours, administrative meetings, and the film series I agreed to sponsor this week, and the only time I've been alone is when I'm asleep. I can run down the people that can vouch for me, if you'd like?"

"That would be helpful," Arnett said, and jotted down the names, events, and time periods she offered.

"Is there anything else I can help you with?" she asked when they'd finished.

"That's it for now." Jo handed her a card as they stood up. "If you think of anything that might help, please let us know."

CHAPTER TWENTY-FIVE

"Three missed calls from Rockney," Arnett said as they walked back across the lawn toward the car.

Jo winced, and pulled out her phone to find the same. "My dad's treatment should be done by now, I'm gonna give him a call first."

"I fully support that decision," Arnett said.

She dialed her father's number when they got into the car, but again the call went straight to voicemail. She left a message, hung up, then started the car. "Beth's take on the Kerlands' marriage was interesting. Maybe there wasn't quite as much domestic bliss as the tarot card would have us believe?"

"Lends credence to the possibility she may have been unhappy about something Arthur was up to. At the very least, it means we need to take a closer look at that relationship." Arnett drained his coffee cup.

Jo eyed the cup with a shudder. "I'll never understand how you drink your coffee when it's cold like that."

"I'm a macho, macho man," he quipped, straight-faced.

Jo's phone rang, and when she answered it Lopez's voice burst over speakerphone. "Man, do I have news for you. But first, a little housekeeping. Nancy Kerland's phone records, computer, everything—so boring I had to slam two Rockstars just to stay awake. She called her sister, her niece, her doctor, and her husband—lather, rinse, repeat. She read biographies, used her Netflix account so much I hope she had stock in the company, and loved to cross-stitch. And before you ask, no, she didn't play any MMORPGs."

Jo laughed. "Got it."

"The alibis weren't much more exciting. Camilla Whorton had appointments out of state throughout the day on Wednesday that make it hard for her to get to the Berkshires during the right time period. While I wouldn't go so far as to say it rules her out completely since we don't know when the killer was there, she'd have had to haul some major ass to make it work. Crawley's day on both Wednesday and Thursday was filled with classes and such, but he still had plenty of slots where he could have run out there and taken care of business. And when I asked for Shawnessy's whereabouts, I got another litany of vague. Working from home on some consulting project, and a few errands where he paid cash, of course."

"Gotcha," Arnett said.

"But my morning took a turn for the dramatic once I started looking at Whorton's financial records. I picked up where you left off with the stuff Camilla Whorton gave us from his home office, and I realized immediately they're an entirely different set of records. Or should I say, a more extensive set, because the ones in the university office were clearly carefully selected to present only a portion of the business he was doing with the corporations."

"His wife mentioned that the bulk of his income came from industry work on the side."

"Ha! If she means illegal side deals, she's correct."

Jo's pulse picked up. "Oh, please explain."

"I asked Ruth Henderson to send me whatever information they had about his approved relationships with pharmaceutical companies, and the university policies governing those relationships. I can explain in detail if you want to bid goodbye to the same chunk of brain cells I did, but long story short: Whorton was a very bad boy. He had illegal side deals with several companies who gave him cut-rate deals on laboratory equipment and access to biological materials, stuff like stem cells. Deals that were worth six figures, no problem. He had initial invoices that listed the equipment at full price—those were the only ones found at his office, and were the ones submitted to his university accounts—and other invoices that showed the actual, discounted prices he paid. Three guesses where the rest of the money from his university accounts ended up."

"Holy shit," Arnett said.

"But here's where it gets *really* good. It didn't take me long to find quite a few places where the companies in question cited Whorton's research in their applications to relevant federal agencies in order to get products approved. And, in turn, I found quite a few places in Whorton's grant applications where he cites the importance of his research in the production of important pharma treatments."

Jo closed her eyes to concentrate. "Let me make sure I'm keeping up. You're saying that not only did he funnel money from his university accounts, but he padded his research to help the pharma companies get drug approval, and then pointed to those drugs as reason for the government to give him more money?"

"Give or take. I can't say for sure the research was trumped up, his findings may have been legit. That'll take more digging by people who know about his type of research. But, I'd bet cold, hard cash that's the crux of it. First, because *not only* were the deals no-nos with respect to university policies, they were downright illegal as well, which means the research shuffling was at the very least unethical. But second, because I did a quick-and-dirty analysis, and his work is cited significantly more often by the companies he did business with than other pharmaceutical companies who are working on similar products. That is not as is should be. If his research was valuable and viable, all the companies would have been using it."

Arnett flipped through his notebook. "Which companies was he doing business with?"

Lopez tapped a few keys. "Primarily Capwell Laboratories and Hawthorne Therapeutics, but I see traces of a few other burgeoning relationships."

Jo jabbed a finger in the air. "Two companies Shawnessy applied to."

Arnett nodded. "Yep. That would explain why he didn't get the jobs. Neither the companies nor Whorton would have risked him catching wind of what they were up to."

"I don't suppose you noticed Kerland's name in any of those invoices or grant applications? That would explain the cush vacation home in the Berkshires," Jo asked.

"Excellent question. A disproportionate amount of the relevant research is coauthored with Kerland. Which is odd, because Kerland's main line of research is in a completely different area, although that's apparently not unheard of. I'd have to check into his records specifically. But at the very least, it's possible they trumped up a joint line of research so they could both benefit." Lopez paused. "But let's return to Shawnessy, and hold on to your hats. We found his prints on the wall of the Kerlands' basement staircase."

"Holy shit," Arnett said.

"You already said that, and I promise you'll say it again in a minute," Lopez said.

"Are you sure? We had Shawnessy in the system?" Jo asked.

"Positive, there was a full handprint on the wall. And no, we didn't have him in the system. He gave his fingerprints willingly when we asked him this morning."

"He showed up to volunteer them?" Arnett asked.

"Yep, right after we asked."

Jo's brow's knit. "Pretty stupid if he's the murderer."

"We've seen stupider." Arnett shook his head. "Things aren't looking good for Dr. Shawnessy."

"They're about to look a lot worse. Because I also may have found you a reason why Shawnessy wanted Britney dead," Lopez chirped.

Jo stared at the dash screen. "The charming tone of your witty banter normally makes my day, Chris, but right now I just can't. If you're messing with us—"

Lopez's voice took on a more serious tone. "I swear I'm not. I was just on the phone with an old friend verifying some stuff, and I'm not a hundred percent sure, but I'm close. The university sent over Britney Ratliffe's academic records, and after a quick initial look, I figured the best way to get a feel for her research history with the two profs was to compare her CV to Whorton's and Shawnessy's, just to see what I could see. Ratliffe's shows an odd publication about a year after Shawnessy left the department."

"Odd how?" Jo asked.

"It's coauthored with Michael Whorton, but doesn't have anything to do with his area of research. It has to do with the role of regulatory T-cells in treating cancer, which was Shawnessy's research."

"That's not surprising, she worked with Shawnessy during her first year, then switched to Whorton."

"Yup, she did. And there's a line of research with Shawnessy documented in her CV. This publication isn't that. It's a totally different set of studies."

Jo glanced over to Arnett to be sure he was jotting it all down. "Okay, but so what? Don't lots of researchers work on more than one line of research at a time?"

"Not *first-year* graduate students. And, even if she had, there'd be some evidence of it on her CV during that time period, which there isn't. But you're missing the damning part. There are a fair number of related publications on Shawnessy's CV during the period just before, none coauthored with Ratliffe. But, Whorton has never done anything anywhere close to the topic. Because of that, according to my friend, there's no way Whorton's name should be on that paper. She said it might be possible that Shawnessy would give Ratliffe permission to publish the work as a single author if he no longer felt the publication credit was important for his career—which my friend was deeply skeptical about, even without knowing the heavy layer of bitter we're dealing with on Shawnessy's part. But even if he had given permission, there's no way Whorton's name could be on there without Shawnessy's, and I think we can agree Shawnessy didn't okay that. My friend's convinced they stole his research once he was gone and put their names on it. And I think she's right, because it's one of the studies cited in Whorton's and the pharmaceutical companies' grant applications."

Arnett leaned in closer to the phone. "Hold up. Maybe Ratliffe had learned enough about the research while she worked with Shawnessy that she ran her own study and published it after he was gone?"

"My friend was adamant that publications schedules don't work fast enough. Data of that sort would already have had to be collected in order to be put out that fast. And, even if that had been possible, there's still no ethical reason why Whorton's name would be on it and Shawnessy's wouldn't."

"You're sure about this?" Jo asked.

"No, I'm not completely sure about what exactly happened. But I *am* completely sure that whatever happened was jacked up. And the person who got the shaft was Shawnessy."

"Got it. Any other surprises for us?" Jo asked.

"Jeez, what's a girl gotta do to get your approval?" Lopez laughed. "Don't worry, I'm still hard at work."

Jo smiled. "Thanks, my friend. You're a beast."

"Grrowrrr." She disconnected.

"Okay, that's a lot to process," Jo said. "First, on top of everything else, Whorton and possibly Kerland were defrauding the university."

"I wonder if that's related to what Camilla overheard? It certainly fits. If Latimer or some other member of the administration had started to question their income, he'd have looked for a fire to start."

"Would Latimer have just called him up and asked about it? That doesn't seem smart. I'd think he'd start some sort of investigation rather than give away what he knew?"

"I'm not so sure. The dean's approach seems to be 'ignore problems and hope they go away,' and while academics are long on book smarts, that's not the same as street smarts."

Jo considered, then shook her head. "Here's what I'm coming up against. Yes, this is despicable, but would an administrator kill on the basis of this? It seems like it would be the other way around, like Michael or Arthur would kill to keep it all quiet. I can't come up with a scenario where Michael or Arthur ends up dead. The only thing that makes sense if the money's at the heart of this is if Arthur turned on Michael and Britney."

Arnett paused. "Unless we're missing something. Maybe somebody from the pharmaceutical companies took them out?"

"To what purpose? All the records would still be filed with the university, killing them wouldn't stop an investigation. No, if that were the reason for it all, you'd expect Latimer to be the one who ended up dead."

"Yeah, you're right. Either Arthur turned on them, or it's one of our other two theories. Which, with the fingerprints and the stolen research, means Shawnessy has quickly pulled into the lead of our suspect list."

Jo pulled up to a stoplight and turned to Arnett, a frown on her face. "So the story we're looking at is this. First, he kills Whorton, the main impetus behind his failure to get tenure, then he goes after Ratliffe, who apparently co-opted a line of his research as soon as his back was turned. Finally, he strikes out at Kerland and kills Kerland's wife because… why?"

"Because his life has fallen apart and he's pissed and lashing out, and he lost his wife."

"And you think that's a good enough reason to kill someone's wife?"

"I don't, no. But someone who's lost their shit after one too many tragedies in their life just might. And, finally, the tarot cards would make sense," Arnett said. "The Death card for Whorton, who killed his career. Then the Seven of Swords, which shows someone literally stealing, because she stole his research. And the Ten of Cups when he takes someone else's wife because his own wife died."

Jo toyed with the diamond at her throat, still frowning.

"You don't look happy about it," Arnett said.

"It doesn't make sense to me that he'd kill someone else's wife. And I can't shake that feeling I was talking about earlier, that we're being played somehow. Although it sounds less likely that Camilla's our killer, we still only *barely* have a reason to favor Shawnessy over Crawley. And Shawnessy's been inside the Kerlands' Berkshire house before during academic functions, so we'd never get past reasonable doubt that his prints are there for a legitimate reason."

"This many years later?" Arnett asked.

"We'd have to check with Marzillo, but I don't think it's impossible."

"You're probably right. Shit."

"And all that makes me wary of diving in until we talk to someone who knows more about how research works in biology and can verify Britney did something wrong. Doesn't it feel too slick somehow? Or like we're jumping on facts that might justify our theory, rather than the other way around?"

Arnett gave her an incredulous look. "Yeah, no. Not even a little." He searched her face. "Is this about the cancer still? Are you looking for a reason to avoid arresting him because he lost his wife to cancer?"

She took a deep breath, her conversation with Eva filling her mind. She couldn't bring herself to shed any tears over Whorton's death, that much was true. But Britney Ratliffe and Nancy Kerland were another story.

"Of course I don't. If he committed these crimes, I want him behind bars, now. As far as my personal issues with it all go, it's more that I *hope* he didn't do this, because the whole situation has wreaked enough havoc, and I'd like to see him be able to find happiness again. And I'm legitimately still not convinced he did it. Your wife theory doesn't sit well with me, it's just two weird to have a clear-cut reason to kill two people, but a loose, fly-by-the-seat-of-your-pants reason to kill the third. And, I can't come up with an explanation for why he'd leave those tarot cards, and that's why my brain keeps playing ping-pong between the suspects. Can you honestly say you see Shawnessy leaving those cards? It just doesn't fit who he *is*. With Crawley, remember that e-mail he sent to Whorton? I can at least stretch to a place where I can see him leaving the cards. But Shawnessy? They just don't fit."

"I think you're overthinking this. He's pissed, and he wants to make it known."

"Make it known to who? The people he just killed? They can't—" Her phone rang.

ADA Rockney flashed on the screen.

Her jaw tensed. She nodded to Arnett, and he answered the call. "Sir. I have you on speaker."

"I know you and Arnett are getting my calls, Fournier. Problem with *both* your cell phones? Going through a hundred-mile tunnel?" A barely controlled anger simmered in Rockney's voice.

"I apologize, it's just that we needed to get to—"

"Three murders, Fournier. In the space of *three* days."

"Yes, sir." When Rockney was like this, there was no point speaking.

"Can you guess who I get to meet with later today?"

"Someone at the university?"

"Ah, see, *there's* that detection skill we value so much. Not just *someone,* Fournier. The *president.* And guess what? He didn't invite me for tea because he likes the cut of my jib."

Jo rubbed her eyes. "No."

"So I need you to tell me I have good news for him. Tell me we're moments away from making an arrest."

"We have two primary suspects, Terry Shawnessy and Greg Crawley. We have strong reasons to suspect both, and we just found Shawnessy's prints at Kerland's house—"

Rockney interrupted with a growl. "Then what's the hold up?"

"We don't have enough to hold them. We're not sure we even have enough to get search warrants—"

"Prep the paperwork for the warrants. I'll make sure you get them." He hung up.

CHAPTER TWENTY-SIX

Fueled by pressure from the university, Rockney pushed through the two warrants within the hour. As soon as they were finalized, Jo and Arnett drove to Shawnessy's house, forensics team and backup officers in tow.

"You didn't have to get a warrant," Shawnessy said. "Check whatever you want to check. I'm happy to help any way I can."

"Tell us about your relationship with Britney Ratliffe," Arnett asked.

His confused expression deepened. "Britney Ratliffe? I don't have a relationship with her. I haven't spoken with her since I left the university."

"Not even after you found out she'd stolen research from you?"

His face flushed. "No. What would that have accomplished?"

"So you did nothing?"

His eyes flicked back and forth between them. "What could I do? File a complaint against her? I can't say I have much faith in any of that anymore."

"What I think you did is murder her, yesterday morning."

Shawnessy blanched, and took a step back. "Oh God."

Jo weighed his reaction. While his distress seemed genuine, he was scared. But scared because he was guilty, or because he realized he was a prime suspect?

"Detectives, should we get started in here?" Ron Flores, another senior medicolegal from the lab, had come to conduct the search, since Marzillo was still processing Britney Ratliffe's crime scene.

He and his team had finished an initial search of Shawnessy's car, and were ready to move inside.

Jo nodded. Arnett turned back to Terry. "Stand here with Officer Murphy and don't touch anything."

Jo and Arnett suited up. While Ron's team worked their way through the kitchen and bathroom, they started with a writing desk in the corner of the living room, and worked their way systematically around the space. When they found nothing suspicious, they moved to the bedroom.

While Arnett went through the laminate Ikea bureau, Jo flipped back the covers on the bed and checked the pillow, then between the mattresses. She opened the nightstand, and froze. "Bob. Take a look at this."

He glanced up from the drawer he was searching. She lifted out a well-used book, slightly larger than a paperback, with a picture of a tarot card on the cover. She flipped through it; after an introductory section, the book showed each tarot card on the left, with an explanation of the card's meaning on the right.

"Well, well, well. Turns out Terry has a hobby," Arnett said.

Terry appeared in the doorway behind them, red-faced, with Officer Murphy at his side, ready to restrain him. "I bought that yesterday when I heard about the tarot cards at the crime scenes."

Jo stared up at him. "I don't suppose you kept the receipt?"

He shook his head. "I paid cash."

"Of course you did," Arnett mumbled under his breath.

"Where'd you buy it?" she asked.

"Books on Birch," he answered, without hesitation. Jo knew the shop, one of several used bookstores that catered to both university students and the greater Oakhurst population.

"So they'll be able to confirm you bought this yesterday."

The flush on his face deepened further. "I hope so. You know how busy they are."

"Do you remember who took your money?"

He swallowed, hard. "Not her name. But she was a petite girl, early twenties. Blonde."

She handed the book to Arnett, and turned back to the nightstand, disgusted. That description fit a good third of the employees at any store in town.

She pulled out the only other item in the drawer, the type of smallish leather photo album her mother would call a *brag book*. She flipped through the pages, which were filled with pictures of the same woman and young man in the framed photos around Terry's apartment.

"My wife and son," he said.

She glanced up at him again. Pain pulsed from his face. A pang of doubt and shame stabbed at her as she saw the situation through his eyes. She was a stranger, pawing through the only thing he had left of the woman he loved, mementos that were likely far more sacred to him than anything consecrated in a church. If the situation were reversed, and someone was invading her connection with her father, she'd have wanted to rip their arms right off their body.

She straightened, and flipped more quickly through the rest. The book ended with several funeral cards on top of one another. A second pang tore through Jo as she glimpsed a name: *Ellen McCormack Shawnessy*.

Jo's phone rang. She snapped the book shut, replaced it, and checked the phone. She gestured for Arnett to follow her, and stepped outside of the apartment.

She took a deep breath and answered the call. "Fournier."

"What have you found?" Rockney's voice was brisk and urgent.

"Not much. No weapons, no tranquilizer guns, no collection of hunting knives. No evidence he owns any safety deposit boxes or storage rentals, but we may find that on his computer. On the positive side, we did find a book about tarot cards."

"That's something. Enough to get us started, at least."

"We'll bring Shawnessy down to the station, but before we charge him—"

"No buts. I just got my ass handed to me by President Stevens, on behalf of the university. He says, and I quote, that he can't allow his campus to be terrorized by a serial killer, and he wants answers, now, before someone else dies. Charge Shawnessy."

"Not a serial killer, a spree killer," Jo said reflexively, and knew the words were a mistake before she'd finished them. She winced at Arnett's groan behind her.

Rockney paused, then responded in a slow, tight voice. "I'm more than happy for you to call him and explain the difference. Then he can explain to you exactly how much the reputation of the university means to Oakhurst, and exactly how destructive it is for the local economy to have parents and students, current and potential, terrified to send their children here."

"Right. I apologize, sir. I just think due diligence is called for. If we arrest Shawnessy before we execute Crawley's warrant, it will look like we've made up our mind before we do a thorough investigation, and since our evidence is largely circumstantial—"

"Detective. I need you to make an arrest. Shawnessy or Crawley, I don't give a rat's ass. Execute all the search warrants you want. But have a suspect in custody, and a press conference announcing it, in time for the evening news tonight." He ended the call.

Jo drew in a deep breath, and reentered the apartment.

*

Two hours later, they'd read Shawnessy his rights, brought him to the station, and ushered him into an interrogation room.

Arnett led off. "You're here on suspicion of the murder of Michael Whorton, Nancy Kerland, and Britney Ratliffe. We'd like to clear you as soon as possible, starting with your whereabouts on Wednesday, and on Tuesday evening."

Shawnessy's jaw tensed. "I'd like to speak to an attorney."

Arnett glanced at Jo before responding. "Sure, give us his or her number and we'll get them right in. But we'd like to move as quickly as possible on this, since it's late on Friday. We don't want you to have to spend the weekend in jail because we can't get you in front of a judge."

Shawnessy barked a short laugh. "What part of my life situation makes you think I can afford my own attorney?"

The part of Jo that still held doubts about his guilt twisted at her conscience. "We'll see that you have access to a court-appointed attorney as soon as possible, then. But I don't see that happening within the next few hours, and it'll be too late for an arraignment before Monday. If you have a reasonable explanation for what we've found, it's possible we can get you out of here today."

His eyes narrowed at her. "I tried to help you, I answered every question you asked honestly, apparently too honestly. I was up-front about my history with Whorton, everything. I know you have no actual evidence, since I didn't kill any of them, but I also know how easy it is for police to rig up a case once they've decided you're the person they want to send to jail. I've seen *Making a Murderer*, like most of America." He looked down at his hands, folded in his lap. "I'm not saying anything more without an attorney present."

Jo held up both hands in front of her in a conciliatory gesture. "I understand your worry, but that's not what's happening here. I just wanted to avoid a jail stay for you." She stood up. "Can we get you something to eat or drink, make sure you get a good meal? By the time you get booked, they'll have served dinner."

Shawnessy leaned back slightly, but the tension remained in his jaw. "I don't much feel like eating right now."

"Got it. We'll get an attorney to you as soon as possible."

Arnett followed her out of the room, where they signaled for an escort. She rubbed her forehead. "I don't understand the change in demeanor."

Arnett shrugged. "You've seen plenty of people get pissed and clam up when they're arrested."

She rubbed her brow. "Maybe. But this feels different. And I hate feeling like we're rushing an investigation for the sake of optics."

"Agreed as far as optics. But what can it hurt to have him in custody while we sort this out?"

"Fair enough." She sighed again, and looked at the time on her phone. "Well, this leaves us plenty of time to go execute the warrant on Crawley before the evening news."

Arnett motioned toward the door. "After you."

CHAPTER TWENTY-SEVEN

Greg Crawley's reaction to the search warrant was a complete one-eighty from Shawnessy's. He responded with active hostility, threatening retribution to every member of the search team, and the department in general. They found a small cadre of weapons—guns, mace, knives, and even a taser—but no match for the knives used during the two stabbings, no tarot deck, and nothing else related to the murders. Marzillo's team confiscated his computer and his phone for further examination, and they were forced to leave no further along than they'd been when they started.

"How a guy with his history of mental illness is allowed to own guns like that, I'll never understand," Jo said, glancing back as they strode away from Crawley's apartment.

"Thank the NRA," Arnett said.

She pulled open the car door with a sigh, and climbed in. An odd malaise, almost a sense of futility, engulfed her. "Well, that settles that. We have nothing solid on either one, just a bit more circumstantial evidence pointing to Shawnessy. But at least Rockney has a suspect for his press conference, even if it's unlikely to hold up before a jury."

Arnett shot her a glance as he started the car. "So we'll keep digging until we find something that connects one of them directly. Who knows, maybe Britney Ratliffe had DNA under her fingernails. Maybe her phone records will come back with something more concrete."

Jo nodded absently, thoughts of her father, who still hadn't called her back, melding with her dissatisfaction over the case. "Yep. And I'm thinking the next concrete step we can take while we wait for the lab results is to talk to Parminder or Latimer, to find out what we can about that research paper of Ratliffe's."

Arnett made a show of gawking at her. "You kidding me? No way I'm doing that tonight, we've been at this fifteen hours straight."

She waved her hand. "No, of course not, sorry. I meant tomorrow." She made a decision. "But, since we have a suspect in custody and the time pressure's off, how would you feel about me taking a quick trip down to New Orleans to check on my dad?"

"I can hold the fort down here, Lopez is doing most of the work anyway," he joked. "You clear it with Rockney?"

"Not yet, but I'm guessing he'll be fine with it now that he can assure the university there won't be any more bodies. I'm sure he doesn't want to pay both of us weekend overtime if he can avoid it anyway, and he's always on me to take my time off."

Arnett searched her face. "You're more scared than I realized."

"I am. That funeral card I saw today was a little too real. One day you're happily married, then the next day your spouse is wracked with cancer, and she's gone."

"That doesn't mean the same thing's going to happen to your father."

"But it could. My father has always been an unstoppable force, if you know what I mean? This huge, looming presence who can fix anything and build anything and who's always been there. But that's because I still see him through little girl eyes. Intellectually, I know he's over the hump of his mid-sixties and he's mortal like the rest of us, but I think this is the first time I'm really realizing that, down deep. He's not going to be in my life forever, even if he beats the cancer."

Arnett nodded, expression soft. "Yeah, I get that. It's a shock when you realize they won't be here forever."

Jo pulled out her phone and called Rockney. She gave him the information he needed about Shawnessy, then cleared her trip to New Orleans.

Arnett gave her hand a quick pat, then fixed his eyes on the road. They spent the rest of the ride to HQ in silence.

*

Jo glanced at the clock on her mantle as she slipped out of her coat. Just past nine. No point hanging up her coat, she'd have to hurry.

She pulled out her phone and called her sister.

"Josie?" Sophie's voice had an incredulous edge that jabbed at her.

"Hi, Soph. Sorry to call so late, I'm not interrupting bedtime, am I?"

"There isn't really a good time in the evenings lately. What's up?"

"I just wanted to let you know I'm heading out on a red-eye to go see Dad."

There was a long moment of silence before Sophie replied, her voice icy. "How'd you manage that?"

Confusion and fatigue washed over Jo. Why did Sophie sound pissed, when this was what she'd wanted? "We made an arrest in the case, so we have some breathing room. I figured I'd better take advantage while I can."

There was another pause. "You already cleared it with your boss?"

Jo's confusion turned to frustration. "Yes, Sophie, it's cleared. This way you can work with David's schedule and go down when you can, without worrying that Dad's alone."

"Yeah, great. Except that I already made arrangements to go down because I didn't think you could."

"I said I'd talk to my ADA about it."

"Two days ago. I couldn't wait forever."

Jo bit back her gut response. Her sister was being somewhat unfair, yes, but Jo was also reaping what she'd sowed. She was the one who'd made her career a top priority all these years, and who hadn't called her sister back sooner. "Okay, well, if the flights aren't refundable, I guess Dad will get to see both of us at once. He'd love that. And I'd love to spend some time with you myself."

Her sister barked a sharp laugh. "Happy family time. The tickets are refundable, it's just the pain in the ass of changing up all of the details."

Jo's grasp on her patience slipped. "What details? Mom isn't going to care if she watches the girls this week or next, and you said David preferred you to go next week. That's the whole point of me going now."

"That was two days ago. If you'd called me back like you should have, that would have been perfect. But you didn't, and so now things have changed. The world doesn't revolve around you, you know."

"Apparently it does," Jo mumbled under her breath.

"What was that?" Sophie snapped.

"Nothing. Fine. If this doesn't work, I'll get clearance to go next weekend, and into the following week. Does that work better for you?"

"I'll believe that when I see it. Between now and then some emergency will come up. But at least that will give me time to make backup plans."

Jo felt like she'd been punched in the gut. "Wow. There's just no winning with you, is there?"

"You just don't get it, Josie, and you never will."

Jo felt like a bottomless pit had appeared under her and she was falling through it at an ever-accelerating rate. Her brain spun for a moment, then hit on a realization. "No, I think I *do* get it. You're pissed that I stepped up to the plate. Because it cramps your ability to be the good daughter who makes all the sacrifices, and look good for both Mom and Dad. If I come through and take some of the burden off you, you can't play martyr. Well, newsflash, Sophie, this isn't about your insecurities, this is about Dad."

Jo listened to the sounds of Sophie's girls playing in the background as Sophie sat in shocked silence. Finally, Sophie responded. "Fuck you, Josette." Then she hung up.

Jo stared at the phone. That confirmed it. No way Sophie would have risked her daughters hearing that sort of language if she hadn't struck a nerve.

She crossed to the kitchen and pulled down the snifter and bottle of calvados. She poured two fingers, and tossed them back. Years ago her therapist had told her that every family had a dynamic. Everyone in the family had a role to play, whether they liked it or not. And even if they didn't like it, or didn't *think* they liked it, there was some reason why they kept acting in accord with those expectations. Something about it filled a need for them, even if it was simply keeping the peace of the status quo.

She'd just sent a quiver through her family dynamic, shaken up the assigned roles. And that terrified Sophie, because if she couldn't be the good one, the long-suffering, dedicated daughter, where would that leave her?

Jo poured herself another drink, then picked up her phone again. She left a message requesting a change in vacation time, and called the airline to change her flight to the following week. Then she made a final call.

"Eric. Any plans for the evening?"

"I always have time for you. Your place or mine?"

*

Jo woke Saturday morning to the heavenly, but confusing, smell of coffee and bacon wafting in from the kitchen, then remembered with a regretful pang in her stomach that Eric had spent the night.

She groaned into her pillow. This was why she rarely allowed men to stay over; there was no easy way to escape in the morning. And, she realized with a jolt of panic, she had two empty days stretching in front of her. With Shawnessy behind bars and no other pressing cases, Rockney wouldn't okay any overtime, and if she showed up off the clock, she'd have to explain to everyone what happened to her trip. She could dive into the recent batch of Golden Gate suicide files, but that wouldn't take more than a couple of hours to go through, no matter how closely she scoured them. And the thought of filling an entire weekend, especially one where all she could think about was her father's cancer treatments, terrified her.

Arnett told her regularly she needed a hobby. Maybe he was right.

She flipped back the covers, slipped into a robe, pasted a smile on her face, and padded out to the kitchen. Eric looked up from the skillet where he was scrambling eggs at her approach, disappointment flooding his face. "Oh, dammit. I was going to bring you breakfast in bed."

She reached up to kiss him, pushing down the claustrophobia that gripped at her, and the annoyance of having her space invaded. "That's very sweet, but there's no need. I hate to eat in bed, anyway." She grabbed two mugs from the cabinet and filled them from the coffeepot. "How do you take your coffee?"

"Just black is fine."

She slid the mug over to him, then poured a heavy glug of milk from the carton on the counter into her own cup. She plopped into a chair at the kitchen table and sipped from the mug with both hands, relishing the taste as she watched him cook.

He must have felt the weight of her eyes on him. "Don't worry, I'll clean it all up when we're done."

But he wouldn't clean it right. "No need. My rule is, if you cook, you don't clean." She took another large swallow from the mug.

He divided the eggs between two plates, and turned to pull a sheet of bacon from the oven. "Eh, it's not a problem. I'm glad to have the chance to do something nice for you after what you did for me last night." He winked at her.

She smiled at the memory despite herself.

He placed the plate in front of her. "You didn't have any bread, otherwise I'd've made toast."

She picked up a mound of eggs with her fork, and sniffed them. "God only knows how old these eggs are. And where did you find bacon?"

"In the freezer."

"Huh." She considered. "Ah well, it all smells amazing." She shoveled the pile into her mouth.

"Bon appetit." He bit into a strip of bacon.

She moaned with pleasure as the eggs dissolved in her mouth. "These are amazing. What did you do to them?"

He smiled through his full mouth, chewed and swallowed. "You had an old block of cheddar. After I scraped off the mold, there was enough left over to give them some zip."

She met his eyes and burst out laughing. "I'm so, so sorry."

He raised his eyebrows. "After you finish your breakfast, I'll come up with a way you can make it up to me."

CHAPTER TWENTY-EIGHT

While the police focused their energy on Terry Shawnessy, I focused mine on the next task at hand: Dreta Kline, OakhurstU Ombudsperson.

A deceitful, disgusting excuse for a human being.

And focusing on the task wasn't easy, because the thought alone of pretending to be attracted to her made me literally retch—I could barely look at her face. When the time came to act, I almost couldn't face it, and nearly abandoned the plan for an easier way. But that's how mistakes are made, and it was far too risky to go out on an unnecessary limb.

I'd followed her for several months, noting where she went and what she did and who caught her eye. I discovered quickly how pathetic her life was, and how trashy, just like her. Every Saturday night she drove far out of town to a different dive bar, always one with food and live music. Smart of her to go out of town, since any place in Oakhurst would be stuffed to the gills with students or staff, and she'd be recognized in an instant. And quickly become a university joke.

Smart of her, and very helpful to me.

Once she'd selected her dive du jour, she'd eat a little and drink a lot. She'd survey her field of options, pick a target, and flirt with them so egregiously it was embarrassing and uncomfortable to watch. Then, without fail, she'd go back to their place for her weekly dose of illicit sex.

Not that I'm judging. I don't give a shit who she slept with or what else she did with her life. I just find it ironic.

I watched her through windows when I could. We'd never met in person, only talked over the phone, so it was unlikely she knew what I looked like. But I couldn't be sure, and even if she didn't know who I was, I couldn't risk her noticing the same face hanging out at more than one of her destinations. If she became suspicious, I was done. So I used the dark parking lots for cover when I needed to, and when the bars were smoky or dark, I donned a disguise and tucked myself into a darkened corner. I learned quickly what drinks she liked, how fast she got drunk, which come-ons worked and which didn't—and most important, what her type was.

Then, when the time arrived, I became that.

Still, I was nervous as I watched her get out of her car and head into the Atomic Raccoon, so nervous I waited a full half hour before following her in. I dodged the cloud of smoke and the tang of spilled beer that assailed me when I pushed through the wooden door, and stifled a cough. An '80s metal cover band was pumping out AC/DC's 'You Shook Me All Night Long' from a rickety platform in the far corner, and I let the music seep in as I scanned the room and pull me in to the character I was playing. I spotted Dreta perched on one of the cracked-leather bar stools that faced the dance floor, lip-syncing the words between sips of her Long Island iced tea. She eyed the people on the dance floor, her shoulders bouncing to the music, begging someone to ask her to dance.

I chose a stool on the short end of the bar's L-shape, diagonal to her. I ordered a Coke and waited. When she turned around to order her next drink, I caught her eye and smiled, praying all the while that my true feelings weren't written all over my face. Or that if they were, the first iced tea had impaired her judgment enough to miss them. And that two more drinks would seal the deal.

I sidled up to her and told her how beautiful she was, then asked for the honor of buying her next drink. I made the typical small talk, and asked her to dance. She shook her hips at me during 'Rock You Like A Hurricane,' *then ground them into me during* 'Pour Some Sugar On Me.' *I laughed, flirted, and ran my hands over her hips for another set, then, during the next ballad, took her in my arms and leaned in for an ever-so-bashful first kiss.*

She practically ran to my car when I asked her to come back to my place.

I disguised my nervous energy as excitement, laughing and kissing her hand as we pulled out of the parking lot and took off down the main street.

Then, as soon as we turned down the first dark side road, I chloroformed her.

CHAPTER TWENTY-NINE

Dreta jerked awake, head pounding like someone was slamming a refrigerator door on it. She squinted into the dim light, trying to get a handle on where she was, and shifted up off the cold hard floor for a better look. Her head rebelled, and when her right arm reflexively rose to grasp it, she met rattling resistance.

She was shackled to an iron ring cemented into the floor.

Adrenaline counteracted the lingering effects of alcohol in her system. She bolted the rest of the way to a sitting position, wincing from the explosion of pain in her skull, eyes strafing every inch of the room. Small and rectangular, it had worn beige walls, and the entire floor was cement. There was no furniture, no wall hangings, no rug. On the longer wall across from her, thick wooden beams boarded up two windows, while the shorter wall to her left had a door with a deadbolt, and a small camera mounted near the ceiling. A single touch-on wireless lamp in the far corner of the floor gave the only source of light.

Relief flooded her as she recognized her phone in the same corner, battery removed and placed beside it. She leapt to grab it, and cried out in pain when the shackle jolted her arm.

She scooted back against the wall and startled as her hip brushed against something. She whipped around to find a box cutter, and a voice recorder. She scrambled, hand shaking, to pick up the recorder and press play.

The voice that poured out was metallic and mechanical, like she was listening to Stephen Hawking:

Welcome, Dreta Kline.

"I want you to understand what desperation feels like, Ms. Kline. To find yourself in a torturous situation, with nobody to help you but yourself.

"You're miles from the nearest road, so you can scream for hours, but nobody save the rats will ever hear you. I will not return. If you take no action, you'll die a horrible death of thirst over the next few days. It's not a pleasant way to die, I promise you. But all is not lost! All you need do is take the box cutter and sever the hand that's shackled to the wall. That will free you to reach your phone.

"The worst part, I assure you, will be the time you spend making the decision. I've made sure the blade itself is razor sharp, so slicing through muscles and tendon will be as fast and easy as possible. But the going back and forth in your mind, between fighting the inevitable and giving in to what you must do, knowing only you can save yourself—believe me when I tell you, I know just how soul-crushing that psychological battle is. And I can also assure you, the act will only get more difficult as you get weaker.

"I wonder, have you figured out who's doing this to you? Are you searching your memory desperately for a name? Should I tell you? No. If you know my name, you'll just give it to the police should you escape. So I'll say nothing more, except wish you the very best of luck.

Dreta sat in paralyzed silence for a long moment, forcing her brain to process what she'd just heard. She rewound the tape, and played it again.

When it finished the second time, she began to scream.

CHAPTER THIRTY

Jo arrived at work on Monday half an hour late. Arnett made a show of checking his watch when she entered the large common area that housed the detectives' desks. "I don't think you've ever been late before. Looks like the weekend off did you good."

She raised her eyebrows, and shrugged. "Yes and no." She explained her plans had been canceled. "Then the Crawley vs. Shawnessy debate kept playing through my mind, and I had to force myself not to call my father every few hours to check up on him, so that all drove me a little nuts. But for the most part I managed to distract myself."

"Do I know him?"

She narrowed her eyes at him. "Ha, ha. Do you really want to know the details?"

He thought for a moment, and gave an exaggerated grimace. "No, I really don't."

"Good choice. Not that I was going to tell you anyway." Primarily because the whole weekend had been confusing for her. By the time she and Eric had finished eating breakfast, she'd stopped searching for ways to get him out of the house without offending him. She'd forgotten how much she enjoyed sex in the morning, and by the time they finished with that, they were hungry again. And so the weekend went, alternating between bouts of eating, having sex, and when they were too tired to do either, binge-watching *Game of Thrones*.

Jo found herself drawn into Eric's favorite show. The power dynamics were fascinating, even if she still couldn't keep everyone straight after finishing season one. And Eric turned out to be a whiz at making wondrous meals from the next-to-nothing in her larder. She'd been glad to avoid being alone, scuttling around an empty house obsessing about her father and the university killer. Still, by the time Sunday night came, she was relieved when Eric announced he had to go.

She plopped down into her chair. "Anyway. Sorry I'm late. If I remember correctly, our next step was to find out if someone on campus would clarify Ratliffe's odd-duck research article. Since Latimer wasn't a drop more forthcoming than we forced him to be, I think our best bet is Parminder. He'd probably have more insight into the research and Ratliffe's history with Shawnessy, regardless."

"Agreed. And maybe we can find a graduate student or two to give their perspective. But you caught me right in the middle of clearing out our backlog of paperwork. Lend me a hand and we can get out of here faster."

But it was well past two in the afternoon before Jo shrugged back into her blazer. They were halfway out of the building when her phone buzzed again. She glanced at it, and answered. "We're just on our way to your campus, Dean Latimer. What can I do for you?"

"The campus ombudsperson, Dreta Kline, didn't show up to work today. Her office called to check on her, but her phone went straight to voicemail. Given everything that's happened, the campus is on high alert, and they called me right away. Nobody was aware of any tarot card, but I didn't want to take any chances. I checked her incoming mail for today, and sure enough, I found one."

An icy cold filled Jo as she reached for her notebook and paused at an empty desk. "What's her home address and phone number?"

Latimer gave them to her. "Her administrative assistant drove to Dreta's house on her lunch break, but nobody answered her knock, and Dreta's car isn't there."

"Which card did you find?"

"It shows a person laying face down on the ground, with swords sticking out of his back." Jo heard him counting. "Ten of them."

"Was she at work on Friday? All day?"

She listened as Latimer asked the question to someone near him, then came back on the line. "Yes. In fact, she was here Saturday morning catching up on paperwork. Her administrative assistant says they were here until noon."

Jo tore off the page and shoved the address into Arnett's hands. "Okay, we're on our way to her house now." She ended the call, and summarized for Arnett as they dashed for the car. Then she called Dreta Kline's cell phone, and verified that the call went directly to voicemail.

"Let's not panic, she could be just fine, off on some overnight trip with friends." Arnett programmed the address into the GPS as Jo tapped Dreta Kline's information into their search engine.

"Maybe the card was in the mail before we arrested him Friday night, and she's just off somewhere," Arnett said, tires squealing as he pulled out into the road.

"You don't believe that, and neither do I. Shawnessy had absolutely no motive for killing the ombudsperson. But *Crawley* did." Jo scanned the screen in front of her with laser focus. "Okay, found her. Single. Lives alone as far as I can tell, nobody else comes up at the same address. License says she's thirty-seven, brown hair, brown eyes, five-five, a hundred thirty-five pounds." She picked up the phone again, dialed Lopez, and caught her up on the situation. "I need you to run her plates, and see if we can find her via her cell signal. The calls are going directly to voicemail, so it's probably turned off, but I read something the other day about the feds tracking terrorists' cell phones even when they're off."

"Keeping up on your tech, Jo! Very impressive. But to do that, they have to install a Trojan in the phone first, so unless our ombudsperson has been a *very* bad girl, that's not relevant. Luckily,

GPS signals function even when the phone is turned off, as long as there's even a residual trace of battery power."

"Great, thank you. Find out anything else you can, too. If you've got any tricks up your sleeve, now's the time to use them."

"Don't-ask-don't-tell, got it."

They rounded the corner onto Ash Street, and Arnett took pains to ease the car casually up in front of Dreta's house. The canary-yellow, two-story colonial was lined with marigolds in the last throes of their bloom, on a spacious lot of rolling lawn ringed with oak and pine trees.

Jo and Arnett cased the house and surrounding area while they approached. Nothing seemed out of place, no broken windows or other signs of an altercation. "The computer said the plates belong to a 2016 Honda Accord, which I'm not seeing anywhere," Jo said.

Arnett headed toward the side of the house. "I'll check around back."

While Arnett circled the property, Jo scanned the neighbors' houses. A face peered out from the curtains of the next house down.

Arnett reappeared. "Don't see anything back there, either."

Jo pointed to the twitching curtain. "Her neighbor seems to keep a watch on things. Should we talk to her first?"

"Never a bad idea to double-check before excepting the Fourth Amendment," Arnett answered.

A seventy-something woman in a turquoise tracksuit opened the door as they strode up the driveway. "Can I help you?"

Jo held out her badge. "I'm Detective Josette Fournier, and this is Detective Bob Arnett, Oakhurst County SPDU. When was the last time you saw your neighbor?"

Sharp blue eyes flicked between them. "Dreta? What's this about?"

"We received a call from a citizen worried about her welfare. Have you seen her today?" Jo asked.

"Nope. Last time I saw her was Saturday night, before she went out for her weekly tomcatting."

"You're certain not yesterday or today?" Jo asked.

The woman tossed her helmet of silver hair, and pointed at a pair of binoculars on her hall table. "I'm sure. She didn't come home Saturday night. She usually doesn't, so I'd've noticed if she had. She normally does her walk of shame late Sunday morning, then mows her lawn with some form of hair-of-the-dog in one hand while she steers her John Deere with the other." She jutted her chin toward the house. "See for yourselves, it hasn't been cut."

Jo turned to politely appraise the lawn. "With fall moving in, maybe she decided to skip a week?"

"She never skips until the snow comes. Besides, she always leaves for work at 7:15 a.m. on the dot, but she wasn't here this morning. If I hadn't seen her by tomorrow, I'd've called you myself."

Jo nodded. "Does she normally park in the garage?"

"Nope. Garage is packed to the gills. Always parks in the driveway."

"Any idea where she goes on Saturday nights?" Arnett asked.

"Nope."

"Thanks for your help, Mrs...?" Jo paused for the answer.

"Garcia. Rose Garcia."

Jo handed her a card. "Thank you, Mrs. Garcia. If you see her, or remember anything else, can you let us know?"

"Will do."

As they made their way back to Dreta's house, Arnett stopped to grab a truncheon from their trunk. They climbed the porch stairs, hands on their weapons, then Arnett rapped on the door. "Dreta Kline? SPDU, welfare check."

When there was no reply, Jo tried. "SPDU, welfare check. If anyone's home, please respond or we will enter the premises."

No response.

Arnett jabbed the truncheon through the window, tapped out the glass, then reached around to unlock the deadbolt and pulled the door open.

They drew their weapons and entered, greeted by stale air, and secured each room as they searched. The house was lived in but neat, and the only sign of recent activities were several discarded outfits on her bed. The landline in the kitchen showed no missed calls, and as Rose had assured them, the garage contained only boxes and old furniture.

Jo's phone rang. "Fournier."

Lopez spoke. "Any sign of her?"

"None. What did you find out?"

"Bad news is, something's up with her phone, because I can't get any sort of GPS tracking on it. Good news is, I have the location of the last cell tower it pinged. In Hillsdale, about twenty miles west on the Pike. And the last charge on her credit cards was also in Hillsdale, at a place called the Atomic Raccoon Bar and Grill. Eleven-forty-two p.m. Saturday night."

"Thanks. We'll head over there. Keep looking for anything that can help us."

CHAPTER THIRTY-ONE

I enjoyed watching her struggle.

She screamed until her throat turned raw. Next, she tugged and yanked at the manacle, trying to force her hand through. But I'd made sure the metal was so tight around her wrist it bit into her skin.

When she gave up on that, she turned to the iron ring. She grabbed it with both hands, feet braced on the wall, and pulled so hard I could see her muscles strain. She removed one of her booties, and smashed the heel against it. When the heel flew off without budging the ring even the tiniest bit, she grabbed the box cutter, and started to dig at the cement base—but stopped almost immediately. She peered at the blade so long I thought the feed had frozen, then set the knife aside.

Because whatever she is, she's not stupid. As soon as it hit that impenetrable cement, she must have realized she needed to keep the blade as sharp as possible.

Then as abruptly as she'd stopped, she erupted into frantic screams. She grabbed the recorder, and smashed it against the base of the ring until it shattered.

Her screams morphed into jagged cries. A sort of glowing energy took me over as I watched her curl up into a ball, gasping for breath as the sobs wracked her body. I actually caught myself talking to her then, asking her if it had been worth it, if she regretted what she'd done, if she now had an understanding of the pain she'd inflicted.

And then, even though she had no way to hear my questions, she answered them. She pushed herself back up, stared directly into the camera, and begged for her life. Told me that however it was she wronged me, she'd do anything—anything—to make it right if I let her out.

I enjoyed that part even more.

She curled back up, begging and crying herself to sleep. I slept when she slept, the app set to wake me when the camera sensed motion again.

Her movements were slow when she woke back up, and the one time she tried to stand, she nearly fell. She talked a bit to herself, voice hoarse, but it made her cough.

People worry about starving to death, but humans can live weeks without food. The real danger is running out of water. Without it, humans will die in three days. And while she'd only been confined for just under two days, she'd started out with two strikes against her—all the alcohol she'd consumed had dehydrated her before I locked her in, and her crying had made it worse still.

She wouldn't last much longer, and she knew it.

After she fell, she sat for nearly an hour, shoulders sagging, head drooped. I tried to guess what was going through her head. Fantasies of the perfect bank shot, made with the largest piece of recorder shrapnel that would push her phone within reach? Prayers that someone would find her if she just held out long enough? Or was she regretting the time she would now never have with loved ones, maybe the mother I'd seen her visit during my surveillance?

Then she picked up the blade.

I leaned forward, eyes glued to the screen.

She cut.

I'm not sure what I expected. Maybe that she'd jump in, stabbing or slashing, trying to make it as fast and easy as possible. But she didn't. She made a small cut, no bigger than a paper cut as best I could tell. Then she went over it again and again, making it bigger, then bigger still, blood slowly dripping onto the cement. She whimpered as she cut, interspersed with a low, animal braying.

Without warning, she slashed faster and harder, and the noises morphed to a series of guttural, war-cry howls. Then, finally, into primal screams until the blade tinked as it hit the cement.

She scuffled across the room, trying to keep her balance, and I retched as I caught sight of the white, disembodied flesh sticking up from the pool of blood like a cresting whale behind her. I focused my attention back on her, in the far corner now, scrambling to get the battery back into her phone. She forgot for a moment she now only had one hand, and screamed when her bleeding stump smacked the glass. Her fingers slipped on the blood left behind as she braced the phone against the wall and used leverage to click the battery into place.

The phone lit up, and the power-up initiated.

Then, it beeped, and the screen went blank again.

And the sobs when she realized the battery was dead—that was the part I enjoyed the most.

CHAPTER THIRTY-TWO

Jo and Arnett spotted the Atomic Raccoon Bar and Grill's neon sign peeking out of the surrounding trees, a beacon to motorists looking for a meal or a drink. The building itself was a large cabin set half a mile down a dirt road off the highway, bordered with a rustic wooden-and-stone fence. An eclectic array of beer signs dotted the windows.

They pulled into the gravel parking lot, got out of the car, and scanned the area as they crossed to the entrance. "Nestled into the woods. Picturesque, and the perfect place to abduct someone," Arnett said.

"No lights in the parking lot, no streetlights in the surrounds." Jo swung open the wooden door, and motioned for Arnett to enter first.

"We're not open for another half hour." A middle-aged blond man hunched over a palette of glasses, polishing them and lining them up behind the bar.

Arnett flashed his badge. "Detectives Arnett and Fournier, SPDU. You the owner?"

The man dropped his towel onto the bar. "I am. Pete Rankovits. What's the problem?"

Jo held up the picture she'd had Latimer send to her. "We're here about a missing woman, Dreta Kline. Last known location was here, Saturday night. You remember seeing her?"

Pete Rankovits studied the picture and shook his head. "You're sure she was here?"

"Charged something on her card just before midnight, possibly a bar tab," Arnett said.

"Teresa was tending bar Saturday." He called out, and a woman appeared through the swinging door from the kitchen. Jo estimated her age at around thirty, with long black hair, and a tight black shirt over skinny jeans.

She set down the bowl of limes in her hand, gaze moving from Arnett, to Jo, to her boss. "What's up?"

"These cops want to know if you've seen some woman. Dreta Kline?" He glanced back to Jo.

"Correct." She held up the phone. "Do you remember seeing this woman?"

Teresa peered at the phone, and wagged her head side to side. "Looks familiar—yeah, I do remember her. She downed a Long Island iced tea like it was nothing, and I do *not* short my drinks. Was her hair longer than this?"

Jo kept her expression blank. "It's possible. Do you remember her leaving?"

Teresa frowned in concentration. "I don't. Saturdays are busy, I'm sure you get that. I know she had at least one more drink, because I was worried I'd have to cut her off after the way she downed the first one. Oh, and I do remember seeing her on the dance floor. She was wearing this mustard and red tunic bright enough to make God cry, and her dancing didn't improve it."

"Was she dancing with someone?" Jo asked.

Teresa shrugged. "I'm sure she was dancing with *someone*, but if you're asking if I saw who, no, I didn't."

Jo pulled up a picture of Crawley. "What about this guy? You ever seen him in here?"

She bent to peer at the picture. "Not that I remember, but I can't be sure. Why?"

"What about these?" She showed Teresa pictures of Latimer, Kerland, Parminder, and Shawnessy.

She considered. "Can't say for sure, but I don't think so."

"Have you ever seen Dreta Kline in here other than this past Saturday?" Arnett asked.

"Not for certain, but again, I can't rule it out. And I don't work every Saturday." Her brow creased. "Hey, Pete, didn't you have a car towed yesterday?"

"Yeah. So?"

Jo exchanged a look with Arnett. "2016 Honda Accord?"

"I'm not sure, but that sounds about right. I can check the paperwork."

Arnett shook his head and turned his face away. Jo said, "Don't just check it. Bring it here, we'll need to see it."

Jo's cell rang. She glanced down at it, tugged Arnett's coat to let him know she was going, and stepped away. "Fournier."

Lopez's voice had an excited edge. "Kline's phone is sending a GPS signal again."

CHAPTER THIRTY-THREE

"How is that possible?"

"I can't be sure. Usually even a dead battery has enough charge to keep the GPS signal going, so all I can think is maybe someone took the battery out and tossed the phone, then someone found it and reassembled it?"

"We have a location yet?"

"I'm downloading the position to your car's computer. It's out in the middle of the boonies, but only about twenty minutes from where you are. Google Earth shows some sort of shack about half a mile in from the nearest dirt road, hidden among the trees. Looks like it might fall down at any second, and since the pic is from 2015, it may already have. There's a foot path leading back from the road, might be big enough to drive on if it's not overgrown by now. I'm doing a search to see who owns the property as we speak—looks like somebody named Doris Pentiger. Want me to track her down?"

Jo made her way back to Arnett. "Yes, find out what you can and see if you can reach her. See if you can get some locals out to the site, too. We'll call you when we get there."

*

Exactly nineteen minutes later, they parked next to the path leading from the road. While not completely overrun, foliage obscured much of the path, except for two rough trenches where tire tracks compressed the undergrowth. Arnett eyed it warily. "Shit, great way to get Lyme disease. How far did she say?"

"About half a mile."

"I vote we drive as far in as we can."

Jo shook her head and laughed. "Remind me to never invite you on a camping trip."

They climbed back into the car and drove carefully down the path. "The coordinates Lopez sent are right here, this has to be it."

They got out of the car and drew their weapons. "That's odd. Lopez said it was falling down," Arnett said.

They approached the structure, a rough rectangle large enough to have once been a family vacation cabin. Although covered with a mélange of weather-beaten planks, one corner of the house was braced with newer two-by-fours, and perched on a fresh cement foundation. The windows were boarded up from the inside, but both the front and back doors were solid, framed with new, substantial beams. "Looks like someone's done some work on it." He raised his voice. "State police detective unit! Is anyone there? Dreta Kline?"

They circled the cabin, repeating the call as they went, but found no other exits, nor any open windows.

Back at the front, they flanked the door. Arnett tried the knob, but the door didn't move. Arnett pounded on it. "SPDU! Open up!"

Nobody answered.

"Door's solid, no way we're knocking it down."

Jo holstered her gun and pulled out her phone. "Okay, I'll—"

A siren whined behind them, and, as they stared down the road, twirling lights broke through the trees.

"Oh, no. Please tell me they're not stupid enough to—" Arnett started.

But they were. Three black-and-whites screeched to a halt in front of the cabin. Jo and Arnett pulled out their badges as six officers jumped out of the three cars. "Detectives Fournier and Arnett?"

Arnett rushed forward "What the hell? Haven't you ever heard of preserving a crime scene?"

The first closest officer drew himself up to his full six-foot-plus height, stepped toward Arnett, and narrowed his brown eyes. "I was told there's an emergency situation here."

Jo stepped in front of Arnett and checked the officer's name. Time was of the essence, and a pissing match wasn't going to help. "Sergeant Temple. We appreciate your help. We don't know what the situation is yet." She caught him up. "We need to get in there ASAP."

Temple called back to the other officers. "Battering ram, now!"

Two burly officers opened their trunk and extracted the ram. Jo pulled out her firearm again, and the others followed. The officers hefted the ram into position, and in a single fluid motion, caved in the wood.

Jo and Arnett eased forward, shined their flashlights around the dark cabin, then stepped in and flipped on the lights. The room was dusty and the furniture covered with sheets, like the family who owned it had shut it up for the season and never returned. They proceeded through the main room, past several others branching off the side. At the back of the house, in the corner that had been reinforced with beams and cement outside, they found another, thinner, locked door.

One of the officers kicked it down, and peered inside. Almost immediately, he retched.

"Take that outside!" Arnett yelled, and he and Jo stepped into the room.

In front of them, against the back wall, a human hand rested amid congealed blood. And in the far corner, Dreta Kline lay curled around a cell phone.

*

The Berkshire County SPDU again happily turned jurisdiction over to Oakhurst County, and Marzillo's team again processed the scene late into the night. Jo stumbled home well past midnight, and after a fitful five hours of sleep, hurried in for an update.

Both Marzillo and Lopez were uncharacteristically somber, and tension hung over the room.

"Probably best to start with what we found on the shattered recorder. You'll understand why in a minute." Marzillo pointed to Lopez, who pulled up a file on her laptop and hit play.

"This guy's even sicker than I thought," Jo said, once they'd listened to it three times.

Marzillo continued. "The ME hasn't done the autopsy yet, but based on the recording and what I saw, it's safe to say Kline cut off her own hand and bled out. The cement made the room relatively easy to analyze. There were no prints on anything in the room other than Kline's, and the prints we got from the rest of the house don't match any we've collected, or anything in IAFIS. No hairs or fibers not associated with Kline, even on her clothing. Since there were no signs of a struggle prior to her death, my guess is she was carried in unconscious. Accordingly, we're running some tests for DNA where he's likely to have touched her. But it's a needle in a haystack—you said she was dancing, so who knows how many people touched her on that dance floor, accidentally or otherwise. And, given the lack of fingerprints, I'd guess our killer was smart enough to wear gloves when transporting her."

"You said no struggle, so no chance of defensive action, something under the fingernails or such?" Jo asked.

Marzillo shrugged. "The ME will do the equivalent of a rape kit, so something might show up there. But I didn't see signs of anything that give me hope."

Everyone was silent for a beat.

"Dreta's car?"

"We're bringing it here from the impound lot. But my guess is that since it was still in the lot, the killer transported her in his car, and was never anywhere near it."

"What about the camera, we must know where it was sending the signal?" Arnett asked.

"Nope. It's wireless. Anybody with the password can tap into the signal."

Jo turned to Lopez. "There must be some way to trace back the IP address of whoever tapped into it, right?"

Lopez pulled her legs up under her, fingers winding through her long, black ponytail. "I already tried. They used a proxy."

"Any chance we have Dreta's phone records yet?"

"Yep. Easy to summarize, because she hadn't made a call or sent a text since Friday, and those were all work related. Last personal call I could find was Tuesday night, to her mother. There are three incoming calls after she disappeared, one from her administrative assistant, with relevant voicemail, calling to find out where she was. The other from Latimer, about two hours later. Then one from you about forty-five minutes after that," Lopez said.

"So she didn't make a call once she turned it back on?"

"Nope. There wasn't enough battery power."

"So how did the GPS start transmitting?"

"You only need a small amount of residual battery power for the GPS to work, far less than you need to power up the phone," Lopez said.

Jo's instincts perked up. "So why leave the battery at all? I get that the phone was bait, so she'd think she had a shot at rescue. But she'd have never known the battery was missing until it was too late. Why remove it from the phone just to let her put it back in?"

"Maybe he knew it didn't matter, that she'd bleed out before an ambulance could get there, regardless," Marzillo shrugged.

"Any luck finding the property owner?" Jo asked.

"Yep, Doris Pentiger lives in Colorado. She inherited the property seven years ago when her father died. He lived in Springfield, used the cabin as a getaway. She hired a local realtor to sell his main property in Springfield, but didn't find a taker for the other property. She said she keeps meaning to get out here and figure out what to do with it, but she's not as young as she used to be, either."

"Any proof she was in Colorado over the weekend?" Arnett asked.

"I'm checking into it. She claims she works a nine-to-five shift both weekend days in a bank, so that should be easy enough to check. She's not married and has no kids, and I haven't found anything that connects her or her father to any of the vics or the suspects, or OakhurstU at all, for that matter."

"Keep digging. There has to be a connection of some sort. The house is so far from any regular road, I can't see how you'd realize it was essentially abandoned unless you were looking for it. There has to be some reason our killer knew about it, and we need to find out what that is."

"Time to pull out that behavioral targeting again." Lopez twirled her ponytail, the gleam returning to her eyes.

"Someday you're going to have to show me how you do that. In the meantime, we'll also need to check into Pentiger's realtor, and any realtors that specialize in that area." Jo rubbed a hand over her eyes, and sighed. "Which leads to the elephant in the room. There's no way Shawnessy did this. She disappeared from the bar on Saturday night, when he had several hundred witnesses that he was present and accounted for in the cell block. Which leads us back to Crawley. Although the killer had to know we'd recover the recorder. Not the smartest move."

"He's a depressive paranoid schizophrenic, Jo. Good choices aren't his strong suit," Lopez said, expression grim.

"Fair enough. Still, I don't think we should close the door on other suspects too quickly again. And I think we need to consider there may be a suspect we haven't even considered yet, because nothing fits the way it should. I'd like to look into Dreta's work records, see if we can find anything we've missed. We need to dig deep."

"Anybody who'd have reason to contact the ombudsperson would be affiliated with the university, so we're looking at staff, faculty, or students. And that tape rules out the infidelity angle, at least," Arnett said.

Jo shook her head. "Not if Whorton was having an affair with the ombudsperson. I'd bet Camilla Whorton would describe the situation Michael put her in as tortuous, and if she killed him and his lovers, she probably felt like she was alone and that was the only way to save herself. And, like I said, the killer had to know we'd recover the recording. It could very well be intended to mislead us."

Arnett's eyebrows shot up. "Touché. Guess infidelity is still my blind spot."

"You trust the people you love. There's nothing wrong with that. Far too many cops aren't able to shake off what they see on the job, and take it home to their detriment." Jo sighed. "In the meantime, we need to have another chat with Crawley, and talk to the other employees at the Atomic Raccoon."

Marzillo choked on her coffee. "The Atomic Raccoon?"

Lopez pointed at Marzillo. "Don't even pretend you wouldn't hang out there."

"Are you kidding? I wish I'd thought of the name myself. When I'm famous on the poker circuit, I'll need a handle."

"Totally badass." Lopez nodded.

Jo shook her head and stood up. "It's time to eat crow. Let's get Shawnessy released before his lawyer takes action against the department."

CHAPTER THIRTY-FOUR

Their visit to Crawley's apartment was short.

"This has become harassment. I still don't have my computer back, and your people came today and took the loaner I got from the library, and the burner phone I had to buy. When I don't return that computer tomorrow, I'm going to have to pay a fine I can't afford." He held out a card to them. "I've had enough. I have nothing to say to you. Direct any questions you have to my lawyer."

"How the hell can he afford a lawyer?" Arnett asked as they walked back to the car.

Jo shrugged. "Got me. Who knows, maybe it's an old army buddy."

She dialed the number as soon as she settled into the car. The woman who answered sounded young, and Jo could have sworn she heard gum popping. She exchanged a skeptical look with Arnett. "This is Detective Josette Fournier, SPDU. I'm calling for Roderick Duncan."

The gum chewing paused. "One moment, please."

The line was silent for several minutes. Then, a man's voice, also relatively young, picked up the line. "Detective. I assume you're calling about Gregory Crawley."

"I am. I should tell you, you're on speakerphone. I'm here with another detective, Bob Arnett."

"Gotcha. What can I help you with?"

"We're outside your client's apartment building right now. Another university-affiliated person was found murdered yesterday, and we need to talk to your client about his alibi. When can you bring him in to make a statement?"

"Right, we heard about that all over the news. I can certainly bring Mr. Crawley in to make a statement, but I'm not sure there's any need, I should be able to answer any questions you have."

"We'd prefer to speak with him."

"That's fine, but even if we're at the station, I'll be the one answering your questions."

"I'm sure it'll be a pleasure to meet you in person, Mr. Duncan. This afternoon, if possible."

"I believe he has classes this afternoon."

"We'll be happy to work around his class schedule. Four people are dead now, so as I'm sure you can appreciate, time is of the essence. And the department tends to look unfavorably on citizens who aren't cooperative in the face of such events."

The attorney gave an exaggerated sigh. "Let me call him. I'll find a time he can meet me at the station later today."

"We appreciate that."

Jo hung up the phone. "Parminder next? He's out of class in forty-five minutes."

"Let's do it." Arnett pulled away from the curb toward the university. "Sal's is right on the way, and who knows when we'll get to eat again the way things are going. Meatball sub?"

"I might need two to get through this day," Jo said.

Jo's phone rang again just as they slid into a parking spot outside of Sal's. "That was fast, Mr. Duncan. Good to hear from you."

"Mr. Crawley can be at the station in half an hour."

Jo stared longingly at the big red "Sal's" sign facing her. "Perfect. See you in half an hour."

"You know," Arnett said, also staring up at the sign, "when everything kept getting in the way of us interviewing Latimer and Parminder, that was almost funny. But if it starts happening with Sal's, this is gonna get real personal."

*

Ronald Duncan, Esq. was pretty much exactly what Jo had pictured. His suit was a cheap polyester blend with haphazard stitching that ensured nothing hung correctly, his black hair was slicked straight back from his forehead, and the attaché he carried into the interrogation room had worn edges. As she watched him carefully place the case beside the table in an attempt to hide a nasty brown stain, she made a mental note to check whether he was actually an attorney at all.

Jo sat across from Duncan, leaving the seat across from Crawley for Arnett. Crawley stared at both of them with open hostility.

Duncan spoke before Jo got a chance to. "Mr. Crawley has a class in an hour and a half that he doesn't want to miss, so let's get started. Yes, we realize you're recording this, and yes, we're fine with it. On to the matter at hand. My client attended classes during the day yesterday, then was at work until midnight last night. One of his classes was a discussion section where the TA takes roll, so she can confirm he was there, and of course his boss can confirm his work hours."

Jo leaned back in her chair. "I appreciate that information. But we actually need to know where he was on Saturday, specifically Saturday evening."

The attorney paused, and confusion flitted over his face. "Why? I thought Ms. Kline was killed yesterday?"

Jo weighed her options. They wouldn't be able to keep the basic information about the murder quiet for long, regardless—she might as well explain. She chose her words carefully. "She died yesterday, but she was abducted Saturday night."

Mr. Duncan paused again. "I can't see how that matters if Mr. Crawley has a solid alibi for the time when Ms. Kline was killed?"

Jo kept her face blank. She hadn't chosen her words carefully enough. This guy might be young and bargain basement, but he wasn't stupid. She felt Arnett shift in the chair next to her, and reached for a favorite fail-safe. "That's all I can say at the current time. We need to know where Mr. Crawley was Saturday afternoon and evening."

Duncan leaned over to Crawley, who whispered in his ear.

Jo watched the exchange, wondering if she'd been caught inside a pulp noir novel. The kid really couldn't answer for himself? She exchanged a supercilious glance with Arnett, and watched anger flash on Crawley's face.

Duncan straightened back up. "Mr. Crawley worked until five Saturday evening. Then he went to Hill of Beans to study for an exam he has later this week."

"Do you have anyone who can verify that, Mr. Crawley?" Jo asked.

Crawley continued his malevolent stare, while Duncan responded. "Unfortunately, no. But the computer you confiscated today should show activity during that time period."

"He could have used it anywhere, that proves nothing."

"I don't know anything about that, but if it becomes necessary, I'll have computer experts of my own evaluate what the computer does and does not prove."

Jo kept her face blank. She couldn't wrap her head around this guy—he was smart enough to parry her thrusts and keep the wall up between them and Crawley, but with every word he said, it became harder for her to take him seriously. She met Crawley's eyes. "And on Sunday?"

They consulted again in whispers. "He worked a shift from eight in the morning until two. Then he went to Hill of Beans to study for several hours. He paid cash for his coffee, but the barista on duty has a crush on him, so she should remember him."

"Her name?" If the girl had a crush on Crawley, Jo would eat her own teeth.

"Delima."

"Have you ever gone to see Dreta Kline for any reason?"

"I believe that information is confidential," Duncan said, and his jaw tensed.

Aha. She'd hit a nerve. "Do you mean that Mr. Crawley is asserting his Fifth Amendment rights? Because we won't have any problem accessing the university's records on this. The confidentiality promised to those who consult the ombudsperson is university policy only, it doesn't extend to cases where law enforcement is involved."

Duncan and Crawley conducted an impressively contentious whispered exchange, then he turned back to respond. "My client did consult with the campus ombudsperson regarding discrimination he was facing from Dr. Michael Whorton."

"How long ago was that?"

"Last semester. He doesn't remember the exact date."

It was a stupid roadblock to put up, they'd get the answer without a problem. Why was he stonewalling? "And what was the outcome of that consultation?"

"Ms. Kline intervened with the administration on Mr. Crawley's behalf. She suggested that the grades on his tests and assignments be reexamined and justified. The dean agreed that was reasonable, and followed through with Whorton."

She redirected her gaze back to Crawley. "My understanding is that the reexamination didn't come out in your favor, and you were upset about that."

Crawley narrowed his eyes at her, but didn't speak. Duncan nodded. "He was, understandably so. The university was covering its ass."

Arnett spoke, drawing Crawley's gaze from Jo. "Did you contact Ms. Kline again after that evaluation?"

"He did. At that time she told him there was no more she could do for him," Duncan responded.

Arnett laughed. "Shut you down, huh? Let you know how insignificant you were?"

Crawley's face flushed.

Duncan tapped the table with his index finger. "The situation was upsetting for him, yes. But if you're insinuating he'd hurt Ms. Kline because of it, he did no such thing."

Jo took back over. "Greg, do you know anyone with a house or a cabin out in the Berkshires, particularly in the area of Granton?" She watched him flinch when she used his first name.

"What relevance does that have?" Duncan asked.

Jo kept her eyes on Crawley. "I'm not at liberty to discuss that. Please answer my question, Greg."

Crawley opened his mouth to speak, but Duncan placed a hand on Crawley's arm, and leaned in for another whispered consultation. "He's not immediately aware of anyone that owns such a house, but it isn't impossible."

Jo swore silently—Crawley'd been *so close* to losing his temper. "Has he ever been to the Granton area?"

"Not that he's aware of. But his father took him and his brothers hunting and camping regularly when he was younger, so it's possible." He removed his hand from Crawley's arm. "Any other questions, Detectives?"

"For the moment, no, but we'll have more later. We'll transcribe the information you've given us into a statement for your signature. You're still a person of interest, so please don't leave the area without letting us know."

"We have no problem with that. But, we'd like to know when Mr. Crawley's computers and phones will be returned to him. He has exams to take, and after the biased discrimination from Dr. Whorton last term, he's fighting an uphill battle to get his GPA back in order. He can't afford to fail another class, or the fines for the borrowed computer."

"I can't give you an ETA, since we're still processing them. However, if you show the receipt we gave you to the library, they should be willing to waive the fee. They can call me to confirm if they like." She pushed her card across the table.

"Surely the burner phone at least should be cleared shortly?"

"We'll make every effort."

Crawley snorted.

Jo and Arnett stood up. "We'll send someone back as soon as possible with the statement so you can be on your way."

Jo turned to Arnett once they heard the door click into place behind them. "There you go. He admits he went to her, even though he denied it when we talked to him. Why did he lie?"

"It wasn't lie. You asked if he went to anyone after they evaluated his exams, and he said there was no point." He raised his hand as she started to object. "But yes, he didn't tell us, and I'm not clear why. And, if he got off work at five, he had plenty of time to do a few internet searches on the borrowed computer and then drive out to the Atomic Raccoon. And plenty of time to get Kline up in the death cabin and still be home in time to grab some sleep before work the next morning."

Jo nodded, but didn't speak.

"What?" Arnett asked.

"I'm still trying to wrap my head around that interaction."

"Clear as a summer's day. Incompetence. Duncan got his law degree from the same site where he found that suit."

Jo smiled. "What gets me is, most of the answers were rehearsed, but a few seemed to catch them both off guard, like the alibi on Saturday."

"So he played stupid about the timing. They could have rehearsed that, too." He shook his head. "First you didn't want it to be Shawnessy, now it seems like you don't want it to be Crawley."

She shook her head to clear it. "Yeah, you're right. I don't know why I'm second-guessing everything in this case. We need to keep our eyes open, double-check Camilla Whorton's whereabouts, all that, but Crawley fits the facts best. He's insane—I don't know what brand of insane, but definitely insane. We just need to find the evidence that proves it."

"I think we also need to start being proactive about this. Who knows how long that to-do list of his is? Until we can get him put away, I think we need to put him under surveillance."

"Agreed."

They finalized the arrangements for Crawley's statement, then grabbed their jackets. "Sal's then Parminder?" Jo asked.

"Yup."

Jo froze when her phone rang.

CHAPTER THIRTY-FIVE

Fifteen minutes later, Jo and Arnett rushed into Steve Parminder's office. He sat completely still, face sickly pale, while Roger Latimer paced the length of the small office.

Latimer pointed at an envelope on the desk. "It came in today's mail."

"How much did you handle it?"

Parminder looked up at her like a deer caught in headlights, then stared back at the envelope. "Um. I'm not sure. I was sorting through my mail as usual. I saw this one was manually typed rather than machine printed, so I opened it first." He gestured to a letter opener out on the desk.

"And you took out the card?"

He nodded. "I reached in, then pulled it out. The next thing I remember I was on the phone with Dean Latimer. I must have stuffed it back in and dropped it there."

Jo snapped several pictures while Arnett tugged on gloves and readied an evidence bag from the satchel they'd brought with them. "Very cute. Postmarked Saturday, out of Granton," she said.

"Must have dropped this off on his way to kill Dreta." Arnett lifted the envelope with tweezers, and extracted the card with a second pair. "Same markings as the other card, almost certainly from the same deck." He flipped it over.

The words *The Moon* were centered at the bottom, and the card featured two dogs howling up at a hybrid moon and sun that had flames dropping from it. Behind them, a lobster crawled toward them, out of a pond. A path led from the pond out between two gray towers, and disappeared into mountains in the distance.

"Any clue what this one means?" Arnett asked.

Jo racked her brains. The card had a dark, unsettling feel to it, but she couldn't conjure any meaning more specific than that. She shook her head. "We'll have to look it up."

"You're sure it came today?" Arnett asked.

"It might have come yesterday. I was out of town giving a keynote address. I didn't get back until late last night." Parminder's gaze flicked back and forth between the two of them. "They told us to report it immediately if we received or found a tarot card. They didn't say why, but I'm not stupid—I'm next. But I thought you arrested Terry Shawnessy?"

Jo closed her eyes briefly and nodded. She cleared her throat. "We did arrest Terry Shawnessy, but we released him earlier today."

"Why—"

"Because he can't be our killer. We have several very viable suspects, and we initially believed he was the most likely, until Dreta Kline was murdered while he was in custody. Here's the crux of the matter, Dr. Parminder—"

"Steve, please," he said, reflexively.

She nodded acknowledgement. "Steve. The killer sent or left a tarot card for each victim. So yes, I believe this is a threat." Parminder went a shade paler, and she hurried to focus his attention. "Do you know of anybody with a grudge against you, especially anybody who also had a history with the other victims?"

He gazed up at her, eyes wide. "No, nobody."

Arnett asked, "How about Greg Crawley, was he ever a student of yours?"

Steve nodded. "Yes. I know he struggled, but I had no problem with him. He passed my class."

She hadn't expected that answer. But then, Michael Whorton hadn't discriminated against Greg Crawley, but Greg certainly believed he had—that was the dangerous thing about paranoia, it didn't need a legitimate basis.

Steve's eyes were widening still farther, and she needed to calm him down. "There's actually good news here. This is the first time we've found the card before anyone was harmed, and that gives us the upper hand. My guess is you upset the killer's plan by not being here yesterday. Most likely he'll abandon his plan, because he'll know we're waiting for him. But we're not going to risk anything. We'll do whatever we need to do to keep you and your family safe."

Parminder sat forward in his chair, and Jo saw his hands were shaking. "My family?"

She groaned inwardly—she should have put that more delicately. But, the reality was, pussyfooting around the issue wasn't going to solve anything. She stood as tall as she was able, hoping to send a subconscious message of protection. "Yes. The killer may have already targeted family members. We'll need to assign a protective detail immediately." She gestured to the picture on his desk. "You're married, with two daughters?"

"Married, two daughters, yes," Parminder repeated with flat intonation, staring at the picture.

"We'll send an officer to your daughters' school to escort them home safely, and do the same for your wife—"

Parminder's eyes stayed on the picture. "My wife is a stay-at-home mother."

"Even better, because the best thing will be to keep them out of school until we arrest the killer. We'll assign a pair of officers to monitor your home until we do. Do you have a graduate student who can take over your teaching for the short term?"

Parminder didn't respond.

Jo waited, giving him a moment to digest. "Dr. Parminder?"

His eyes flew back to her face, and he bolted up out of his chair. "No, Detective, I'm sorry. I will not wait here for my family to be slaughtered. You can have your officers bring my daughters and my wife to the airport, where we'll be on the next flight to New Delhi. We'll stay with my cousins—just let the bastard try to find us in Punjab." His head swung around to face Latimer. "Given the circumstances, I hope you'll grant me an emergency sabbatical. I have enough time on the books for it. And the university has been looking to create more online courses. Mine will have to be that for the rest of the semester."

Latimer immediately looked infinitely less miserable. "I'm sure we can arrange that. I'll talk with your TAs, see how much of the course they can teach for you in class, and we'll sort out the rest of the details. Detectives?"

"That's an excellent idea," Arnett said, then waved a hand below the eyeline of the two men, toward the hall outside.

"I agree. Excuse us a moment." Jo stepped into the hall and closed the door behind her, mind racing.

Arnett leaned close, and whispered to her. "For once we're one step ahead of this asshole, and I hate to give that up."

She smiled. "My thoughts exactly. There has to be some way to turn this to our advantage. He's watching, I'm sure of it. There must be some way to exploit that."

"I say we make him think the Parminders are still here, unprotected, and see if we can get him to make a mistake."

She shook her head. "He's not stupid enough to believe we'd leave them alone after all this. Better to guard the house for a day or two, then make a show of pulling out?"

"Maybe even have a press conference when we do, saying we've made an arrest, give him a false sense of security?"

"It's worth a shot."

CHAPTER THIRTY-SIX

I settled in to watch the Parminder residence and wait. When the first police car rolled up the driveway, I decided I could allow myself a single glass of wine to help with the anxiety. I uncorked a bottle of increasingly misnamed Two-Buck Chuck, grabbed the burner phone, and settled into the couch.

Several members of some tactical team in protective gear scoured the yard. Fascinating to watch, really—so methodical. Every tree, every shrub, metal detectors, even a bomb-sniffing dog. An hour later they were still radiating out, farther and farther, and I began to wonder if I'd done too good a job. I could have sworn one of them found the camera—he looked me right in the eye, and I was certain the feed would end any second when they pulled the camera and the solar power source from their hiding place in the tree. But he simply moved on, behind my field of view, and I lost sight of him until he strode back toward the house ten minutes later.

Not good. My anxiety exploded like a Bouncing Betty in my chest, and I forced myself to take several deep breaths. I needed to logically analyze the options and their implications.

Option one: he hadn't seen the camera. But did that matter? They had to know I was watching, did it really change my plans if they didn't know exactly how? As far as I could tell, no.

Option two, he'd seen the camera, but had been instructed to leave whatever he found. If so, why? Were they hoping to track the feed back to me somehow? If so, good luck to them.

Or—they had something they wanted me to see.

Which would be very clever on their part. And from what I'd seen of Fournier and Arnett, I'd come to expect no less. But did that possibility change anything? Possibly, possibly not. I wouldn't be able to puzzle that out until I saw whatever it was they wanted me to see.

Once the area was cleared, a caravan of marked and unmarked cars dropped the Parminders home, along with a small security detail. Fournier and Arnett drove off as soon as the detail was in place, which surprised me. Fournier especially is so hands on, like a child who won't let go of her favorite stuffed animal—I expected her to stick around and see to their safety herself.

But those are the moments, the unaccounted for elements that keep you grounded and humble. Which ensures you don't slip up and make a mistake.

I thought for a while longer, and concluded there was nothing more I could do. So I closed out the one app so the other camera could fill my screen.

CHAPTER THIRTY-SEVEN

As the team swept the Parminder residence, Jo and Arnett sent a pair of plainclothes officers to watch Greg Crawley's apartment building, a second to Camilla Whorton's house, and a third to watch Arthur Kerland. Latimer spread the word through the university that for the foreseeable future, Dr. Parminder would be teaching from home, and Parminder made arrangements with the airline and his family in India.

While Jo and Arnett ostensibly set up the security detail, the Parminders quickly packed their suitcases. Once they finished, inside the garage, Jo and Arnett hid the family under dark blankets in the back seats of the two squad cars. When the cars left the premises, they appeared to contain only their pair of uniformed officers. Then, Jo and Arnett left final instructions for the phony security detail to make the house look lived in, waited ten minutes, and drove back to HQ. There they awaited confirmation that the Parminders had been successfully processed through a separate security entrance at the airport and secured into a private lounge to await their flight.

By the time the Parminders' plane was in the air, everyone had settled in to wait.

CHAPTER THIRTY-EIGHT

For the next several days, Jo and Arnett checked alibis, pored over phone records, and dug deep into devices. Greg Crawley's computer and smart phone showed a fair amount of disturbing activity and scores of deeply alarming journal entries, but nothing that could tie him to the murders or justify any sort of arrest. They tracked down all the attendants and other employees who might have seen Camilla Whorton take a train or bus from Maine back to Massachusetts, and checked rental car records in the area. The Office of the Ombudsperson verified that Crawley had sought help from Dreta Kline, and her work phone records showed the two conversations Crawley had reported, plus an additional one that he hadn't. They found no contact between her and Terry Shawnessy, Camilla Whorton, or Arthur Kerland.

Dreta Kline turned out to be something of an enigma. She'd been closed-mouthed about her personal life at work. Her mother, Irene Kline, turned out to be suffering from the early stages of dementia, but they caught her on a good day. She confirmed what the phone records suggested, that Dreta hadn't been in a long-term relationship in years. In fact, Irene told them, Dreta had never been in a long-term relationship, much to her dismay. She'd been unlucky in love early on in high school, and gave up on relationships, preferring to focus on her career. Thank goodness Irene had a second daughter who'd given her grandchildren. Jo ignored the parallels to her own life, and bit her tongue to keep from asking if Irene's other daughter was named Sophie.

The contents of Dreta's house, particularly her ten brimming bookcases, revealed nothing other than her love of reading. As best they could tell, Kline's life had been simple. She worked, she visited her mother three nights a week, was an avid reader, and went out dancing every Saturday night until early in the day on Sunday.

If she'd been having an affair with Whorton, her phone and laptop didn't show any evidence of it. She had, however, been in contact with Whorton via her office phone several times over the previous semester. Those were likely related to his situation with Greg Crawley, but given Whorton's history, it was possible something had sprung up between them during that time, and that the affair had otherwise been conducted via in-person contact on campus.

They located Doris Pentiger's realtor, but couldn't find any evidence that she or her father was known to any of the suspects. Camilla Whorton owned property in the Berkshires, but it was in the same area as the Kerland house, and far enough away from Granton to make it unlikely she, or the Kerlands, would have stumbled on Doris Pentiger's cabin.

In the meantime, the killer was maddeningly silent. Whether their ruse had been unsuccessful or the killer had been spooked by his failed attempt on Parminder, he was keeping his distance now. In light of that, ADA Rockney could no longer justify twenty-four-hour surveillance teams on the suspects, and pulled them. Whether the university liked it or not, the county SPDU, and the Oakhurst Police, had responsibilities other than a single killer.

Lunchtime Thursday found them in a corner booth at Sal's, frustrated with their lack of progress.

Jo tapped her finger on the table. "I think the time has come to pull the fake protective detail. Flush Crawley out, make him think everything's safe."

Arnett shook his head, and spoke through a mouthful of pizza. "This would be the worst possible time, with you flying out tonight to see your father."

Jo halted the forkful of eggplant Parmesan she'd been about to eat. "That's why I'm thinking I'll cancel the trip."

Arnett shook his head again. "Bullshit. You just don't want to deal with your sister. We've done everything we can do for the moment. Until the killer makes his next move, we're in a holding pattern anyway."

"And what if he goes after the Parminder house, or goes after someone else? We've gone three days now with nothing, after four murders in a week. It's only a matter of time before Rockney has to pull the team, anyway."

Arnett shrugged. "Maybe Parminder was last on his list. But if he does go anywhere near the Parminder house, we have him dead to rights, and I'm fully capable of making an arrest without you. If he goes after someone else, guess what, those planes fly both ways. You'd be back practically before Marzillo finishes processing the scene."

He was right, she didn't want to face Sophie. Her father's guilt-laden stares and silences were enough to handle, add her sister into the mix and she might as well wear a sign that said *whipping post here*. The closer the trip got, the more justifications she generated for staying put. But until the DNA results came back from the lab, or the killer made another move, she was spinning her wheels.

"You're stronger than that, Jo," Arnett said, apparently reading her mind. "I've seen you face down six-foot-plus gang-bangers. I can't believe you're gonna let a five-seven homemaker keep you from being there for your father."

"Ouch."

He jabbed his pizza wedge at her, a smile on the corners of his mouth. "That's right. Suck it up, Jo. We all have relatives we wanna punch in the neck. You're not that special."

She sighed, and set her fork down on her plate. "Uh-huh. Just don't complain when you have to bail me out."

*

The police and I had entered into some strange stalemate, which worried me—I didn't know what traps they'd put into place, and that made every step I took fraught with another layer of anxiety. I had every reason to feel confident I had the upper hand, but couldn't take that for granted.

So, imagine my apprehension when I got an alert for the camera I'd placed outside Detective Fournier's house. And imagine my subsequent pleasure when I watched her, dressed in distinctly civilian jeans and houndstooth coat, wheeling a suitcase to her car. With the darkness, I had to double-check that I'd seen correctly. Yes, I had.

Fournier was going on some sort of trip.

Trust, but verify.

I strolled out to the old, neglected maintenance shed. I slipped open the broken lock and ducked inside, then shifted the boxes and defunct equipment as quietly as possible until I uncovered the firesafe I'd buried there. I tapped in my combination, pulled out one of the burner phones and my voice modifier, then reversed the procedure behind me.

Back inside, I called the DA's headquarters. I navigated through the automated answering system until I found the right division. A bored woman answered, "Oakhurst County State Police Detective Unit."

"Hello, I need to speak with Detective Josette Fournier. Is she in?"

"Hold, please."

I listened to a song about pina coladas and walks in the rain until she came back on the line. "I'm sorry, she's not available. Do you want to speak to someone else, or leave a message?"

"Do you know when she'll return?"

"She's out on vacation for a few days, so the best thing to do would be to talk with her partner, Bob Arnett."

"No, that's fine, thank you. I'll try her when she gets back." I hung up before she could ask me any awkward questions, then pulled the battery out of the phone—she'd alert someone about the call, and they'd trace the number.

I returned the phone to the firesafe. I would have much rather disposed of it right away, but I couldn't risk being followed by an undercover unit who'd grab anything I threw out, regardless.

Discomfiting, yes. But a small price to pay for the peace of knowing that Detective Fournier would be far away during the final kill.

CHAPTER THIRTY-NINE

One lesson I've learned through all of this is people are mind-bogglingly predictable. It's far easier to get a handle on people's day-to-day habits than one would think, and if one did think about it, one would never sleep well again.

Even with two well-placed cameras on him, I expected to have to watch for months, and began the surveillance early in accord with that. His activities changed every day due to the vagaries of academic life, which complicated things slightly, but not for long. He had three classes on Monday, with a gym visit sandwiched in before lunch. Two classes on Tuesday, gym visit after the second; same on Thursday, but with a very late lab Thursday night. No classes on Friday, gym visit replaced by a long run around a trail near Quabbin. Parties or pub hops on Friday night and Saturday, hangover recuperation on Sunday, followed by a trip to Mom and Dad's house to get his laundry done and a home-cooked meal.

Two strong possibilities emerged by week three: his run on the trail, or after his lab. Thankfully, the extra time I'd padded into the schedule allowed me to discover he didn't always run alone. He did, however, always come home well after dark on Thursday night, and his parking space was tucked around by his apartment building's storage unit. Out of street view, and away from the apartment windows.

And there was another advantage to my extended surveillance—I came to learn just how horrible a human being he is.

It sounds like I'm self-justifying, I know. But I have no reason to. His father's actions had damned him, regardless—they were the crucial factor. But, discovering that the apple truly didn't fall far from the tree made what I had to do far easier. He's not the sort of man the world would miss.

In the course of that few weeks, I watched him bully freshmen and hit on women aggressively, try to ply them with alcohol, then become abusive when they told him no. I watched him steal from a café, throw pennies at a homeless woman, and key someone's car for parking too close to his Lexus. He was exactly the sort of entitled prick that didn't give a shit about anybody other than himself. Morally bereft, just like his father.

I used the nearby campus webcam to be sure he entered his lab that final time. When the class let out I watched him leave, to be sure he hadn't talked some naive girl into coming home with him, or decided to bring back a buddy for late night "brewskis." Then I drove to his apartment. I sat in the cold car and waited, my breath fogging up the windows, praying he hadn't gone to visit a friend. I didn't want to have to resort to my far riskier backup plan the following day.

I needn't have worried. His headlights appeared around the corner right on time. He drove past me to get to his parking space, grabbed his backpack out of the car, and started toward me. I got out of my car and stepped toward the sidewalk, but he barely looked at me. Typical of his frat-boy, upper-crust privilege—why would you fear the world around you when you own it?

I timed my stride so our paths would cross, or, more precisely, so I'd block his path. He had no choice but to notice me at that point, and he bobbed his chin toward me, said, "S'up," and shifted to walk around me.

I reached out with the taser. As it made contact, recognition crossed his face.

Too late.

CHAPTER FORTY

Jo landed in New Orleans just before six the next morning, and ran through the airport while praying the line at the Hertz counter would be short. Her father's appointment was at eight-thirty, and it would take her at least half an hour to drive from the airport into the city, *if* traffic was cooperating. Her sister was already on a plane home, so if Jo didn't arrive in time, he'd have to go alone.

Luck was with her. Half an hour later she pulled out of the rental lot in an avocado-green Chevrolet Spark, unable to relax about the pending hospital visit. Hospitals themselves didn't generally upset her, but they gave her the heebie-jeebies when someone she cared about was involved. When that was the case, a low-level panic set in and she felt like fire ants were crawling all over her until she was able to leave. She couldn't decide if she hoped her father would want her to stay in the waiting room, or ask her to come inside with him while he received his treatment. Waiting alone would be akin to wandering endlessly in a seventh-circle-of-hell purgatory, but seeing him on any sort of machine, or a hospital bed, or being poked with needles, would be more than she could bear. Since there were so many different types of chemo, she hadn't even been able to research and prep herself for what she'd see, and her father was maddeningly reticent about it all. As always.

Traffic was also on her side, so she stopped at a drive-thru Starbucks to grab a venti mocha for herself, and a venti latte for her father. But as soon as she pulled out onto the road again, she swore aloud—was he allowed to have coffee before the treatment?

Would he be honest with her if he wasn't? She yanked the car over to the side of the road, did a Google search, and swore again. The patient could eat and drink, but needed to avoid caffeine. She flipped around, went back into the drive-thru, and got him a decaffeinated version.

She pulled the mobile eyesore up to her father's house at seven-twenty, and fished her house key out of her overnight bag. Just as she reached the door, it opened.

Sophie.

"I thought you had a flight this morning?"

"I figured it would be best to make sure someone was here for Dad, so I had them put me on standby for the later flights."

Jo pushed past her. "I managed to run an entire county's detective unit, Sophie. I can be trusted to take our father to an appointment."

"Don't take everything so personally, Josette. I know the detective unit couldn't possibly run without you, but even you can't control flight delays, weather, or traffic accidents."

Jo paused, trying to judge if she was being too defensive. But when she glanced back at her sister, there was a smug superiority under the raised eyebrows. Sophie was enjoying this. That flared Jo's temper, but she reined it in, refusing to give Sophie any more satisfaction. "Excellent point, Soph. Thanks for changing your flight."

"Josette." Her dad appeared on the landing at the top of the stairs, a huge smile on his face, and started down. "Right on time."

From the corner of her eye, Jo watched Sophie's expression deflate.

"Dad, you're looking good." Jo stepped forward to embrace him.

It wasn't a lie. His chestnut hair refused to show more than a few errant gray hairs, and his olive eyes were sharp as ever. He moved down the stairs quickly, and when he pulled her in to kiss her cheek, his grip was iron.

"Take more dan a few jabs of a needle to slow me down." He reached for his keys on the nearby table.

Sophie's voice took on an ever-so-slight whine. "Dad, it doesn't help anybody if you lie." She pointed toward the blue-and-yellow country-French kitchen. "He's been vomiting, and he's been constipated. You know how he is, he won't be honest with you. You'll have to monitor it all. He's got a stack of medications."

Her father grunted, and brushed Sophie away. "Your sister's a drama queen, Josette. Anybody ever tell you dat?"

Jo couldn't resist the low-hanging fruit. "I grew up with her, Dad."

He laughed, her sister's jaw tightened, and she instantly regretted falling into the old habits and roles. Her father would use Jo to make Sophie feel bad, then use Sophie to make Jo feel bad once Sophie was gone. And here she was, playing right into it.

"If I leave now, I may be able to make the next flight." Sophie turned and hugged their father. "Do what the doctor says, Dad. You're only hurting all of us if you don't." She managed to give Jo a perfunctory hug with barely the tips of her fingers, picked up her suitcase, and left without another word.

Jo sighed. Why did it have to be so hard?

She gestured her father toward the door.

"I'll drive," he said.

*

Four hours later, Josette pushed back through the door and dropped her father's keys into the ceramic bowl on the entryway table. The jingling lasted longer than it should have, and she turned to find he'd picked them back up, and was dangling them off his index finger. "Go grab the overnight bag I have waiting in the dining room, Josette. We're going for a drive."

She fought to keep her patience. "Overnight bag? The doctor said you need to rest."

"I can rest on the way, and I can rest when we get there same as I can here. Now, get on. We're already late."

"Late for what? Look, Dad, I need you to listen. I came out here to help you, and—"

"And you're helping me by doing the driving. You can come or not, baby girl, but I'm going. So what's it gonna be?"

No words would change his mind when he was like this. So she stared at him, willing herself to remain silent. He stared back, unblinking.

She sighed, and fought back the adolescent urge to stomp across the parquet floor. She bristled when she found the suitcase tucked onto the farthest chair under the dining-room table—he must have hidden it there from Sophie, knowing she'd never allow it. Jo pulled it open, and rifled through. Two pairs of pants and two shirts, a toiletry bag, a book, and a gallon Ziplock bag full of medications. She twirled, strode into the kitchen, and pulled open the cabinet to double-check. It was empty except for Advil and Excedrin Migraine. At least he wasn't in complete denial about what was going on, no matter how much he wanted to pretend he was.

She peered around the garage for a cooler. The smart thing would have been to just ask him where it was, but somehow that felt like capitulation. She opened and closed several of the floor-to-ceiling cabinets that lined the wall, and on her third try, found one. She grabbed it, filled it halfway with ice in the kitchen, then stuffed in as many bottles of water as she could fit.

He appeared next to her. "We gotta get a move on."

"The doctor said eight ounces of fluid every hour, Dad."

"They got water where we goin'," he said.

"Where exactly is that, Dad?"

He turned on his heel. "Lock up the house. I'll be in the car."

She gritted her teeth, and took a deep breath. She grabbed the cooler with one hand and the overnight bag with the other, then dropped it again. She reached up into the cabinet and grabbed the Excedrin Migraine.

She loaded up the car, then transferred her roller bag from the trunk of the rental. She climbed in the driver's seat. "Are you gonna tell me where we're going now?"

He reached down to adjust the passenger seat backward. "I programmed the GPS. I'm gonna take a nap."

"Good." She started the car, wincing at the petulance in her voice and her need to have the last word. Even if he wouldn't admit it, her father was scared and tired—no way he'd take a nap otherwise. It was childish to make things harder than they already were for him. But this was the long-established cycle that always caught them up. His *tête dure* brought out her own pig-headedness, no matter how often she prepared herself beforehand or chastised herself after.

She shook her head and clicked the back button on the GPS. The address was in Brenneville. Two hours outside of New Orleans with traffic, Brenneville was a little town that housed a large percentage of her father's family. Or more precisely, a large percentage of the inhabitants of Brenneville were her father's family. And, of course, her family.

Contradictory emotions swirled through her. Annoyance and anger at her father for being difficult, but also the burgeoning of something akin to anticipation. Her memories of Brenneville revolved around food and music and fun. She had gone with her father every year when she visited as a teenager, and she'd always been welcomed like she never left, like she was a necessary piece of some grand puzzle that they slid right into place. Aunts and uncles thrust baby cousins into her hands to watch while they worked on other tasks, or thrust utensils into her hands and assigned her chores like she was their own child. There was an intoxicating warmth associated with that unconditional sense of belonging—it didn't matter what she did or what mistakes she made, she belonged.

She didn't get much of that in New England, where her mother's family was scattered and sparse, and most holidays were spent with her stepfather's family. They were always kind to her, yes, but it wasn't quite the same. She wasn't *theirs*, and they weren't *hers*, and no matter how many Christmases they spent together, it remained a pastiche rather than a seamless blend.

But her last trip to Brenneville was twenty years ago. A year away didn't break the bond, but twenty years was a very different animal. Would her absence be seen as a rejection of them?

She sighed, and reminded herself she was far too old to care about being accepted, or where she fit.

Besides, no matter what else happened, the food would be good.

CHAPTER FORTY-ONE

I kept the boy awake for the drive. I don't like chloroform regardless, it's too easy to kill someone if you use too much, or have them wake prematurely if you use too little. But that was irrelevant. I needed him awake, fully aware of what was happening. Anything less defeated the whole purpose.

After an initial bout of thrashing, he was quiet during the ride. I imagine—hope—he was desperately plotting, trying to come up with some escape.

When I pulled him out of the car, I approached with extreme caution, my Beretta at the ready. He's younger and stronger than I, after all, and it wasn't far out of the realm of possibility that he'd manage to overpower me. But I needn't have worried. When I slid him out of the car and unwrapped the blanket, the smell of urine nearly caused me to vomit.

In retrospect, now that I'm not faced with the smell, it amuses me no end that he pissed himself. It's so perfectly ironic. The nastiest bastards in this world, the ones who delight in making life difficult for everyone else, are the biggest cowards. Callous, pitiless and destructive when they're hiding behind artificial power structures, or when buttressed by safety in numbers. Bold and brash when attacking women, or anyone younger, anybody with a whiff of helplessness, but sniveling and pathetic when facing a real fight. Of course this is so, of course weaker people attract them as light attracts moths, because they can only feel strong and important when standing on someone's neck.

And for most of my life, knowing that was enough. Recognizing the cowardice that underlies that behavior actually inspired compassion from me for many, many years. I even said prayers when I was young asking God to help heal their wounds. But then I realized those wounds can't be healed, and treating such people with compassion only enables their behavior.

"Get up," I told him.

He stared up at me, fear and pride battling on his face, and didn't move. I kicked him in the ribs, and waved the gun in his face. "I said get up. You won't like what happens if you don't."

He struggled, but managed to right himself despite the duct tape and zip ties. I shoved him toward the cabin. His restraints limited how fast he could move, and I watched him take advantage of the time to analyze his surroundings. He scanned the forest, probably hoping it wasn't as dense as it looked and we weren't as isolated as it appeared. He did the same inside, probably committing the layout to memory, not that there was much to remember.

I shoved him into the back bedroom and shackled him to the wall. Once he was safely restrained, I clipped the zip ties holding his hands, which dropped the rope between his wrists and his thighs. Then I ripped the duct tape from his head.

I left him to spend some time alone with his thoughts that first evening. I made a show of leaving the house, allowing him to think I was gone, then drove a short way down the path and slept in my car.

The next morning I made a show of slamming the car and rattling the house door. I crossed into the kitchen, grabbed a beer and a Coke from the refrigerator, and returned to the bedroom. I popped the top of the beer and set it where he could reach it, then sat down in the folding chair I'd placed on the other side of the room. I opened my Coke and lifted it in a toast. "Drink up."

He eyed the beer suspiciously.

I laughed. "You're smarter than that. You watched me open it, there's nothing wrong with it. And if I wanted to poison you, I'd inject you and you'd have nothing to say about it. Now drink."

I could practically see his brain whirring and clunking, trying to get a handle on what was happening to him. Had he heard the standard advice about humanizing yourself to your captor? How you should keep them talking? That the smartest thing to do was take any chance to fight back and escape, since kidnappers rarely left their victims alive to bear witness against them?

I could only hope.

"Why? What's this about?" he finally asked.

"You don't need to know that. Your father understands, and that's all that matters."

"My father knows what? He'll be looking for me soon, you know. I have breakfast with my mother every Friday morning."

I smiled at the lie. "Excellent. The sooner the better."

CHAPTER FORTY-TWO

As the drive settled into flat green fields outside the city, Jo took solace in her father's snoring. She turned up the zydeco on the radio—no way could it compete with his volume otherwise—and was surprised to notice the tension drain ever so slightly out of her shoulders.

Until her mind returned to the university killer case. She hated being backed into a corner, waiting for him to make another move, needing him to slip up because they had too many suspects and not enough evidence. She'd gone over it all so many times the logic danced around her head unbidden. Greg Crawley fit the evidence best, with a clear motive against Michael Whorton, Britney Ratliffe, and Dreta Kline, and a potential motive against Arthur Kerland. He was unstable in exactly the sort of way that would lead to these sorts of killings, with the dramatic flourish of the tarot cards. The difficulty was why he'd choose to kill *Nancy* Kerland, and why he'd hold a grudge against Parminder. Even if he'd been trying to kill Arthur rather than Nancy, Parminder was still a wild card.

She could also make a reasonable case for Camilla Whorton, if Michael Whorton's infidelity was the motive. Many men and women had murdered over far less infidelity than she'd suffered, and almost everything fit if she was killing off his lovers. Maybe she had reason to believe he'd had an affair with Parminder's wife, as well. But, there were no phone or e-mail records to support the theory, and without evidence, they'd never convince a jury.

Arthur Kerland was even muddier, for the same reasons. And, what possible motive could he have against Dreta Kline or Steve Parminder?

None of them spoke to her instincts the way they should, and she couldn't figure out why. Worse, she still had a sense, especially when she considered the tarot cards, that she was missing something central to the case.

She had no resolution by the time the fields and roads were replaced by bayous and bridges. Her father woke as though he had some sort of internal sensor. "Turn left up here."

"That's not what the GPS says," Jo said.

He shot her a glare and canceled the GPS route. She turned left.

"How are you feeling?" Jo asked.

"Fine. A little tired is all."

When translated from Frank-speak, it meant the treatment was hitting him hard. "Should we stop somewhere for a bathroom break? The doctor said that constipation medicine could make diarrhea come on fast—"

He flicked a hand at her. "I was there, Josette, I don't need to hear it again. After you cross that bridge, turn right."

She bit back her response and turned where he indicated, down a forest-lined road. Several minutes later, a small white clapboard cottage came into view through gaps in the dense trees. As she caught glimpses of the short red-brick columns setting it off the ground and the small porch jutting off the front, something tugged at her memory. "Aunt Rosalie's place?"

"Was when you were last here. Now her son Nick owns it. She sold it to him and moved in with her daughter after her back surgery."

"I didn't realize she had back surgery. Did you tell me about it?"

He shook his head and shrugged, staring out the windshield. "You don't remember nothin' anyway."

She turned down the long dirt path leading to the cottage. "We have a lot of cousins and aunts and uncles to remember, Dad. I do my best. It doesn't help when you don't tell me things."

He shrugged again.

Before she was halfway down the path, a stream of people spilled out the front door, and from around the side of the house. Her father pointed toward a section of grass, and she pulled the car to a stop there.

The tall man leading the pack pulled open her father's door. "Nonc Frank! Ça va?"

"Ça va." Her father got out and the men embraced. "You got everything ready?"

"You know it." The man turned. "Josette! You look just the same. Always was pretty as a bluebell."

Another glimmer of memory kicked in. "Nick?"

Nicolas had been a small boy the last time she saw him, about five years younger than she. Too young to have any interests in common, but his glowing blue eyes and broad smile showed a remaining glint of the mischievous child he'd been. Now the five years that separated them barely made a noticeable difference.

"Bingo. This is my beautiful bride Lydia, and our kids, Robert, Jacqueline, Raymond, George and Emily." He tapped each on the head as he named them off.

She hugged and kissed him and his wife, then the children one by one. The older girl, Jacqueline, handed her a small, mashed bundle of ironweed and goldenrod. "Thank you, cherie," Jo said, and bent to hug her.

Nick reached in the backseat and grabbed her father's duffel. "Come on now, let's get you set up inside. We got a lot to do for tomorrow, no time just to veiller."

Jo grabbed her bag from the trunk and followed, confused. Isn't that exactly what they were there for, to sit and visit? "What's going on?"

"Your father didn't tell you?"

Jo kept the frustration off her face. "No."

He laughed, and shook his head. "Some tings never change. We got a boucherie tomorrow out at Paul's place, starting at first light."

A boucherie! Despite everything, excitement bubbled up inside her. She'd been to two, maybe three of these large Cajun parties as a child when her parents were still married, and her memories of them were nearly as good as Christmas. She'd always thought of them as similar to a barn raising, except rather than build a barn, the community came together to slaughter and cook a pig. She'd been too young to help much with the cooking, but she ate and danced and sang and played and explored the mysteries of the bayou with her cousins until she made herself sick. For some reason, her mother hadn't liked boucheries, so they stopped going. Her mother's face flashed in her memory, and she was suddenly sure that something about her mother's position on them went part and parcel with the decline of her parents' marriage.

Jacqueline and Emily led her to the room she'd be sharing with them. She deposited her bag, then carried her father's duffel to the room allocated to him. She made sure he had another bottle of water in his hand, then hurried to the kitchen to see how she could help.

One look around, and another flash of memory returned. The night before a boucherie was itself a busy pre-party partying event. They'd need to prepare food and drink to take with them to augment what would be prepared the next day, and to keep them going while everyone worked.

The rest of the evening passed in a blur of talking, music, and cooking: alligator jambalaya, court-bouillon, corn hash. She kept a close eye on her father, and soaked in as much of everything as she could.

*

Even though she was smart enough to stay away from the potent homemade wine, she slept hard, and the next morning came far too quickly. The girls woke her while the first slits of light were breaking through the dense trees, and she threw back a cup of strong, thick coffee as they all piled into the airboat. "I'm guessing this is faster than driving?"

"Pfft. 'Course not. But your father asked specifically," Lydia said.

Jo nodded, tears back in her throat. It was kind of them to cater to him.

The boat took off, the light bright enough now to transform the still water from black to deep green, trees ghostly with hanging moss reflected on the surface. Jo settled back into the ride, allowing the calm to take her over, as though the vibrations of the boat shook free something in her soul. The day was already warm, and she caught sight of a heron perched in the tree limbs, watching their progress with heat-induced laziness. Periodic splashes reminded her that despite the apparent stillness, frogs and turtles, even alligators, lurked out of sight all around them, moving only when forced.

The boat pulled into a dock several hundred yards from a large two-story gray barn, already surrounded by people. Nick helped her out of the boat, then they both tried to help her father.

"Get away, I'm not a child," he barked.

The smell of pig assailed her as they approached the barn, followed closely by grunts and scuffles. The largest hog she'd ever seen waited, gazing at them. A ceramic bathtub sat closer to the front of the barn, and next to it, a huge heater boiled water to fill it. A least a dozen tables were scattered around the perimeter of the barn, the closest blanketed with knives and other tools that looked like they belonged in a nineteenth-century dentist office.

In that moment the reality hit, with the shock of childhood memories snapping into the lens of an adult mind. To know from an intellectual perspective that the purpose of this event was to butcher a pig was one thing. It was another entirely to look the

animal in the eye as it stood next to the instruments of its impend-
ing death. She glanced at a small saw on the table, and her mind
flew to Dreta Kline's hand.

Another crowd of relatives surrounded her, dragging her attention back to the present. Cousin Paul, whose pig they'd come to
slaughter, stood next to his wife and children; her uncle Euclid,
a confirmed bachelor; her uncle Raymond and her aunt Odette.
Other 'aunts' and 'uncles' who were really cousins of aunts and
uncles, along with their children. Within minutes, Jo lost hope
of remembering any but a minority of the names.

When the round of greetings, kisses, hugs, and teases were
finished, Paul clapped her on the back proudly. "Josette, you're a cop,
you know your way around a gun. You gonna do da honor today?"

Her stomach churned. "No way, Paul. I'm off-duty. Besides,
unless it's self-defense, I'm supposed to de-escalate the situation."

To her relief, everyone laughed, and for reasons she didn't fully
understand, she felt like she'd passed a test. Lydia linked an arm
through hers, and led her to one of the tables. "We over here,"
Lydia said. "Nick's making the *boudin*."

She felt a tug at her arm, and turned to find everyone's head
bowed. Someone started the Lord's Prayer, and everyone joined in.

Seconds after they finished, a gunshot echoed through the air.
Jo's stomach lurched again, and tears pricked her eyes. No, she
couldn't imagine her mother enjoying this.

Three men pulled up chairs, fiddles and accordion in hand,
and warmed up their instruments. By the time they were in full
throng, four men appeared around the corner carrying the hog.
They angled the carcass into the tub of boiling water, artfully
minimizing any splash. They chatted and joked with one eye on
their watches, and when time ran out, they pulled the pig out and
slung it up on a nearby table. They shaved the pig's hair, then let
its blood into a bucket. For a moment, the warm, coppery scent

lingered in the air, then was replaced by odors of flesh and feces as the animal was cleaned.

In a matter of minutes, a tag-team of men and women completely rendered the pig into component parts, each taking away a portion to one of the waiting tables. As they began cooking, the smell of ingredients overtook the smells of abattoir.

A cousin whose name she'd forgotten held the blood out to her. "This is for Nick."

"Right." She carried the bucket to Nick. "I'm told this is for you."

"Yes, ma'am," he said, and noticed her grimace. "You didn't know boudin was made with blood?"

"I knew it, but I didn't *know* it."

He laughed, and dumped what looked like half a pound of salt into the blood. "I get it. Like when a little one realizes the chicken in the yard is the same as the chicken on the plate."

She gave him a friendly shove. "Thanks for making me feel like a city slicker."

"Cherie, you got city stamped all over you. Nothing wrong with dat, it's a part of who you are." He shrugged. "But it's good you here, so you don't forget the other part."

His words landed hard. "Oh, I see."

"See what?"

She turned to look at her father, sitting alongside the musicians, talking with the elder Euclid. "That's what this is about. That's why we're here. I thought it was because he was feeling sentimental." She turned back to Nick. "But that's not it, is it?"

He shook his head. "He out here maybe once a month. Came to Ti-Euclid's boucherie not two months ago. Probably still has some boudin left in his freezer."

"Got it." She closed her eyes for a moment, reopened them, and nodded. "What can I do now?"

"Nothing here yet." Lydia glanced around, then pointed. "But it looks like Jimmy could use a break from stirring the cracklins."

Jo walked over to the cauldron and offered to take over. He thanked her graciously and promised to return in a few minutes.

"Take your time," she said, glad for something to do with her hands.

She surveyed the scene as she leaned back, trying to avoid the waves of heat coming off the pot. Fifty adults scattered around the tables, hard at work on various parts of the pig with a skilled purpose. She'd heard the phrases 'tip to tail' and 'farm to table' more times than she cared to think about, but here the principles were being enacted in dramatic and complete fashion. Every part of the pig was being used, from the head boiling away at one station to the intestines and stomach being cleaned at another. The hive of activity was hypnotic, like the huge glockenspiel she'd seen in Germany with dozens of figures performing different activities simultaneously. Everybody knew their roles and enacted them in a synchrony of ingredients, recipes and skills that had been perfected over generations.

"Impressive, no?" Paul appeared by her side and handed her a cup of homemade wine.

"It really is," she said.

He threw back what was left in his cup, and nodded. "You know the history, right?"

"I don't."

He refilled his cup from the jug and topped off hers. "Back in the day, nobody had freezers, right? You slaughtered a pig, you only had a short time to eat it or preserve it. And only certain people had certain tools. So families came together to make sure all of the pig got used, and used well. Everybody contributes, everybody shares in the result. You eat off your pig one month, you eat off someone else's another."

"And not one bit gets wasted." She jutted her chin toward a cousin cleaning out pig intestine.

"You gotta honor the sacrifice of the animal. He gave his life to feed us, that matters around here. Nothing pisses me off more than bastards that shoot a deer in the woods and leave half of it to rot." He nodded toward the intestines. "Claire's making *andouille*, and I promise it'll be the best you ever had. Over there, Rene's making hog's head cheese pie. Ponce over there from the stomach, *fraisseurs* with the organs. Gumbo, of course. Backbone stew. Not to mention at least five different kinds of sausage, and more barbeque than you can shake a stick at."

Jo shook her head. "Amazing. An animal that big, turned into a restaurant of different food by the end of the day. No way one person could do this alone, freezer or no."

Paul nodded. "Without a doubt. That's the power of community. People working together can accomplish far more than they can alone."

His words froze her in place.

"Don't stop stirrin' now, girl, you—"

"Paul, I'm sorry, but can you take over for me for a minute?"

"Of course. You okay?"

"I'm fine, I just need to make a quick phone call."

"Go on. Looks like Jimmy's heading back anyway."

"Thanks." She set down her cup and hurried to where she'd stashed her bag. She grabbed her phone, then walked away from the noise, praying she could get a signal.

Relief flooded her when Arnett picked up on the first ring.

His voice was tight. "I was about to call you—"

She cut him off. "They did it together, Bob. They're working together."

CHAPTER FORTY-THREE

"Back up. Who did what together?"

An array of facts fell into place in her mind. "Shawnessy and Crawley. They did it together. That's why neither feels right, why some of the victims seem to fit and some don't, why it never made sense why Crawley would want Kerland's wife dead, or why Shawnessy would want Dreta Klein dead. They both wanted Whorton dead, that must be what brought them together somehow, maybe Britney too. I haven't figured out which of them would have a vendetta against Parminder, but—"

"That's what I'm calling to tell you. Nobody's come for Parminder's family, but the dean's son, Jason Latimer, is missing."

The trees spun around her as the words sunk in. "Dean Latimer's son?"

"Yep, nobody's seen him since his lab meeting Thursday night. His roommate called Latimer this morning."

"What took him so long?"

"He goes to bed before Jason comes home on Thursday, and when he didn't see Jason Friday night, he just figured Jason had plans. But they were supposed to help prep their frat house for a party tonight, so he went into Jason's room to wake him. Jason wasn't there, and didn't answer his texts or calls. With the deaths on campus he got worried."

"Did he find a tarot card?"

"No, Latimer had him check Jason's mail first thing."

Jo paused. "Then maybe it's just a coincidence, maybe he crashed somewhere after whatever he did Friday night?"

"That's what I thought, too, but the kid's car is in the apartment parking lot. And, the roommate started calling people, and Jason didn't show up to a study group Friday afternoon and was supposed to be at a party Friday night. And when I went down there, I found another camera up in a tree, pointed right toward the kid's parking spot—the exact same kind of camera we found across from Parminder's."

More pieces fell into place. "Holy shit, he played us."

"What do you mean?"

"That's what the cards were about, *that's* why it never made sense. Don't you see? He played us. All along they've confused us, right? It's the sort of thing a killer does either to frighten their victims, or that a serial killer does because they want to leave a calling card. But this isn't a serial, and the cards couldn't have been used to frighten the victims."

"With you."

"So what else did they accomplish? When the card for Parminder arrived, we sure jumped, didn't we? Threw all our resources at the Parminders, got us all looking where he wanted us to look, then boom, someone else goes missing. They were never after the Parminders at all. And—Oh, God."

"What?"

"What would have happened if we hadn't found a card at the Kerland house? We'd have chalked it up to weird timing, and walked away."

"So?"

"They needed to be sure we connected the killings, to confuse us." Nausea washed over her. "And—oh, God, I can't believe I didn't see it—they *wanted* us to arrest Terry Shawnessy. Remember how he was so helpful, then all of a sudden snapped shut, wouldn't say a word? He *needed* to be in jail during that time period so he'd have an alibi. *That's* why his demeanor suddenly changed, and he refused to talk to us. What murderer is stupid enough to hide the tarot deck, but leave out a book on tarot? He spoon-fed us. And—oh, hell—*that's* why they left the battery for Dreta to put back in the phone. They needed us to find her, so we'd let Shawnessy back out. And I'll bet they hoped we'd take Crawley into custody after we found Dreta, so we'd be forced to release *him* once Jason was killed."

"Motherfuck."

"Hey, Auntie Josette!" Jacqueline's voice pulled her back into the present.

"I'll be right there, cherie. Do me a favor? Go fetch Nonc Frank for me?" she asked.

As the little girl turned back around, Josette heard Arnett snort. "What?" she asked.

"Your turbo-charged accent, that's all. Thanks for that, I needed a comic moment."

"Be glad I'm not slipping full-on into French. One last thing. Didn't Shawnessy have a son? We saw pictures of him, right? And I saw several funeral cards in Shawnessy's photo album, but I assumed they were all his wife's. If I'm right and Shawnessy's a part of this, it's no coincidence the dean's son is missing. We need to find out where Shawnessy's son is, and if he's alive."

"On it."

Josie checked the time on her watch. Eight-thirty. "I'm hell and gone from the closest airport out here, but I'm on the first flight back that I can reach."

"Lopez and I are on our way to the Pentiger cabin now—who knows if they were stupid enough to take Jason there, but it's the only lead we have. If luck is on our side, we'll have him safe and sound by the time your plane touches down."

CHAPTER FORTY-FOUR

I've never been a good liar, and I certainly never considered myself a good actor. Before all of this, I don't think I've told more than a handful of lies in my adult life. I wasn't looking forward to playing the part of a psychopath, or of trying to bluff my way through psychological torture. I don't think I could have convinced Jason the sky was blue if he hadn't been drunk out of his mind during all of it.

I timed out everything as best I could beforehand, based on an approximation of Jason's height and his weight. I was fighting mutually exclusive needs—to inflict as much pain as possible for as long as possible, without running out the clock. But I didn't have to be perfect—I only needed to keep the police off my trail a little longer until I reached the conclusion.

I started him off with three beers in that first hour. Enough for a solid foundation to take the edge off, and make him a bit more amenable.

After that, I switched to shots of tequila. Six in the next hour, each followed by a beer chaser. We chatted as I doled them out, his attempts to get in my head becoming more and more clumsy as the alcohol kicked in, my attempts to get in his easier and more insidious. He turned out to be an aggressive drunk—why was I not surprised?—and turned to threats around the fifth shot. When he finally passed out, I laid him on his side and left a bucket for him to vomit and urinate in, and left.

When the timer woke me the next morning, I pulled up the camera in his room to check on him. Then I grabbed a beer from the refrigerator and took it to his room. He was just waking up, groggy and moaning. I slammed the door behind me, and he winced. I laughed. "You're not looking well."

He squinted up at me. "Fuck you."

I tsk-tsk-tsked. "Is that any way to treat your host? And after I showed you such a fun time last night?"

"Look, man, what the hell is going on here? You kidnapped me to get me drunk? No way that's all this is. If you're gonna rape me or kill me or whatever, just get on with it."

"You made your position on that very clear last night. Thank you for the offer, but I'm going to pass on the rape, and hold off on killing you for now." I put the beer down next to him. "Here. Hair of the dog."

"What the fuck?" he said, but he reached for it, popped it open, and downed most of it in a single go. He paused for breath, finished the rest, then crushed the can and threw it at me. Or, rather, he tried to throw it at me—his chained arm impaired his aim.

"There you go. You'll be feeling better in no time." I reached down into the black canvas duffel bag I'd dropped by the door and pulled out my laptop. "Hey, what do you say we drink a few brewskis and watch a movie?"

His eyes darted around the room. "Yeah. Sure. Whatever floats your boat."

The pacing issue was a little more complicated than the day before, when all I'd really needed to do was get him drunk enough fast enough to give him a nasty hangover without giving him alcohol poisoning. But now I needed to be sure he was drunk, but still able to process what I was about to do to him.

I handed him a second beer, and slipped a DVD into the laptop's player. "Have you seen any of the Saw movies?"

He went rigid, and slid back crab-style against the wall.

"Don't worry, we're not going to reenact them." I laughed and pointed at his beer. "Drink up."

He shook his head. "Nah, man, I'm alright. That first one is hitting me pretty good, I'm feeling a lot better. Any chance I could get some water?"

I lifted the Beretta out of the bag. "Entirely my fault if I let you think you had a choice. Drink up."

He lifted the beer and took a small sip.

"Oh, come now, Jason. You showed me yesterday just how fast you can pound a beer. Don't get shy now."

He reached for the beer and downed it, watching my face the entire time.

I gave him two more beers and a shot during the course of the first movie, followed by a privacy break for the bathroom, then stuck in Saw II.

"I've never seen the second one, I'm looking forward to it. That trap around her head in that first one, that's just diabolical, isn't it?"

He stared at me. "Yeah. Really gross."

I slipped him another shot of tequila, along with his beer chaser. "I remember after these movies started coming out, everyone called it 'torture porn'." I pointed to the shot, and waited for him to toss it back. "I remember thinking, what could that possibly mean, 'torture porn'? I'm quite sure there are a few people in the world that get off on seeing someone tortured, but millions of people went to see these movies, and they can't all be like that. So what does it mean?" I shook my head. "What do you think?"

His faced scrunched in concentration, and his words had a slight slur. "I mean, I don't know... Like, I guess maybe they're just glad it's not them? Maybe it makes them feel glad to be alive, like the guy says?"

*I pretended to consider. "Yeah, I guess that makes sense."
I smiled, and lifted my Coke. "Here's to being alive."*

He took a pull off his beer, his eyes never leaving mine.

*I reined the alcohol in as we watched the second movie,
doling out only one more shot and one more beer. When the
credits started to roll, I closed the laptop, and shook my head.
"Wow, I think I need a break before we watch any more. But
you know, I have a theory now about why it's called torture
porn. Want to hear it?"*

*"Whatever, dude. I don't give a fuck about anything you
have to say."*

*I smiled—the aggression was back. "That hurts my
feelings. And I don't think it's true, I think you very much
want to hear what I have to say. But if you don't, you will
soon." I took a sip of my Coke. "So, my theory. I think
people enjoy watching movies like this because we all have
someone we'd like to see in these situations." I smiled a
we're-buddies-we-can-be-honest smile. "I'm sure you know
somebody'd you'd like to put in one of those reverse bear-trap
hats, right?"*

*The fear sprang back into his eyes. "I've never done
anything to you. I barely even know you."*

"That's not what I asked."

His brow knit in confusion. "I mean, no, not really."

*"Nobody? Not some guy who stole your girlfriend or beat
you out for first string on the football team?"*

"Football players are pussies." He laughed at his wit.

*I made a mental note to postpone his next shot. "Basket-
ball? Baseball?"*

*"Hockey. But you don't torture people for shit like that.
Thass fucked up," he slurred.*

*"No, you're right. But still, we all think about it from
time to time, don't we? Or maybe not you, maybe you're too*

forgiving. Or maybe nobody's ever done anything bad enough to you." I smiled.

I reached into my duffel bag again and pretended I'd had an idea. "Hey, while we're taking a break from the movie, let's play a game." I slid three pictures over to him. "Take a look at what I did last night."

He picked up the pictures and flipped through them. I watched his face change from vaguely clueless to confused, and finally to horrified. He dropped the pictures like they were on fire, and backed as far away from them as he could. "Fuck you, you sick fuck, that looks like my mother!"

I gathered the pictures back up. "It looks like your mother because it is your mother. And I'm sure you noticed the chain on her wrist, just like yours. She's not here, of course, that would be too cruel."

He stared at the pictures in my hand, trying to make sense of what I just told him. When the information penetrated, he tore at the chain and screamed, saliva flying from his mouth. "Rat fuck fucker, what the fuck? You better be fucking lying or I'm gonna fucking kill you, you motherfucker!"

I waited until he calmed down, then put a shocked look on my face at his final insult. "Motherfucker? No." I spread a lascivious smile over my face. "Well, at least not yet. In fact, I need to go pay her a visit now. But one thing before I do." I poured him another shot, and slid the cup over to him. "Drink that."

He slapped the cup across the room, spraying tequila over the floor. "Fuck you, you sick bastard! I'm not doing another fucking thing you say!"

I held the pictures upright so he could see the top one. He froze.

"Listen up, you entitled little prick. Here's how this goes, starting right now. You're going to do everything I say, exactly

when I say it, or I'm going to go cut off your mother's head and bring it back to you in a bucket. You got that?"

He remained frozen, and tears slipped from the corners of his eyes.

I poured out another shot.

"Now, let's try this again. Drink."

He drank. And then he curled up in a ball and cried.

CHAPTER FORTY-FIVE

Arnett and Lopez flew down the highway toward Hillsdale, sirens blaring, two backup cars behind them.

Arnett's phone rang, and he answered through the car's panel.

"Good news, we got Crawley. We're bringing him down to the station now." Officer Dailey of the Oakhurst PD came over the line.

"You search the house?"

"We just started, but our quick once-over didn't find anything."

"Thanks. Keep us updated." He ended the call. "Right. That's everybody in custody except Shawnessy. Call Hernandez."

"He'd have called by now if he found Shawnessy."

Arnett glared at her.

"Fine, just keep your eyes on the road." She texted Hernandez, and got a response immediately. "Still no luck."

Arnett flipped off the lights and sirens as they neared the Granton exit. The two backups followed suit. His knuckles, already white, tightened as they went around the bend to the main road. Once he had a straight stretch in front of him, he clicked the walkie. "We're only a few minutes out. Keep your eyes open."

He drove as fast as he could manage until he spotted the path turn off, then forced himself to slow, eyes sweeping the trees as they passed for any movement.

Lopez unholstered her weapon, checked the safety, then held it toward the floor, eyes also glued to the woods around them.

The cabin sprung out of the woods and Arnett braked sharply to a halt, tires crunching into the gravel just outside it.

As he and Lopez climbed out of the car, weapons pointed at the ground, the other two cars screeched up behind them. He gestured at two of the officers to circle around the building.

Arnett gestured Lopez to the right side of the door, and crept to the left. "SPDU, open up!"

No response.

He reached for the doorknob. The latch clicked, and the door swung open with a creak.

He nodded to Lopez, raised his weapon, and stepped through the door.

Nothing.

The cabin was dark despite the time of day, due to the boarded-up windows. Arnett pulled out his flashlight and strafed the room, checking behind the minimal furniture as they progressed. Lopez's beam crisscrossed his as she covered him and checked the two rooms that branched off either side.

They eased through the kitchen to the final room at the back, where they'd found Dreta Kline. Arnett again waved Lopez to one side of the door, but this time stayed in front of it. She listened, then shook her head. He braced himself, and nodded.

She turned the knob, and again the door swung without resistance.

His beam swept the room.

"Son of a bitch!" Arnett spat, and tapped on the light inside.

Undisturbed fingerprint powder spotted the walls. Nobody'd been there since they left.

CHAPTER FORTY-SIX

With a well-finessed appeal to the decency of a gate agent, Jo managed to get a seat on the next flight to Hartford, and arrived at just before four that afternoon. She arranged with airport security beforehand to deplane immediately after landing, while the rest of the passengers were still required to have their seatbelt fastened. She pulled out her phone as she raced through the airport.

"I just landed. Have you found any leads on where Jason might be? Any information on Shawnessy's son?"

Arnett's voice was tense. "Nothing. We did find his son, Patrick Shawnessy, but he died in a car accident a year ago. I can't see how he can possibly blame that on Roger Latimer or Michael Whorton or anyone else. Nobody else was even involved in the accident, he took a turn too sharply and broke over the guardrail into a ravine. So we're back to square one. We're trying every lead we can, going back over all the work we've done since day one, looking for anything we've missed. Granton PD is looking for any suspicious activity in the area, but who knows if he's even there? He could be in Canada by now for all we know."

"I'll get there as fast as I can," she said.

When she arrived an hour later, she found Lopez hunched over her computer, one hand mousing furiously, the other wrapped around a Rockstar. "Where's Arnett?"

"Interrogating Crawley for the third time, trying to get him to slip up. That kid may be a complete head case, but he *will not* crack. I even tried the empathetic approach, good cop after

Arnett's bad cop. Crawley lost his shit completely at me, flew off the handle and screamed until he was red in the face, but still stuck to his story. He knows nothing, he's never even met Terry Shawnessy, yada yada." She gestured to the computer. "I'm pulling every public record I can find on Shawnessy and Crawley, hoping something will pop out."

"No luck, I'm guessing, or you wouldn't be sitting here."

Lopez leaned back in her chair and rubbed her neck. "Nope, nothing new, and all the property searches are a dead end. Crawley's never owned property, and his family's isn't anywhere near the Berkshires. Shawnessy's only ever owned one house, in Oakhurst. I can't find anything that connects either of them to the cabin, or Granton, or the Berkshires at all, for that matter. I even did a data recovery search on both their computers, but couldn't find anything suspicious or otherwise helpful. We were just about to take their phone records back another year if you want to help."

"Hand 'em over."

Arnett joined in when he came back from interrogation. Two hours and two pots of coffee later, they finished. "I got nothing," Jo said, and gestured to Lopez. "You? Anything in Shawnessy's records?"

Lopez crushed her third Rockstar can and hurled it across the room. "Not a single fucking thing. Plenty of calls, but all to businesses. I don't think I found a single personal call in any of it."

"I didn't find many in Crawley's records, either, but at least there were some to family," Arnett said.

"So they're not using their phones to communicate with each other. They have to be coordinating somehow. What are they doing, some Skype account we haven't found? Smoke signals? Carrier pigeon?" Jo said.

"My money's on additional burner phones we haven't found yet." Lopez pointed at Jo. "Not least because someone called looking for you from a burner."

"What?" Jo leaned forward.

"You're just mentioning this?" Arnett said.

She waved her hand at her desk. "Sorry, I forgot, what with all this. Someone called asking to talk to you Thursday, not long after you left. When they relayed to me that someone had called and didn't want to talk to anyone else, I thought I'd better have them trace it."

"Why would they call here looking for me?"

Lopez leaned in to her computer, clicking open several browser tabs. "Based on the timing, my guess is he wanted to be sure you were leaving town."

"How the hell would he even know that was a possibility?"

Lopez shot her an incredulous look. "He's got cameras on everyone. At the Parminder residence, Jason Latimer's apartment building, Dreta Kline's death cabin. My guess is he has one on all of us."

A chill shot up Jo's spine. "Unless you have a better idea, I think now might be time for that lesson on behavioral targeting. Since we can't find a clue in anything else, their online behavior is the last shot we have."

Jo and Arnett pushed their roller chairs over to Lopez, who shifted her computer so they could see. "I just pulled up Shawnessy's Facebook page. Earlier I went through his timeline for the last couple of years, which wasn't hard, because he rarely posts anymore. I also checked his activity to see if he's been on at all, and he has, but not much. From what I can tell, only to check out potential places of employment."

"No personal phone calls, no interaction with friends on Facebook. Sounds like he's something of a recluse."

"He didn't used to be. Back a few years ago, his activity level was pretty typical."

Jo nodded. "Let me guess, before he left the university—wait, hold on, you aren't looking *at* his account, you're *in* his account."

Lopez gave her another *well-duh* look. "His account was set to private, so I hacked it. Perfectly legal in an emergency situation, which this is."

Jo wasn't convinced she was right about that, and if she were wrong, anything they learned as a result of the information might be fruit from a poisonous tree. But while Jason Latimer's life was on the line, finding him was the main priority. "So what next?"

"I looked through all of his photos earlier, and his friends' list, to see if anything there jumped out at me. But nothing did. So the next step is to widen the circle. I'm going to pull up each one of his friends, and look at *their* friends' lists, and *their* photos. It's a shot in the dark, but I've had success with it before, mostly with cheating boyfriends. And what other leads do we have?"

What else, indeed? Jo rolled her chair back over to her desk, and logged on to her terminal. "Can you log us into his account on our computers? We can break up the alphabet between the three of us?"

For the next hour, they settled into a rhythm, clicking and scrolling. "Amazing what people put on the internet," Jo said, after scrolling past several borderline-racist rants on one person's page.

"Isn't it? Makes you lose faith in the future of humanity if you do it for too long. But then, that's the entire internet. I recommend an antidote of an hour or two with the Disney channel at your earliest opportunity."

Jo half-smiled, and clicked back to Shawnessy's friend list. As she scrolled, she caught sight of his late wife's page. She pushed down the OCD urge to stick to a strict order and clicked on Ellen's picture.

Her timeline was covered with tributes from friends and family since her death, posting their most cherished memories with her. Pictures of parties and events they'd attended with Ellen, with attached comments about how their hearts were broken, and how much they missed her. As she scrolled back through time, these were replaced by shocked comments left in the aftermath of her death, then before that, pictures documenting her battle with cancer. Ellen smiling optimistically before her first chemo treatment. Reports of bad news about Rh factors and hormone therapies. Ellen making a fun occasion with friends out of choosing wigs to wear, since her hair had started to fall out. Then, before that, post-op posts describing her mastectomy, and her hope they'd caught the cancer in time. Early posts about how treatable breast cancer was, and how good her chances were of beating it.

Jo rose from her chair with as much calm as she could muster, and strode out of the room. As soon as she was out of sight, she sprinted for the bathroom, wiping away the tears now pouring from her eyes.

She shut herself into one of the stalls, then shoved her mouth and nose into the crook of her elbow to muffle her sobs.

Would her father have those same pictures and milestones, moving from a relatively positive prognosis to pain, suffering, then death? How had she justified leaving him yet again, rushing home to worry about someone else's tragedy in the middle of his? She wasn't Wonder Woman, Arnett and Lopez didn't need her to solve this case. What had she done? Maybe her sister was right. Maybe at her core she was selfish and uncaring, and just didn't understand how family worked. Maybe it was all just an excuse to run away from pain, to protect herself from having to truly care about anyone or anything.

The bathroom door opened and shut. She held her breath to keep from making another sound, and forced herself to pull it together.

She was overreacting, feeling sorry for herself, allowing herself to play the victim. There was nothing she could do to help her father today, he was handling the chemotherapy well and all there was to do was wait. Cousin Nick had agreed to take her father to his next two treatments, claiming he had to go to New Orleans anyway, and that this would be doing him a favor by saving him the cost of a hotel. Even her father had given his blessing, after she promised to come back the very day the case was over. He'd kissed her with a smile and toasted "to my brave daughter, who fights to make this world a better place," the first time he'd indicated any degree of pride in her, even if it was undeniably underscored by homemade wine. She couldn't let her own pain take her over—that's what Shawnessy had done. He'd let his anger and his helplessness warp and twist him until only taking revenge could ease his pain.

And while she couldn't help her father today, someone's innocent child desperately needed her help, if it wasn't already too late. And every minute she spent crying in the bathroom made his circumstances that much more dire.

She splashed water on her face, then strode back to her desk. She forced herself to return to Ellen's posts and comments, scrolling back up in the hopes that chronological order would shed the light of different context—and saw a comment she'd missed, which made her nausea roil back.

"Can we do a Kickstarter or a GoFundMe for you, since you don't have medical insurance?"

She scrolled through the replies to the comments, trying to process the implications. No medical insurance? No wonder Ellen's treatment had bankrupted them.

But it was worse than that. As she scrolled back up and checked the comments in greater detail, she found several that referenced treatment options the Shawnessys hadn't been able to afford.

How had they not put that together before? Ellen was a homemaker, and Terry had lost his job. Whorton made sure he didn't get another—so of course he'd lost his medical benefits. He might have had COBRA for the same eighteen months he was on unemployment, but even then it was prohibitively expensive—no way the family could have afforded it long term. It was the causal link they'd been missing—of course Terry Shawnessy would blame Whorton and Kerland for the loss of his benefits, and so the death of his wife.

She returned to her search with renewed vigor—if there was a connection to Terry's wife here, there must be one to his son. She scoured Ellen's friends' list for Patrick Shawnessy, then clicked through to his profile.

And froze.

At the very top of his wall was a tribute left by what appeared to be a childhood friend:

A year ago today I lost my closest friend. Patrick, you were always there for me, through good times and bad, and I let you down. I wasn't there when you needed me the most, I tried my best, but I just didn't know how to help you. I miss you more than I can say. I don't know how I'm going to make it through today.

She checked the date—it had been posted earlier that morning. She scrolled down quickly, looking for confirmation. When she found it, her voice was a strangled cry. "Look." Arnett and Lopez hurried over. "Look at what?"

"Shawnessy's son died a year ago to the day." Jo pointed to the screen and stared up at them, her expression horrified. "I think Shawnessy's going to kill Jason *today*."

*

Arnett squinted at the screen. "No way the timing's a coincidence. But how could he possibly blame anyone for his son's death?"

Something pulled at Jo's memory "Wait a minute." She scrolled back up to one of the posts she'd just speed-read. "Here it says he was in a drunk-driving accident."

"It was a single car accident. I checked," Arnett said.

"Do you have the accident report?" Lopez asked.

"I can pull it." Arnett jumped back over to his desk.

Jo scrolled down to the posts before Patrick's death. Several posts from friends, mentioning they hadn't seen him in a while, then a slew of posts commenting how trashed he'd been at one event or another, most joking about it, a few mentioning how it wasn't like him.

"Click on his DMs," Lopez said.

Jo did so, then zeroed in on the third one down, from the same friend that had left the anniversary tribute post.

> I know you're pissed at me, but I was only trying to help. The three of us all agree, your drinking is just out of control. You're trashed all day, every day since your mother died. I'm not saying I blame you, I know how close you were to your mother. But this isn't going to help, it's just going to make things worse. Your mom wouldn't want you throwing your life away like this. So be as pissed as you want, but I couldn't live with myself if I wasn't honest with you.

"Sounds like he was drinking himself to death over the loss of his mother," Lopez said.

Jo checked the timing. "It fits—the posts about the drinking all come after his mother's death. Not a single comment about it before that. There's our connection. Whorton and Kerland killed his career, and tanked his ability to get another job. That left him without health insurance, which lead to the death of his wife, which caused his son to start drinking excessively. And that lead to a drunk-driving accident."

"Shit," Arnett said, staring at the accident report. "Zero-point-two-five blood alcohol level at the time of the accident."

Lopez whistled. "At that level, he was probably blacked out. But, I still don't understand why Shawnessy would kidnap *Latimer's* son."

Jo squeezed her eyes shut and rubbed her brow, trying to remember as much as she could about their interview with Roger Latimer. "He didn't want to tell us much of anything. He tried to pretend he didn't know all of the ins and outs of the political situation in the department, which was bullshit. And he was more than willing to turn his back on the possibility that Whorton was harassing women." She opened her eyes again, wide. "I'll bet anything Shawnessy went to Latimer when he realized Whorton and Kerland were coming for him. That would be the sensible thing, since the dean was the next person in the hierarchy if the chair was engaging in unethical behavior."

"So Latimer sided with them somehow?" Lopez said.

"Maybe. But everything we've seen about Latimer and the university indicates a culture of sweeping things under the rug to maintain the status quo. I think it's more likely he just didn't step in to protect Shawnessy," Jo said.

"But we don't have any evidence of that," Lopez said.

"Other than his kid is missing, on the same weekend Shawnessy's kid died." Arnett jabbed his finger at the screen, toward a picture of Patrick standing in a group in front of a dense copse of trees. "He obviously has some sort of grudge against Latimer."

Jo stared at the group in the picture. "Hang on a second, that woman there, she looks familiar. And so do those woods." She scrolled carefully back up the page, but didn't find what she was looking for. She clicked back to Ellen Shawnessy's profile, and scrolled down. "I'll be damned. Look at this."

Arnett and Lopez leaned in again. "What are we looking at?"

Jo pointed to another picture of a similar group standing in front of similar trees. "These woods. They could be the Berkshires, couldn't they? And this guy and this woman, they were also in that picture with Patrick in the woods. And look at Patrick's comment: 'Thanks for always being such great hosts.'"

"Click on the picture, see if the people are tagged," Lopez said.

Several names popped up, including those for the two people Jo had pointed at. "Ginny and Sean McCormack. McCormack—didn't Ellen's funeral card list her full name as Ellen McCormack Shawnessy?"

Jo clicked on the 'relationships' tab on Ellen's profile. Sean McCormack was listed as one of her cousins. Her pulse raced. "This is it, this is our connection. We need to find out if Sean and Ginny McCormack have a vacation house out in that area of the Berkshires, and get the address if so. Hold on." She clicked on Sean's friends list, and scrolled through. "And there it is. Doris Pentiger."

"Nicely done." Lopez held up a fist.

Jo bumped it. "Arnett, does that accident report have a time of death?"

He scanned back over the screen. "They approximated 10:30 p.m."

Jo checked the time. "Shit, if our theory's right, Shawnessy's going to kill Jason Latimer sometime tonight. It's almost nine, and it'll take us almost an hour to get out there. Let's hope he's a stickler for timing, otherwise we may already be too late."

CHAPTER FORTY-SEVEN

Jason Latimer cried until he threw up. Then Professor Shawnessy made him drink two more shots.

He tried to focus, but every thought seemed to be moving through a thick layer of custard.

The asshole had his mother. That thought kept cutting through, followed by flashes of rage and panic that made him rush forward, only to have the shackle around his wrist snap him back. Then helplessness washed over him, and he just wanted to curl up and cry again.

But he couldn't. He couldn't. He had to force himself to think

Mom—Mom—Mom. The word circled his slush-filled head. He had to try to help her, had to try to figure out what was happening. Why was he here? Why would a professor kidnap him and his mother? He didn't understand, and he needed desperately to understand. What the fuck was this?

What the FUCK?!

Rage bolted through him again. He struggled against the chain again, and then collapsed under the wave of helplessness again.

He had to get out of there. That also kept pounding through his brain. He had to get out. OUT.

Another flash of rage. Another wave of helplessness.

Maybe he should just give up. Ask for more tequila, drink until he passed out and maybe he'd die and that would be just fine because he couldn't do anything anyway.

No. No, no, no. He shook his head and forced himself to focus again. He'd had a brilliant idea, when the professor left him to piss in private. He'd shoved his finger down his throat and made himself throw up, hoping to flush out the alcohol, but Shawnessy heard him and made him drink more shots to make up for it. And after that, no more privacy. No more pee-pee priva-cee, he thought, and laughed, then caught himself, and dropped his face in his hands. It wasn't funny. This wasn't funny. He needed to focus.

Focus. Think. Focus. But the asshole kept pouring alcohol down his throat so he *couldn't* focus.

But so what? He could beat it. He drank way more than this when he rushed the frat, they got him so trashed, oh man he was trashed, but he still managed to find his way home from the woods where they'd left him and the other pledges, even after he'd had a whole fifth of Jack all by himself. They'd been so cold dressed only in their boxers and he'd tripped and almost broken his arm, but he wore a sling for a week and he was fine and all the girls wanted to make him feel better so he'd laid a different girl every night that week, it was so awesome and—

"What'd you think of that one, Jason? I gotta say, after that, I'm never gonna stay in a European hostel again." The professor poured another shot, a double, and slid it to Jason. "The violence in that one was just gratuitous. I don't like gratuitous violence. Violence is a last resort."

Jason squinted at the laptop screen, and rubbed his face with his free hand. When he opened his eyes again, they took a moment to focus. "Whatever you want, my dad'll give it to you. My grampa hassa shitton of money." He heard his words slur, and shook his head again, trying to clear it.

"I don't want money, Jason."

The helplessness ripped through Jason again, and his eyes teared up. "Then what the fuck d'you want?" he sobbed.

Shawnessy reached into his bag for something. Adrenaline shot through Jason—nothing the asshole pulled out of the bag had been good. He backed away until he hit the wall, and screamed, "What do you want!"

Shawnessy watched him for a moment. Jason squinted again, tried to make sense of the look on the professor's face, but couldn't. The room had started to spin, and his eyes struggled to focus. He rubbed them, hard.

"I want you to hurt, Jason."

Jason gestured toward the laptop, but he misjudged and swung so hard he fell forward and had to right himself. "What are you gonna do, cut my feet off like that guy in the thing? Just fucking do it then!"

"No, Jason, I don't want to hurt you physically. I want to hurt you psychologically. I've decided I'm a really, really big fan of torture porn." He slid several photos across the floor.

"I'm not looking at those again, you sick fuck."

Shawnessy tsk-ed at him again. "Remember our agreement."

Fear froze Jason in place for a moment, then he forced himself to lean over to the photos. He wouldn't really look at them, his eyes weren't focusing well anyway, he'd just pretend. But then he saw his mother again and he needed to see, needed to know if she was okay, so he struggled to make the pictures out, but this time the shot was taken from farther away so it showed the whole room and it was harder to see so he squinted and leaned in further—

She was lying on the floor in a pool of blood. Her hand cut off, away from her.

"Oh God she's dead, is she dead? She's dead, you killed her—you fucking killed her you fuck—" Saliva flew from his lips as he yelled and his chest heaved like he was going to vomit and he gasped for breath and strained against the chain but it didn't matter, this time he'd pull his arm out if he had to, he was going to kill this—

Shawnessy lifted the gun, and fired a shot in Jason's direction. Jason dropped to the floor, and something warm soaked through his pants. "You shot me, I'm bleeding!"

"I didn't shoot you, you ridiculous moron. You just pissed yourself. Again." He laughed. "Now listen up. Your mother's dead, thanks to your little vomiting trick earlier. So shut up and listen to me."

But Jason couldn't stop crying. He wanted to, but his body was convulsing like he was in the throes of dry heaves. Shawnessy came over to him, gun pulled back out of reach but still pointed at him, and grabbed his face. "Look at me. Look at me. Look."

Jason managed to look up into the professor's eyes, and his wrenching sobs subsided slightly.

"Good. Calm down. Breathe. Good." Shawnessy let go and stepped back, and waited until Jason had regained control. "I need you to listen to me. I need to go chop some wood now so we don't freeze tonight. Now you know I'm serious, and you know I'll kill you if you try that little vomiting trick again while I'm gone. Don't make me go kidnap one of your sisters, too. Got it?"

Jason nodded his head and tried to wipe the threads of snot cascading from his nose.

"Great. I think we need to lighten the mood a little, don't you? So I'm gonna put on an episode of *Friends* for you. I'll be back by the time it's over."

The professor stood back up, slid a new DVD in the laptop, and left the room.

Jason reached down and pulled up his shirt to wipe his face. He was still crying, he realized, and rocking back and forth. He needed to pull himself together. To focus. To think.

But his head felt so heavy, he just want to curl up and sleep because what was the point anyway, and it was so hard to focus his eyes. He rubbed them again and looked over toward the door, the colors from the laptop screen streaking as his eyes swept across it, and past a flash of silver. Out the door, he couldn't see Shawnessy anymore, but he heard a door slam in the distance and—

A flash of silver. What flash of silver?

He swung his head back, his movement too big so he overshot and had to swing it around again. Toward the laptop. Where was the silver?

Keys. On the floor.

Keys?

Another jolt of adrenaline shot through him. He reached out, but misjudged again and fell on his face.

He pushed himself up and reached again and—

His fingers closed over them.

His head whipped toward the door and back again, bringing up a wave of nausea. Oh my God oh my God oh my God how did they get there? Right where the professor had been sitting when he came over and grabbed Jason's face, they must have fallen out of those lame-ass khakis that made him look like an ancient loser.

Jason lifted the keys, and winced when they clanked. "Shhhhh," he said out loud, then laughed, then told himself to stop laughing because what if Shawnessy heard him

He reached up with his empty hand and slapped himself hard, trying to sober himself. He barely felt it, but the action jolted his shoulder and sent searing pain through his arm.

He swung his head around again, expecting to see Shawnessy coming back, alerted by the noise. But nobody was there.

Jason studied the keys in his palm. Five keys, or six? It didn't matter. The shackle, the chain, he needed the key, was the key on this ring? If he could get it off, he could run, he could get far away by the time Shawnessy got back, they were in the woods, but there had to be a road so he needed to find the key—

One was smaller than the others, was that it? He pinched two fingers together and closed one eye to see better and carefully slid his fingers on either side of the key and gripped it and lifted slowly to make sure the keys didn't clink. Then he moved the fingers close to the lock, closer, but how could he get the key in the lock with only one hand and his fingers were over the key—

He squeezed his eyes shut. He had to focus. He could do this. He *had* to do this.

The *Friends* theme song twanged out of the laptop. The intro was coming to an end so at least five minutes gone. The professor would be back before it was over and he needed time to run—

The floor, he could use the floor. He set his arm down and then set the keys on the floor next to the lock, then picked up the key from the bottom and tried to slide it into the lock—

He missed.

His eyes strained as he tried again. He could feel the tip of the key scraping against the metal of the lock, he just had to keep steady—

The key slipped in.

He turned it, felt the tumblers clicking with the movement. The top of the lock popped up.

He yanked at it and slipped it off, and then the shackle was off his wrist with a *clang*—

He swung his head toward the door, expecting to see Shawnessy there or to feel a bullet bite into his chest. But the doorway was empty and he couldn't see anyone beyond it.

He gasped and grabbed the keys again, then scrambled up, using his legs for the first time in—how long had it been? How long had he been in this room? He didn't know, but it didn't matter—the cold cement bit into his feet and he looked down at them like they belonged to someone else. They were bare, and it was gonna hurt like hell to run through the woods with no shoes, maybe his shoes were here somewhere? But no, there wasn't anything else in the room and he didn't have time to look for them, he had to *get out*.

He stumbled toward the door, then turned the opposite way from where the professor had gone. He tripped, went down on his knees, caught himself on the edge of a couch, pulled himself up. He could see the front door, he just had to get to it, but he fell a second time and struggled to get up again, this time knocking over a chair in the process.

"Shit!" he cried, and winced at the sound of his own voice. He looked over his shoulder, but no, Shawnessy still wasn't there, thank God. He must have had to go far away to cut wood, but Jason needed to be more careful.

He took one step, then another. With several more careful strides, he was at the door, his hand grasping the cool knob and twisting. And it opened, and he was so relieved he almost started crying again, but he winced, half-expecting the professor to be standing on the other side.

He wasn't there. Jason lurched forward across the porch to the steps, then down onto the gravel—dammit, of course there would have to be gravel—and he sunk to his knees as the rocks bit into his bare feet. He gazed out, and the gravel stretched out for yards as far as his eyes could focus and he nearly sobbed with frustration. It didn't matter, there was nothing he could do but suck it up, so he pushed himself up and the gravel cut into his hands, but that didn't hurt as much, and he was up again, and—

The professor's car. Right there, a few feet away.

He looked down at the keys. Yes, one was big, and attached to a remote. He wouldn't be able to run fast enough without shoes, fucking gravel! He needed to drive. If he drove slowly it would still be faster than running anyway and the professor wouldn't be able to catch him because he wouldn't have his car. Jason pictured Shawnessy running behind him, swinging his fist in the air, screaming for him to stop as he drove away. Jason laughed, because that was wicked funny.

He threw himself forward toward the car, trying to keep his feet from buckling under him, and then he was there. And the door was unlocked, and he swung it open and dove inside.

"Get back here, you little bastard!"

Jason screamed at the sound and his neck wrenched back over his shoulder—the professor was on the porch, heading toward him. He fumbled for the button to lock the door and then scrambled to grab the right key but his hands were slippery—*from blood?*—and he couldn't—

The professor's palms slammed onto the driver's side window. Jason jumped, and the keys plummeted down to the floor.

The professor turned and ran back to the house.

Jason leaned forward and fought a wave of dizziness, desperately feeling for the keys, but he couldn't feel anything but the mat and some plastic and then—*yes!*—the keys were back in his hand, and oh God, the professor was back, running with some big piece of metal, and Jason grabbed the ignition switch with his other hand and used it to help slide the key in, and oh God, the professor was only a few feet away. The key slipped in and turned, and he shifted and slammed his bare foot onto the gas pedal and the tires spun into the gravel, sending up a shower onto the professor as the car hurtled forward.

The line of trees on each side of the road danced before Jason's eyes, and he squinted to try to make them be still, but they wouldn't. But it was okay because the road was wide, and in a minute, Shawnessy was a small figure in the rearview mirror, and he was able to slow down a bit so the trees didn't have to dance as much. Then, in another minute, he couldn't even see the house anymore, so he slowed down a little bit more, and the trees calmed even more.

"Take that you psycho fuck!" he yelled, and flipped his middle finger up, and laughed hysterically with relief. He leaned forward, bracing himself on the steering wheel for better control, and continued, slowly and carefully, down the dirt road.

Then the glow of headlights appeared in his rearview mirror.

*

Jason stared at the lights, trying to make sense of them. There couldn't be any cars behind him because the house was at the end of the road and—oh God—did the professor have another car? How could that be?

Trees sprung up in front of his eyes and he yanked the wheel just in time back toward the center of the road, heart pounding in his chest, but he overshot and had to correct again. He had to calm down. He had to focus on the road.

Once he got the car straight again, he looked back in the rearview mirror.

The headlights were getting closer.

"Fuck me, fuck me, fuck, fuck, *fuck!*" He didn't know what to do, except he really didn't have a choice anyway, the only way he could go was forward. There had to be a main road or another house or something—

But the professor was catching up.

Jason stepped on the gas.

He leaned forward again, chin braced on the steering wheel, trying to concentrate, trying to keep the dancing trees on either side of his eyes, focusing on the white spot from his headlights.

Until they lit up a huge black tree blocking the road in front of him.

CHAPTER FORTY-EIGHT

He took the bait, hook, line and sinker.

Only a drunken fool could think I dropped my keys onto a cement floor without noticing. Or that I couldn't hear all his clanking and furniture tumbling. Or the doors slamming. Or his screams.

I had fun chasing him down the road. I knew that part would be fun—I'd even prepped a song to play, Eric Clapton's 'Catch Me If You Can'. I turned it up and sang out the lyrics like my own little soundtrack, and settled in to enjoy. I replayed his face in my mind, the terror in his eyes when I appeared on the porch and then at the car window, and contemplated whether he'd urinated all over himself yet again.

The real moment of truth was still coming. What would he do when he reached the log? I revved the engine to speed him along and savored the buffet of possibilities. In endgame terms, it didn't really matter how he reacted. If he saw the log in time, he'd swerve down the road toward the ravine, and I'd continue to chase, pushing his speed until there was no chance he'd see it before careening over. But if he didn't see the log in time, that was fine, too. He'd barrel into it or the trees by the road, and likely kill himself outright. If the crash only injured him, I'd finish the job with a syringe filled with enough Connecticut Everclear to send his blood alcohol soaring and kill him within minutes.

Of course, I preferred the ravine, for the poetic parallel to Patrick's death.

But at the end of the day—six of one, half a dozen of the other.

CHAPTER FORTY-NINE

Arnett and Jo sped down the Pike toward Scranby, backup following closely behind.

They'd tracked down Sean and Ginny McCormack within minutes, and were able to reach Sean's cell phone. He gave them the address of their vacation home in Scranby, located about fifteen minutes away from Granton, and verified that the Shawnessys had visited for several weeks each year since before Patrick was born. Sean's and Ellen's grandparents had owned the house before him, and while all the cousins now shared it during the summer, it lay empty during the fall and winter. He also confirmed that Patrick had been drinking so heavily before his accident that Terry had asked to borrow money to send him to rehab—but Patrick died before they'd been able to take him.

The GPS router signaled their turnoff. They switched off the sirens as they exited the highway, but kept their speed high.

"The good thing about driving fast is you fly right over the potholes," Arnett said, the pained concentration on his face belying the tone of his words.

Jo scanned the police report of Patrick's accident. "So Patrick was speeding down a rural road when he broke through the guardrail and crashed down into a ravine. He was alive when the paramedics got there, but died shortly after while they were extracting him from the car."

"Shitty way to go," Arnett said. "We're getting close, the next turn is about a mile up."

Jo snapped the cover of her phone shut and scanned the woods around them. "It's black as pitch out there, I can't see a damned thing. Should I turn on the spotlight?"

Arnett wagged his head. "Probably, yeah. I can't see these roads until I'm on top of them, and it's not like we can sneak up on him anyway, he'll hear us a mile away with the quiet out here."

She flipped the light on, and angled it in partly off to the side of the road, in the direction of the house. The backup behind them followed suit.

"What time is it?" Arnett asked.

"Ten-fifteen."

"Shit, we're cutting it close. If he's looking to kill Jason at the same time his son died…"

Jo studied the GPS display. "Right up here there's a side road that cuts through the property. That should save us a few minutes."

Arnett risked a quick glance over. "For all we know, that's a dirt footpath."

"True, but that's why we grabbed a Crown Vic. She can handle it."

A smile turned up one corner of his mouth. "Let's do it."

Jo called the backup car. "See the side path on the map that branches off up here? We're gonna take that. You guys take the main road in case we get stuck."

The turn came up quickly, and Arnett yanked the wheel, tires squealing as they made it through the break in the plank-and-stone fence lining the road.

Jo continued to trace the road on the map, up to the house, then past it. "Oh, God. Look."

Arnett followed her finger to a point about two miles down the path.

"A ravine."

CHAPTER FIFTY

Jason yanked away from the log, then swerved past an oak tree, missing it by inches.

He tried to center himself in the middle of the road again, but this one was narrower and the trees seemed to be reaching out toward his car. He checked the rearview. The headlights hadn't followed him. Maybe the professor hadn't seen the tree fast enough, and had crashed into it? But he couldn't risk that, he had to keep going until he found a house, a main road, something.

His vision was clearing slightly, and his movements felt a little more fluid, maybe he was sobering up. But as he picked up speed again, the blurriness returned, and his eyes kept swaying as he struggled to keep them on the road. Or maybe that was his head? Or his whole body? Whatever it was, the nausea returned, and he fought to keep from vomiting. He sent up a prayer that he could just hold out long enough, keep the wheel straight enough, until he found something or someone.

The trees leapt out at him again, and he barely swerved in time. He slowed down. The professor was gone, it should be safe now.

The headlights appeared in the rearview again.

He sobbed with frustration. He couldn't go any faster, the trees kept coming too close as it was. He had to swerve again and this time he swerved too hard and almost hit the trees on the other side. He gripped the wheel and straightened out, then glanced in the rearview again.

The lights were closing in.

The tears and snot streaming down his face made it nearly impossible to see. He squinted hard to resolve the double images into one.

But it was no use. There was no way out of this. The professor would catch up and run him off the road, or he'd crash into the trees.

He was going to die.

CHAPTER FIFTY-ONE

"What's that?" Jo peered into the distance, not sure if what she was seeing was real.

Arnett followed her stare. "I don't know. Turn off the floodlight."

She did, and the pinpoints of red light in the distance popped out of the darkness. "A car."

"Shit. The road to the house is right up there. Do we go to the house, or follow the lights?"

"Another car heading toward the ravine? It has to be him."

"Right." Arnett rammed his foot onto the gas pedal, accelerating to fifty, sixty, then seventy miles an hour within seconds.

"What's he going to do, drive him into a murder-suicide off the edge of the ravine?" Jo asked.

"I don't—"

"Stop!" Jo screamed.

The end of a huge black shape jutted partially into the intersection in front of them.

She braced herself for the impact.

CHAPTER FIFTY-TWO

I watched Jason swerve back and forth. I followed, revving my engine intermittently to push his speed.

Then something pulled my attention.

A set of headlights in the distance behind me? But when I looked again, they were gone.

Was I seeing things? No. I'd seen lights. And there was only one possibility for who'd be out in the middle of nowhere late at night.

The police.

"Dammit!" I slammed my hands into the steering wheel and snapped off the music so I could focus. Why right now, right as I was on the cusp of completing everything?

I forced myself to take a deep breath and think. The lights had disappeared again, which meant they were traveling slower than I was, or they'd crashed into the log. I'd placed it to block the road that led from the house out to the main rural highway, but had also jutted it partway into the perpendicular road that cut across the property, the one we were driving down now, so Jason wouldn't turn the wrong way. Apparently, that choice had had a huge side benefit—hopefully they'd crashed into the end, and that was that. Possibly. Possibly not.

I thrust my foot onto the gas. I couldn't risk it. I needed to get Jason into that ravine, fast.

CHAPTER FIFTY-THREE

Jo and Arnett screeched to a halt inches from the tree.

Arnett threw the car in reverse, backed up, then squeezed the vehicle an inch at a time between the fallen tree and those lining the dirt road. With a horrible metallic shriek, the edge scraped the passenger side door.

As soon as they were past it, Arnett floored the gas again. "Floodlight."

Jo chastised herself for not turning it on sooner. She angled the light directly in front of them, down the dirt road.

The red lights reappeared in front of them, and grew larger as they closed the distance. Jo spotted another pair of lights slightly farther down the road. "There's another car in front of him."

The second pair of lights shifted horizontally as they watched, and Jo froze. "Oh, God. The driver in the first car is drunk. He's trying to recreate the accident." She checked their position on the GPS display. "And the ravine's only about a mile away."

"Got your seatbelt on?" Arnett deadpanned as he hit the gas, hard. Within moments, they were nearly caught up to Shawnessy's car. "Now what? Road's too narrow to get in front of him. How the hell do we stop him?"

Jo scoured the surroundings, mind grasping desperately for a solution. Arnett was right, there was no reason why Shawnessy should stop. He'd have to know there was no way out of this, and what was one more murder going to add to his time in jail?

"Get as close to him as you can," she said.

Arnett plunged the car forward, jaw tight with concentration, only feet away from Shawnessy's fender.

Jo flipped on the loudspeaker. "Jason, can you hear me? Stop the car, now! This is the police, you're safe now!"

Neither car slowed.

Was Jason too far out of range to hear her? Or too drunk? As she watched, the car narrowly missed slamming into the left-hand row of trees.

"Jason, please! Stop the car!"

No reaction.

Arnett forced himself still closer. She screamed as loudly as she could, knowing it would make no difference to the volume output of the loudspeaker. "Jason! You're heading toward a ravine! STOP THE CAR, NOW!"

Jason hit his brakes, and his vehicle fishtailed. Shawnessy's car slammed into the back of it, and both cars careened into an oak tree.

Both Terry Shawnessy and Jason Latimer were unconscious when Jo and Arnett raced to the cars. Both had a pulse and no serious visible injuries, so after ensuring their airways were unobstructed, Jo called for ambulances and backup, and they waited until both were taken to the nearest hospital.

Three hours later, Jo let herself into her house. She dropped, fully clothed, onto her bed.

Her phone rang. Without raising her head, she slid her phone out of her jacket pocket and answered the call.

"Lopez, you need to go get some sleep," she said, half talking into her pillow.

"I'm leaving now, but wanted to give you an update. Jason Latimer is fine, miraculously. Scrapes and bruises of course, and the doctor said he'll be sore tomorrow, but nothing broken and nothing ruptured. For once, the old maxim that the drunk driver walks away worked out in favor of the right guy. They've also been pumping him with fluids and he's pretty sober now. They're going to keep him overnight regardless, and bring in a trauma specialist for him and his parents tomorrow."

"That's a relief. Any news on Shawnessy?"

"Alonzo and Hofstadt are with him at the hospital, waiting for him to be released. He has a few broken ribs because he wasn't wearing a seatbelt. Pretty moronic when you know you're gonna be chasing a drunk guy through the dark woods in the middle of the night."

Jo's brow furrowed into the pillow. "Strange."

"Anyway, he'll be released shortly, and then they'll bring him back to book him. I told them to put him in a holding cell, since you'll wanna have a little chat with him in the morning."

"Thanks. I appreciate it."

"You sound like you're fading fast, that adrenaline crash is a killer."

But Jo was already asleep.

CHAPTER FIFTY-FOUR

The next morning, Jo picked up two dozen donuts and two boxes of coffee on the way to HQ, then delivered them to Marzillo's lab, where Arnett was waiting for her.

"You think you can buy us off with Dunkin' Donuts?" Marzillo laughed, hand on her jutted hip.

Jo set down the coffee and lifted the lid on the top box of donuts. "Yep."

Marzillo's eyes raked over the contents. "You might be right." She grabbed a Boston Kreme and took a huge bite.

Jo poured out coffee for everyone, including a mini-swarm of lab techs who appeared from the inner offices. "Any surprises for us?"

"Nope. This is how I like my crime scenes, cut-and-dried with all of the questions pre-answered, and a pre-determined suspect to compare all the fingerprints and DNA to. Quite a refreshing change of pace."

"I bet." Jo grabbed an extra cup of coffee. "In that case, it's time to talk with Dr. Shawnessy." She hit a number on her phone. "Alonzo. Is Shawnessy's attorney here yet?"

"No attorney, he waived."

Jo paused for a moment, then thanked him and ended the call. "He waived," she said to Arnett. "He's waiting in three."

"You're kidding me. What's our approach, then?" he asked.

Jo twisted her necklace. "How about you start off, not too soft, not too hard. I'm hoping this means he's going to give us Crawley without a fight."

"And if not?" Arnett asked.

"I'll take over. If you get any strange signals or body language from me, ignore it, it's an act. I have an idea."

Arnett pulled open the door to the interrogation room. Shawnessy was sitting at the rectangular table in the middle of the room, one hand chained to the bar in the middle. His short hair was unkempt, probably from a night spent sleeping on a bench in the holding cell, and a black eye marred most of the left side of his face. He leaned back in his chair with an odd air, like a contradictory mix of peace and agitation.

Jo and Arnett sat across from him, back to the camera perched near the ceiling. Arnett started the recording, while Jo slid the cup of coffee across. "Officer Alonzo tells us you waived the right to have an attorney present. Is that correct?"

"It is. I'm happy to tell you anything you want to know."

Arnett shot a raised-eyebrow look at Jo. "Great. Let's jump right in with an overview. We're pretty clear on why you killed Whorton—revenge because he destroyed your career."

Shawnessy nodded. "Of course. Twice. My academic career, then any possibility of an industry career."

Jo barely kept in her gasp. Two stabs, to the kidney and the neck, one for each career.

"Nancy Kerland gets a little bit more complicated. I get that Arthur Kerland partnered with Whorton to tank your tenure. So why not kill him, why kill his wife?"

"Because they killed my wife." Shawnessy leaned back in his chair, favoring his side.

Jo leaned back as well, purposefully mirroring his movements, and watched his face.

"They didn't give your wife cancer," Arnett said.

Shawnessy spoke with exaggerated patience, like he was dealing with a particularly slow student. "No, but without medical benefits, I couldn't get her the treatment she needed."

Arnett's expression was skeptical. "Upsetting, sure, but not exactly a direct causal link."

Contempt flashed across Shawnessy's face. "Completely wrong. When you take someone's job, you take their ability to provide. That's a fact, and it's real." He leaned forward and winced, then put his hand over his ribs. "And even then, destroying my academic career wasn't enough. They had to tank me with every pharmaceutical company in the area, as well." He jabbed his finger on the table. "*That* crosses over from selfish and self-serving into evil."

Jo considered the word, diving into Shawnessy's perspective. She leaned forward. "I get your point. But I'm not sure that's exactly what happened. We have reason to believe Whorton had cut deals with at least two local pharmaceutical companies, trading favorable research for kickbacks. If those companies had hired you, you'd have figured out what was going on almost immediately. He couldn't risk that."

He turned his gaze to her, and smiled. With admiration in his eyes? "Of course he did. But surely you can't believe that makes it any better? He was still willing to cut off my only other lucrative avenue of employment to protect himself. And it proves he would have kept hurting people as long as he needed to for his own benefit. He had to be stopped."

She nodded, primarily to keep up the connection with him. But, she wasn't quite sure she disagreed, either.

Arnett took back over. "Forgive me for being slow, but I still don't understand why you'd kill Kerland's wife rather than just kill him, like you did Whorton. She didn't do anything to hurt you."

Shawnessy shook his head. "The point wasn't just to kill someone, the point was to teach Arthur, and anyone else paying attention, that actions have consequences. This way he felt what it was like to have his wife taken prematurely through a medical condition he could do nothing about. He felt the pain of having the love of his life ripped away too soon, and he gets to experience what it is to wake up every morning without her, and feel her absence like a two-ton weight settled on his chest."

Arnett's eyebrows raised.

"Okay, but why the bullshit with the coyote? Why choose such a ridiculously stupid, risky way to kill her?"

Shawnessy looked away from them both, into the corner of the room. "I suppose it does sound stupid if you haven't thought it through. Cancer *technically* killed my wife. A heart condition complicated by multiple sclerosis *technically* killed his. Somehow, I doubt, that now the shoe's on the other foot, he'll justify my innocence the way he justifies his."

"Poetic justice," Jo said.

He met her eyes. "I'm not surprised you're the most decorated detective in your department."

Jo's mind flashed back to the camera she'd found in her neighbor's birdhouse, and a wave of revulsion flooded her. She fought to keep her face sympathetic.

Arnett made a show of looking at his notebook. "Next is Britney Ratliffe."

"It's not nice to steal. But it's worse to steal the last, best work of someone who's desperately trying to salvage some portion of their career. That paper could have made the difference between someone hiring me or not."

"Seems a little dramatic to kill her, what with your poetic justice theme and all."

Shawnessy took a deep breath and leaned forward, wincing again. "You don't have to agree with what I did, Detective. I hope we'll never know if you'd do the same in my position. I'm owning up to my choices, and I'm here answering your questions. But if you're going to make fun of my pain, it's best we end this interview right now."

The briefest flash of frustration registered on Arnett's face, so hidden only Jo and his wife would have recognized it. Shawnessy wasn't an egomaniac who'd lose control in the face of sarcastic snark. Arnett had overplayed his hand, and he knew it.

He held up both hands in a conciliatory gesture. "I just don't understand how it fits the bigger pattern, is all."

Shawnessy leaned back again. "She helped steal my life from me, I stole her life from her. It's not much deeper than that. Except—his gaze bounced between the two of them—"I was her faculty advisor for a year, remember. She wasn't a good person. She made fun of students, breached their confidentiality, and cheated whenever she could get away with it. She had an affair with a married professor to get a passing grade. I know this because she came on to me when we worked together until I had a talk with her about it, and after that she started complaining about me to anyone that would listen. Discretion wasn't her strong suit. And, she wasn't very smart. She would have been tossed from the program by now if she'd had to rely on her brain rather than her body."

"Why do you assume it was for a grade? Maybe she has a thing for older men in authority over her. Lots of people do," Arnett asked.

"Because the professor contacted me out of professional courtesy about her grade, since she was already on probation. I sat her down to talk with her about it, and a week later one of my undergraduate research assistants came to me to tell me she'd seen them at a restaurant in Springfield, hands all over each other."

Arnett's eyes went up. "So she deserved to die?"

Shawnessy's eyes narrowed. "Not for that. But it did negate any benefit of the doubt. If she'd been a different type of person, if she'd ever shown any integrity, I'd have thought Whorton talked her into stealing this research, or pressured her to do it. But it didn't happen that way. Even if the initial idea was his, he didn't have to coerce her. Because she had to steal the data from my lab computer, which meant she did it while she was still my student."

The implication hit Jo with a rush. Britney had known what Whorton and Kerland were going to do to Shawnessy before they did it.

Arnett looked at his notes again. "Next up is Dreta Kline."

The odd vibe Jo had sensed intensified as Shawnessy's posture went ever so slightly more rigid.

Arnett continued. "Obviously you didn't kidnap and kill her, your accomplice did."

Shawnessy leaned back, and his face went blank. "No accomplice. I hired a hitman."

Jo leaned back, watching.

Arnett rubbed his chin and the side of his face. "A hitman. What's his name?"

"I don't know, I hired him off the dark web."

"How'd you communicate with him off the web?"

"I didn't. I gave him instructions when I hired him out of the market place, and never contacted him again."

"How'd you pay him?"

"I wired the money to an overseas account."

"That couldn't have been cheap. How much?"

"Fifty thousand."

Arnett exchanged a look with Jo, who shook her head imperceptibly.

"I guess that's it for the whole telling-us-whatever-we-want-to-know thing, huh? And we were doing so well."

Shawnessy's face remained frozen. "I don't know what you mean."

Arnett paused, took a large sip of his coffee, and then resumed. "Let's break down all the reasons I know that's bullshit." He ticked a finger off with each point. "First, if there was any sign Tor had ever been on your computer, our techs would have found it.

Second, no way you had fifty thousand dollars to pay a hitman. We've become more familiar with your finances than our own, and you've been living hand to mouth for months. But, first and foremost, check and mate, no hitman good enough to pull off Dreta Kline's kidnapping and torture would be caught anywhere near anything that convoluted."

Shawnessy crossed his arms over his chest and remained silent.

"And, we know you didn't make any calls while you were in jail, so any hit had to have been arranged before. Why? You had no problem taking care of the others yourself."

Shawnessy reached for his coffee, sipped, and put it back down, but didn't respond.

"And you know what else bothers me? You had a very specific reason for doing things the way you did them, especially the coyote. Same thing with Jason, taking your time getting him drunk, showing him doctored pictures of Dreta Kline to make him think his mother was dead, then trying to crash him into the ravine. Perfect parallel to your son's decline and death after the loss of his mother. There's gotta be some important significance to the way Dreta Kline was killed, but you have no reason to want her dead. You never had contact with her, no phone calls between your personal or work phones, no nothing. So, explain it to me. Why kill her, especially like that?"

Shawnessy's entire body was taut, and his face had turned to stone. "I contacted her about my issue with Whorton and Kerland, I don't know why it doesn't show up. I called from my office phone, maybe that shows as belonging to someone else now."

Arnett leaned forward. "Cut the shit. We know you had an accomplice—"

Jo interrupted. "Bob, can I have a minute alone with Terry?"

Arnett balked, and pointed to the door. "Talk outside?"

"No. And turn off the recording when you go out."

She waited while Arnett left, then turned to Shawnessy. "Terry, I'm sure you don't remember me mentioning it, but my father was recently diagnosed with prostate cancer."

Shawnessy's expression softened, but a wariness remained. "Of course I remember. I'm so sorry."

She took a deep breath, and stared into the same corner Shawnessy had. "Thank you. I actually just went to visit him. He's on his second week of chemotherapy, and he needed someone to take him for his treatment." She glanced up into Shawnessy's eyes. "I've never been so scared in my entire life. Everyone keeps telling me that he'll be fine, that the prognosis is good, but…" She allowed the all-too-real tears to spring into her eyes.

Shawnessy's voice was sympathetic. "But no matter how high the recovery rate is, nobody can promise you anything." He shook his head with a desperate frustration. "And you can't believe it's really happening, but it is, and you have no idea how to process it."

She met his eyes. "If someone interfered with my father's ability to get the treatment he needs, I'd lose it. I have absolutely no problem understanding why you did what you did."

His expression turned wary again, and she hurried to explain. "No, I'm not trying to trick you. There's a huge part of me that can't condemn you for what you did to Michael Whorton. I personally agree with you that the world is a better place without him. If you and I were the only two that knew about it, I'm not sure I'd be rushing to turn you in."

"But."

"No but." She took another sip from her cup. "That's how I feel."

He leaned forward and looked into her eyes. "I've always planned to accept the consequences of what I've done, just as I feel it's important for *them* to deal with the consequences of what *they* did."

She nodded. "I can see that in your face, and it's not something I see often. Very few people who end up in this room are willing to take any sort of responsibility for their actions." She leaned forward toward him. "And that's what confuses me. You believe the honorable thing to do is to own up and take responsibility for your actions."

"Why is that confusing?" He searched her eyes as he asked the question.

She furrowed her brow, and kept her voice soft. "Because I don't understand why you'd choose to partner with someone who didn't hold themselves to that same moral standard. I don't understand why you're okay with them not taking responsibility for their part."

He nodded, and gave a wry smile. "Someone has to pay, yes, but I'm okay with it being me. I'm fine with taking the penalty for both of us."

She kept the confused, compassionate look on her face, careful not to react to his admission of a partner. "But that's just it, you don't have to die. Yes, if you stick to the lie that Dreta Kline was a murder-for-hire case, the DA can argue it's a federal crime, but otherwise Massachusetts can't put you to death. You don't have to die if you just tell the truth."

He leaned back in his chair. "Detective Fournier, I appreciate your compassion more than you know. But I have to end this the right way."

Something had shifted. She was losing him.

She laid her hand on his. "Don't do this. He's not worth it. There's no righteousness about Dreta Kline's murder."

Shawnessy looked confused. "What do you mean?"

"Crawley. He wasn't injured in any way, he legitimately failed those tests. His persecution was completely in his head. He doesn't deserve to have you take the rap for him."

Shawnessy's confused expression cleared, replaced by one she didn't understand. He moved his hand out from under hers, and shook his head. "I'm sorry, Detective."

She opened her mouth to try again, but she could see in his eyes that he'd closed off.

She nodded, and stood up. As she opened the door, she looked back at him again.

The strange expression remained on his face, and she realized what it meant.

He was disappointed in her.

*

When she brought Arnett back into the room to try again, Shawnessy refused to answer any more questions. They finished processing him, and arranged to have sheriff's deputies transport him to the county jail.

"Dammit, we were *this* close. I actually thought he was going to give Crawley up for a minute there," Jo said.

"Why're you beating yourself up? You did great. You got him to admit the hitman story was bullshit, and now we have leverage. We'll give him time to stew in county, then have another talk with him. I'll go hard, pound him with that point, maybe even play him the tape we both know I didn't turn off. He'll crack."

"I think you're wrong. I saw something in his eyes, I don't know what, but I do know he believes it's a moral imperative to protect Crawley. The question is, why? Why would he think Crawley had a right to kill Dreta Kline? It doesn't fit with his whole rationalization. We're missing something, somehow, and I don't know what."

"I say we talk to Crawley, and no more Mr. Nice Guy this time."

*

When Roderick Duncan arrived, they brought in Greg Crawley.

"Detectives, there better be a damned good reason why my client is still being held. This is the last time he or I will be speaking to you unless you file charges."

Arnett ignored the comment. "You may have read that we arrested Terry Shawnessy last night for the kidnapping and attempted murder of Jason Latimer."

"Which makes it even more unacceptable that you're continuing to harass my client."

Arnett launched in. "The game's over, Crawley. Shawnessy told us the two of you have been working together. We caught him red-handed with Jason, but he claims you were the one who committed the other murders. Which means you're the one stuck with the murder charges, while he walks away with minimal time. He's cutting a deal with the DA as we speak, so now's your chance to work with us."

Crawley leaned forward, his intense stare burning holes through each of them in turn. "I knew you were gonna try something like this."

"Greg, let me handle this," Duncan said, discomfited.

"Fuck that. I'm gonna have my say, because now I *know* they're dirty. One of two things is going on here. Either Professor Shawnessy is using me as a fall guy, or you two are trying to frame me. What, you have some blood or something that you're planting at my house or in my car right now? I really hope so, because I've got cameras running, recording the video in the cloud, and I'd love to be the one to end your careers." He crossed his arms over his chest triumphantly. "Duncan, you want to tell them the rest?"

Duncan pulled a manila envelope out of his briefcase, and slid out a stack of pictures and a flash drive.

"My client told you he was in a cafe studying the night Dreta Kline was kidnapped. After talking with you, he remembered that a group of regulars had disturbed his studying that night by loudly celebrating a birthday. He and I have spent as much time as possible in the cafe hoping some of the group would return, and luckily, they did. They allowed me to look through their phones at the pictures they took that night, and we found several with my client in the background over the course of three hours that evening. The pictures have all the relevant verifying metadata, and were automatically backed up in the individuals' respective clouds." He slid the pictures across to them. "I also checked with my client's landlord and found out he recently installed two security cameras in his pool area, because tenants were sneaking in to skinny dip after the pool had been closed for the night. The footage clearly shows my client coming home that night just after eleven, and then again carrying his garbage out to the dumpster at twelve thirty." He slid the flash drive forward. "So, unless you're suggesting that my client left the house after that, somehow knew where Ms. Kline was without having followed her, drove the hour out to Hillsdale, arrived at the bar half an hour before closing and still managed to convince her to leave with him despite the fact that she closed out her tab an hour before, I think we're done here. My client has nothing more to say. Either file charges against him, or let him go."

They didn't have much choice. After Crawley and Duncan strutted out of the room, they brought the flash drive and the photos to Lopez for analysis.

Arnett paced in front of Lopez's desk. "They have to be fake, otherwise I have no idea what to believe at this point."

Jo's fingers flew to her necklace. "I didn't see even a tiny flash of fear that Shawnessy might have sold him out. Like he knew it just wasn't possible."

"We've seen psychopaths do the same before."

"Sure, but Duncan made a very good point. The timing doesn't line up, Dreta had already closed out her tab before he got there." She shook her head.

Arnett waved her off and glanced at his watch. "I'm telling you, the photos and video are faked, and Lopez will prove it. I'm heading out. I'm beat, and there's nothing here that won't keep until tomorrow. We'll go at Shawnessy hard, see what that gives us, and start crawling so far up Crawley's ass he'll think he's getting a colonoscopy."

Jo nodded. "I'm beat, too, and that sounds like as good a plan as any."

*

An hour later, Jo dumped an order of takeout Chinese food onto her dining room table, and dropped into the closest chair, still trying to get Shawnessy's and Crawley's reactions out of her head.

She called to check in on her father and update him, but got his voicemail. She left a message, then checked in with Cousin Nick. Her father was asleep, he told her, and all was well. The neighbors had come over and they played *bourré* until her father won everyone's money. His side effects were still minimal, and Nick promised to call her first thing after Frank's next treatment. She thanked him profusely for his help, but he forestalled her.

"My mother went too fast, Josie. Frank has always been one of my favorite uncles, and, if I'm honest with you, I'm really glad I'm getting to spend some time with him."

She knew he hadn't intended to imply time was short with her father, too, but his words added to the weight already pressing her chest. She grabbed a Coke from her fridge and took her food into the living room. While she'd normally eat in the dining room with a little relaxing music, her brain wouldn't relax, so she decided to lose herself in a movie while she ate.

She selected the most recent Amy Schumer vehicle from the on-demand menu. Not normally her cup of tea, but she decided lighthearted and funny might be good distractions. She clicked it on, dumped soy sauce over her garlic prawns, and tried to turn her mind off. The next thing she knew, fifteen minutes had passed obsessing about Shawnessy and Crawley, her shrimp were gone, and she had no idea why Amy Schumer was hiding behind a group of uniformed schoolgirls.

She sighed, turned the TV off, and cleared away the takeout containers. She caught herself washing down the counters in the kitchen even though she hadn't used them, and forced herself to stop the compulsive cleaning. She considered calling Eric, but he didn't know she'd rushed back from New Orleans, and she couldn't face the hassle of explaining everything to him right then. She settled on a long hot shower.

When she got out, her notifications showed a voice message. She pulled it up, hoping her father had returned her call.

But it was from the county jail. She hit play.

"I'm calling to inform you that we just found Terry Shawnessy dead in his cell. He hanged himself with his bed sheets."

CHAPTER FIFTY-FIVE

Jo woke the next morning feeling frustrated and desperate.

Although her father had left her a message assuring her he was fine, she wouldn't believe it until she saw it with her own eyes. She needed to be with him, but to do that, she needed final closure on the case.

But there would be no pushing Terry Shawnessy to give up his partner now. She swore at herself as she did her make-up in the mirror. How had she failed to read the signs? Of course he'd intended to kill himself. He hadn't been wearing a seatbelt in Scranby, and she'd noticed herself at the crash scene that no airbags had deployed. He must have disabled them beforehand, and why would he do that if he hadn't planned on going over the ravine right behind Jason? And the hints he'd dropped during their conversation about taking responsibility and ending it the right way—that was where she normally excelled, reading cues like that. But she'd dropped the ball. She was so focused on mirroring his postures and convincing him she was empathetic that she'd allowed herself to get too close.

As far as Lopez and the other techs could tell, the pictures and video Duncan had left them were authentic. Jo, Arnett, and Lopez spent the next morning reworking every bit of evidence they had, and brainstorming. They scoured Facebook and Twitter and Instagram, but found nothing that brought them any closer to catching Shawnessy's accomplice. This time, the behavioral targeting approach didn't work.

"We're spinning our wheels here, Jo. Lopez and I can do that well enough alone." Arnett pushed a stack of papers on his desk away in frustration. "Go be with your father."

She sighed, and pulled her laptop closer. "You may very well be right." She searched through flights to New Orleans. "But tomorrow's flight is fifteen-hundred bucks more than the same flight on Thursday, so there's no point in me going any sooner than that, anyway."

Arnett shook his head. "It's bullshit what they charge for last-minute flights. They know they have you over a barrel."

"Yep, and I can't stop thinking about how Ellen Shawnessy's treatment bankrupted them. I dropped quite a roll on my last flight out there and back, it might be smart for me to save money where I can." A thought occurred to her. "Besides, there's something I'd like to do tomorrow, and the delay will give me time."

*

She walked into Demers Funeral Parlor the next day wearing a black sheath dress and pumps, trying her best not to look like a detective. Not to fool anyone, but because she didn't want to intrude on Dreta Kline's friends and family any more than she had to.

She slipped into the back-most row of chairs in the viewing room, and glanced around. Dreta Kline hadn't been the social media type, so Lopez's behavioral targeting techniques hadn't helped them get any closer to her or her circle of family and friends. She didn't recognize anyone at the service except Dreta's mother, Irene Kline.

Irene sat in a wheelchair in the front of the room, between the casket and a large collage someone had put together with pictures of Dreta's life. She seemed to be melting into the folds of a full-length black dress that was too large for her, like a child playing dress up. Her eyes were puffed from crying, but she mostly looked confused, like she wasn't quite sure where she was.

Jo waited while several people approached the coffin and knelt before it, then stepped over to Irene and gave their condolences. When the line ran out, she took her turn, stopping first to kneel in front of the casket.

Jo hadn't been to church regularly since she was a teenager, when her mother stopped forcing her to go. She was suspicious of organized religion—maybe the side of humanity she saw as a policewoman had made her too cynical—and she wasn't quite sure how she felt about God. When asked, she said she was agnostic, that she neither believed nor disbelieved. But that wasn't quite right either. It was more that she believed in *something*, but had no idea what that *something* was. And, she was fairly sure that *something* had far better things to do than worry about the petty lives of humans. Certainly not about who won football games or if a streetlight stayed green when you were in a hurry, but most likely also about who got shot or who got cancer. She'd seen far too much random devastation and loss in her life to imagine a higher power that had anything other than a *sort-it-out-yourselves-and-then-we'll-talk* approach to planet earth.

But she said a prayer as she knelt in front of Dreta Kline. She asked for help, guidance to point her in the right direction, because Dreta and Irene and all of these mourners deserved to know that Dreta's murderer would pay for what he'd done to her.

She finished, crossed herself, then stepped over to Irene. "Mrs. Kline?"

The rheumy eyes turned to her. "Oh hello, dear, so good to see you again."

Jo smiled at the recognition, but the blank face marked the comment for what it was: a coping technique for someone embarrassed about losing their memory. Lopez's mother began doing the same thing after losing her short-term memory due to her alcoholism. "I'm Detective Josette Fournier, Oakhurst County SPDU."

Clarity found purchase in the woman's eyes. "You're the one working to find out who hurt my daughter."

"Yes, I am. I wanted to come pay my respects, and tell you how sorry I am for your loss."

Tears filled Irene's eyes. "She and her sister are all I have in the world. And Donna lives so far away."

A brunette woman talking to someone in the corner perked up at the sound of her name, and sidled up to them. She studied Jo's face as she held out her hand. "Hello. Were you a friend of Dreta's?"

Jo explained who she was, and Donna's face stiffened. She waved across to a man sitting in the middle of the room, and gestured to Irene. After he wheeled her away, Donna asked, "Have you caught the killer?"

"We're working on it. I just wanted to come and pay my respects. And to see if I can get a better sense of who your sister was. That can make a difference."

"I see." She waved at the photo collage. "This would be the fastest way. I tried to capture all the main parts of her life here."

They stepped closer to the board. Apart from one studio portrait in the middle, it was arranged in chronological order, starting with baby pictures. Her first birthday, cake smeared across her face. Dreta as a toddler, playing with a cat. Dreta dressed in a tutu as a preschooler. "She liked ballet?" Jo asked.

"Nah, not really. Our parents made both of us take ballet. But she did love to dance. She switched to jazz and hip-hop and loved it."

Jo laughed. "So why not a picture of that?"

Donna shrugged. "You know how it is. Parents have an idea of who you are and what they want you to be. My mother more than most." She pointed to the first birthday picture. "See the cake on her face? Dreta didn't do that. She got the cake into her mouth without a hitch, didn't make any mess at all. My mom smeared it across her face for the purpose of the picture. That sort of sums things up."

Jo nodded her understanding. "Funny how parents do that. And even when you turn out to be what they wanted in the first place, like with Dreta's dancing, somehow it's not right."

Donna met her eyes. "You get it."

"This is prom, I take it? Cute guy. First boyfriend?"

Donna flicked a glance toward her mother, making sure she was out of earshot. "That's the official story, anyway. She hadn't come out to anyone but me yet."

Jo's head snapped to her face. "She was a lesbian?"

Donna nodded. "Mm-hmm. Dreta didn't want Mom to know. We had an uber-religious upbringing, you see, and my mother's firmly in the 'Adam-and-Eve-not-Adam-and-Steve' camp. So is most of our family."

Jo scanned the rest of the pictures. No romantic relationship shots with anybody of either sex. "So her real relationship pictures didn't make it up here."

Donna sent another glance toward her mother. "She never really had any serious relationships. Unfortunately, I think our family's position on homosexuality, particularly my mother's, led to quite a large amount of self-loathing in Dreta. She wanted my mother's approval so desperately. Whatever she did, she hid it well. I'm not aware of a single woman she ever dated long enough to mention her name."

Something clicked in Jo's mind. "That's why she's not on social media."

Donna nodded. "She was deathly afraid of social media. She just knew someone would post something that would get back to the family, who'd report back to our mother."

The final piece fell into place. Jo pulled out her phone and feigned receiving a text. "I'm so sorry, but I have to leave. I'm so sorry for your loss. Please give my regards again to your mother."

CHAPTER FIFTY-SIX

Jo put a call through to Bob as she screeched out of the parking lot. He picked up immediately. "Dreta Kline was a lesbian," she said.

"A lesbian," he repeated.

"So that unidentified man who romanced her at the Atomic Raccoon? That was an unidentified woman. Crawley didn't do this."

"Unfortunately, that doesn't help much. Camilla Whorton has an iron-clad alibi for Kline's murder, and all the other women involved in the case are dead."

"Not all of them. Beth Morlinski. We ruled her out early on because there was no way she could have killed Michael Whorton or Nancy Kerland. But knowing what we know now, it all fits. We need a search warrant for her home and office, and we need to get over there before she gets wind that we're on to her."

*

Two hours later they arrested Morlinski in her academic office. While the other techs searched the rest of the office, Lopez immediately started on the computer. Within minutes, she called Arnett and Jo over to show them a video titled *Happy Fall*. She clicked play, and suddenly Dreta was alive in front of them, bleeding out from what was left of her wrist, desperately trying one-handed to get her battery back in her cell phone.

Jo fought back nausea, and Arnett went a shade paler. He looked away under the pretense of asking Lopez, "How'd you find it so fast with that title?"

Lopez threw him a scornful look. "Amateur. I searched by creation date, not title."

His eyebrows shot up, and with a wan smile and a tepid wink, he said, "I always knew you were smarter than you look."

She reached up and pinched his upper arm.

"Hey, that's assault, and I have a witness." He rubbed the spot.

"No idea what you're talking about. I didn't see anything." Jo's smile broadened. "Great work, Lopez. We got her."

CHAPTER FIFTY-SEVEN

I didn't put up a fight when they came for me. Why would I? They'd already found enough evidence against me, and as soon as they showed my picture around the Atomic Raccoon, someone was bound to recognize me. The only chance I had of hiding my involvement depended on never becoming a viable suspect.

I told them how it all started, how I'd attended Ellen's funeral after she died. How Terry and I met for dinner to catch up. That it dawned on us how much destruction and pain Michael and Arthur had brought into our lives, and other lives they touched. Most of all, we cried over the irony of Terry's inability to afford experimental treatments for Ellen. He'd done so much research trying to help people with cancer, but when it hit his own wife, he was powerless.

That's when the broader implications of what Michael and Arthur had done really sank in. If Terry had been allowed to continue his research, he might have made THE breakthrough, might have saved thousands of lives. And the duplicity with the pharmaceutical companies—how much research money had been channeled away from saving lives, so two egomaniacs could pad their bank accounts? When I explained that to the detectives, I could have sworn the one, Detective Fournier, understood.

During that conversation, I gave Terry the full details about the sexual assault and the lasting impact it had on me. The law would have argued it wasn't rape, because we were interrupted before Michael managed to pull his dick out. And I had no proof, regardless. Too bad I hadn't let him ejaculate inside me, Dreta Kline told me when I went to her. Because as it was, it was his word against mine.

Yes, she actually said that. Just like she told me my best choice was to leave OakhurstU and start over elsewhere. No matter that I'd toiled tirelessly on a program of research that meant everything to me, and I'd likely have to leave that behind. If I stayed and fought, I'd lose, and I was already tainted. Nobody would want to work with me. So there was no point in her fighting for me, it would just take time away from people she could actually help. Her advice was to face the inevitable, sever ties, and get on with my life. "Either way," she'd said, "Best of luck."

Best of luck.

So I left her alone, with nobody to help her and an impossible decision to make, the way she left me alone with no help and an impossible decision in front of me. We both faced a slow, agonizing end, or a quick severing of ties: mine from my research career, hers from the shackle. And she died regardless, just the way my soul has slowly died, regardless.

Because for months I woke screaming from nightmares about being suffocated by Michael. And as I lay in bed trying to catch my breath, I could feel his hand across my mouth and nose, leaving me to gasp for the tiniest trickle of air I could manage as he pressed against me and forced his knee between my legs.

My therapist says it's a form of PTSD, akin to war veterans' flashbacks, and along with the nightmares, a full crop of fears suddenly took over my life. I couldn't bear to be in small spaces. Couldn't bear to have strangers touch me. Couldn't enter a dark room. I washed my hands excessively, obsessed about leaving the stove on or my curling iron plugged in, and suddenly formed an extreme aversion to the number six. I worked with that therapist for a year, and two others after that, but despite them and a slew of medications, it just got worse. My difficulties sleeping and eating grew and I developed daily panic attacks.

Terry and I had had far too much to drink at that point in our conversation, which nudged us toward the macabre. We reveled in declaring that selfish egomaniacs with no consciences should be the ones with ruined careers and dead spouses, terrorized by nightmares. He joked about how he preferred the vengeful God of the Old Testament to the New, because that God understood consequences. How an eye for an eye wasn't just about getting revenge, it was preemptively enforcing a moral code that kept society functioning via fear of retribution.

Neither of us took the conversation seriously. We said our goodbyes that night and went our separate ways.

Then Terry appeared in my office after Patrick died. He asked if I was better, and I told him I wasn't, that in fact I'd been daydreaming on a near daily basis about committing suicide so I could end my pain. He told me what we'd joked about that night wasn't a joke to him anymore. Michael and Arthur and the rest were evil, he said, and they would continue hurting other people until the day they died. Unless we stopped them.

We hatched the plan that night, centered around making a reasonable-doubt burden of proof for either of us impossible. He'd never so much as spoken to Dreta Kline, and I had absolutely no reason to want Britney Ratliffe dead. He also wanted to protect me as much as possible, so he did all the killing save one. And since he'd always found Britney's tattoo to be a perfect symbol of her ridiculously melodramatic personality, he chose tarot cards to link the killings and manipulate the police into looking the wrong way.

But as much as we would have loved to get away with it all scot-free, we knew that was unlikely. And that's the most ironic part. People like Michael and Arthur never seem to realize that a person who's lost everything is extremely dangerous. Terry and I were fighting oppressive depression, each day one step closer to killing ourselves—what did it matter if we were caught and thrown in jail?

But I also believe Terry partially blamed himself for what happened to me, because he filed that complaint. I think he was trying to save me, give me my sanity back, because he hadn't been able to save his wife.

Detective Arnett asked if I had any regrets, at least over Nancy Kerland, who'd never harmed either of us. I laughed. I don't have the smallest scintilla of regret. From the instant we decided to kill them, everything changed for me. I was able to sleep again. I gained back nearly all the weight I'd lost, and I didn't have to obsessively check my stove any longer. I weaned myself off my medications—and caught myself humming as I worked.

Because a person's sense of agency is a deeply powerful thing. When you take that from them, leave them feeling they have no control over their lives or even over their own emotions, their core dies, and it's only a matter of time before their soul rots and dies, too. The murders allowed us to reclaim our agency, and our power. And I learned I have the strength to ensure nobody steals my soul again. With that knowledge and that peace, nothing else matters.

I can survive jail. I wouldn't have survived those demons eating me alive.

CHAPTER FIFTY-EIGHT

Jo's father slept for several hours after his treatment that next Friday. It hit him harder than the previous ones, so hard he even took one of his 'as needed' medications unprompted, something Jo couldn't remember him ever doing without coercion.

While he slept, she took the opportunity to clean his house. Her father was normally almost as meticulously neat as she was, and his pained expressions at the sight of the dishes he hadn't had the energy to wash were an arrow through her heart. They were symbols of his vulnerable state, undeniable reminders that he wasn't all powerful. Neither she nor he needed any more reminders than they were already facing. He woke and came down just as she was finishing up a huge pot of jambalaya. She'd made it in hopes of tempting his appetite; it was his favorite meal, and he'd taught her how to make it.

The smell flashed her back to the food at the boucherie. Food wasn't just biologically necessary fuel for the body; it was connection, and culture, and love. When her father insisted she and Sophie learn to cook, it wasn't because he was afraid they'd starve. It was because he wanted to connect them to their family history, just like the trip to the boucherie hadn't been for his benefit, but hers.

A lot of her relationship with her father was like that, she was coming to understand. His intractable, seemingly random demands and expectations actually signaled something deeper and more intimate. She shook her head and blew out a frustrated puff of air as she dished out the jambalaya. Why couldn't he just tell her why these things mattered? Why go at it sideways, so they ended up spending so many years at cross purposes?

She set a bowl down on the dining table in front of him, then sat down with hers.

"How long you stayin' this time?" He angled an overflowing spoonful of jambalaya into his mouth.

"I told Rockney I was turning my phone off for two weeks, and that unless Massachusetts is invaded by Klingons, I don't want to hear about it."

He nodded, and went silent for a few minutes. Then he said, "You realize today was my last treatment? Short and sweet and then they'll evaluate how effective it was, see if I need more."

The familiar rush of petulant frustration flashed through her. What was he saying, that he didn't need her here after all?

She reminded herself to be patient. "I do."

He lapsed back into silence, attention focused on his plate. She watched his slow, deliberate movements, and searched for something else to say, desperate for any dinner conversation that might be engaging. She came up empty.

When they'd both finished, she cleared the plates, then intercepted her father as he leaned over to grab the remote control. "Hold on a sec, Dad. I have something I wanted to ask you about."

He paused, still clutching the remote.

It wasn't enthusiasm, but it wasn't a refusal, either. She pulled a chair and a small folding table up next to his La-Z-Boy, then opened up her laptop on it. "You're gonna need your reading glasses."

He grimaced. "I got my show to watch, you know."

"It's on DVR, Dad, it's not going anywhere. You can watch it after."

He put on his glasses and glared at her.

She typed an address into her browser. "I started a family tree on Ancestry.com. I put in your information, and everything I know about your parents, here, but then I realized I don't know much past that. What were your grandmothers' maiden names?"

He peered in at the screen, and pointed. "Marie-Madeleine Langlois and Elizabeth Hebert. But you got a mistake here. My mother's name wasn't Angelique. It was Delphine. She hated it, so she used her middle name."

She glanced at his face, lined with concentration.

"You never told me that."

He shrugged. "I don't think *I* knew it until she passed away." He pointed again. "What's that mean?"

A green leaf had popped up when she entered the correct name. "That means they have something in their databases that might help us." She clicked on it, and found several potentially relevant documents. She selected the first, which turned out to be the 1940 census.

"I'll be damned," he said as he studied it. "There she is, before she got married, with her whole family."

Jo examined the list of names. "Who's Charles? I don't remember any Uncle Charles."

"Sure you do. That's Uncle Corky."

Jo stared at him a moment. "How the hell do you get Corky from Charles?"

"You don't, that's how. You know he lost his leg in the war? For a while he had a cork one. Et voilà, everybody called him Corky. It stuck." He shrugged.

Jo narrowed her eyes at him. "You're lying."

He raised his palm up, a huge smile spreading over his face. "Hand to God."

"Hold on." She jumped up and grabbed a notepad out of her computer bag. "I need to write all this down so I don't forget it. I'll add it in later."

As they scoured the documents together, she jotted notes on the pad. Two hours later, television show forgotten, they'd filled the gaps in his memory about his great-grandparents, and were looking through digitized parish documents for marriage records, the easiest way to find the next generation's names.

Out of nowhere, he leaned over and kissed Jo's forehead. She opened her mouth to speak, but he cut her off, staring back at the screen. "This one here—I think that might be it. I think I remember some mention of her people coming from Grenouille."

Jo pushed back the tears in her eyes, and clicked on the link.

A LETTER FROM
M.M. CHOUINARD

Thank you so much for taking the time to read *Taken to the Grave*.
I hope you enjoyed reading it as much as I enjoyed writing it,
and if you did, then you'll love my other Jo Fournier thrillers,
The Dancing Girls, *Her Daughter's Cry* and *The Other Mothers*. If
you'd like to keep up-to-date with Jo Fournier or any of my other
releases, please click the link below to sign up for my newsletter.
Your e-mail will never be shared, and I'll only contact you when
I have news about a new release.

www.bookouture.com/mm-chouinard

When I was a teenager, I read about a man put in jail for
killing his daughter's rapist. Since that day, I've been fascinated
by the question of vigilantism—what sort of injustice would
have to occur for us to take the law into our own hands? What
factors—economic, psychological, egotistical—would aggravate
those circumstances? And why do those lines vary so dramatically
for so many of us? I have no answers, but *Taken to the Grave* allowed
me to push some of the questions to an extreme degree, and to
explore how dangerous self-justification can be.

If you have the time and inclination to leave me a short, honest
review on Amazon, Goodreads, or wherever you purchased the
book, I'd very much appreciate it. Not only do I love getting your

feedback, reviews help me gain the attention of new readers, and allow me to bring you more books. If you know of friends or family that would enjoy the book, I'd love your help there, too!

You can also connect with me via my website, Facebook, Goodreads, and Twitter. I'd love to hear from you.

Thank you again from the bottom of my heart for your support of my books,

M.

www.mmchouinard.com

mmchouinardauthor

author/show/5998529.M_M_Chouinard

@m_m_chouinard

ACKNOWLEDGEMENTS

First and foremost, I'd deeply thankful to everyone who takes the time to read my books—you make what I do worthwhile, and your support allows me to write more of them! Thanks also to those who take the (considerable) time and effort to review them and to blog about them, your support is such a help!

I'm endlessly grateful to the team at Bookouture for helping me make this book what it is. Special thanks go to Leodora Darlington, Alexandra Holmes, Jane Eastgate, Nicky Gyopari and Ramesh Kumar, who all helped edit and produce it—I could spend years poring over the pages and never come close to the amazing job they do catching all my mistakes and making suggestions for improvements. Also, to Kim Nash and Noelle Holten for their tireless promotion of it; Jules Macadam and Alex Crow who helped market it; and Leodora Darlington, Oliver Rhodes, Claire Bord, Jessie Botterill and Natalie Butlin for building the bridge that transported the product to its readers.

Thank you very much to the NWDA Hampshire County Detective Unit, who answered my questions patiently. Any errors/inaccuracies that exist despite their help are my fault entirely.

Also crucial to my success are the BSWs (in general, and Erika Anderson-Bolden specifically with respect to this book), D.K. Dailey, and my fellow Bookouture authors. You're always there for any type of support I need, and have been vital for the maintenance of my sanity!

My husband's support has been irreplaceable. He makes it possible to pursue my dreams—I simply couldn't ask for a better partner and best friend on my path through life.

And as always, thanks to my furbabies, who not-so-patiently keep me tethered to the real world when I get lost in my writing by insistently reminding me it's time for their dinner!

Made in the USA
Las Vegas, NV
12 February 2021

17661129R00184